TREASURE
ATOP THE
MOUNTAIN

Tonya L. Matthews

HALEYA PUBLISHING—Bowling Green, Kentucky.

Cover design by Print Media

Cover photo by Tonya L. Matthews

ISBN: 978-0-578-22240-0

Dedication

To my precious husband,
Todd Matthews

You are the best part of my day.

Gracie's left index finger rested between Ben's teeth and his quirky, yet charming, grin. As she tugged her finger free from her husband's playful grip, his arms tightened around her beneath the sheets. A tear spilled from her thick lashes. She wiped the tear with her hand—her only hand. Though her right arm lay by her side, forever etched with scars, she had never felt more beautiful and complete in her life.

Chapter 1

Gracie Howard watched Gene Carter's beat-up Chevy truck— faded blue hood, red door and missing fender—soar within inches of the front step of Swirly's Ice Cream parlor. Gracie, breathing in deeply, picked up the ice cream scooper.

"One-two-three ..." She held her breath, silently counting from behind the counter.

The smell was worse than usual today. Along with Gene and the squealing load of hogs packed into the trailer out front of Swirly's was his brother, Willy. The two disheveled men entered and peered at the selection of ice cream flavors listed on the chalkboard hanging on the wall behind Gracie. At the count of thirty-nine, unable to hold her breath any longer, she resorted instead to her well-rehearsed, shallow breaths.

Willy streaked his finger across the glass top of the deep freeze pointing to each flavor and asked, "That a new 'un ... Peppermint Pretty?"

1

Gracie chuckled, falling into the conversation they had had more than a dozen times, "Granddaddy made that one for me last spring as a high school graduation gift."

Then turning to Gracie's grandfather with childlike enthusiasm, Willy said, "Thomas! These those new cones that don't get soggy?" Willy jabbed his brother with his elbow, fascinated by the coated ice cream cones protected with a thin oil-and-sugar glaze. The cone tips fit perfectly into the holes of the upside-down milk crate Thomas rigged to hold each cone upright, making it possible for Gracie to serve the customers with her only hand. Her right arm ended near the elbow.

Gracie raised her hand to her face and placed her palm over her mouth, cupping her chin. With her forefinger and ring finger at each side of her nose to help block the smell, she took a few deep breaths. She missed their previous deep freeze that had held only six flavors. Though it had had a heavy lid which was harder for Gracie to lift, Willy had been satisfied with fewer samples. The new deep freeze with a glass sliding display window made it easier for Gracie to get to the ice cream, but Willy took longer with ten flavor options. She waited for Willy to consider his next flavor to taste. Removing her hand, she picked up another spoon and scooped the bite for him. His eyes lit up when he swallowed the Peppermint Pretty.

"Ummm, that one's got candy in it!" Willy looked toward Gene.

Gene pointed to his usual Chocolate Swirl, ignoring Willy.

Willy's and Gene's identical Cartwright jackets, originally navy blue, now pale gray, differed only by Willy's bright "Treasure Festival 1965" button and the cotton crumbs that trailed from its ripped seam.

"Scoop 'a Chocolate Swirl!" Willy declared. Gene nodded in approval. "Oh, give me two of 'em on that fancy cone," Willy decided.

"A fancy cone coming right up," Gracie said indulgently, enjoying the delight that a simple scoop of ice cream could evoke, yet surprised by a twinge of jealousy.

Willy grinned from ear to ear, nodding as if counting the seconds until the cone was in his hand—his tongue's tip out of his mouth, ready for the first lick.

Gracie lowered her eyes to conceal the avalanche of painful emotions that instantly encompassed her. Taken aback by a silly old man's absurd delight about two scoops of Chocolate Swirl, she yearned to once again feel that kind of innocent joy.

*   *   *

Kage reached out to steady the boarding passenger, words of apology on his lips. The man had tripped in the aisle of the bus on Kage's foot, which was helping to cradle the backpack between his legs. The guy jabbed his elbow at Kage's extended hand and cursed. Recovering his footing, he leaned toward Kage, "... blasted ignert!"

Without hesitating, Kage thrust his fist at the stranger's jaw and followed with an immediate uppercut, causing the man to

3

tumble to the opposite side of the bus as it began to pull away. With one last punch to the stomach, Kage laid the stranger onto the lap of an elderly lady who had somehow managed to sleep though the ruckus.

Kage, not afraid of a fight, actually got a sense of satisfaction from the shock in his right arm. He had worked construction since fourteen, pulling the weight of laborers twice his age. With every pick ax swung and scoop of earth shoveled, his arms and upper body had grown stronger.

Living on his own since he was twelve, he had spent the past seven years drifting from town to town learning countless lessons about life. Those who quickly sized up his compact five-foot-seven frame, twenty-nine-inch waist, and cordial demeanor to assume he could be easily taken soon recognized that they had underestimated both the muscle backing his punch and his will to survive.

As the passenger he'd hit scrambled to stand, Kage noticed the stranger's wallet in the aisle. He grabbed his backpack, discretely dipped for the wallet, and rushed to the front of the bus, pushing the door handle open. Mumbling obscenities, the bus driver slammed the door, catching the raveled hem of Kage's pants. Kage tugged his leg, jumped a few small hops and broke free just as the bus pulled away. He hadn't bathed in days. His sandy hair was tangled and matted against his forehead, and his only pair of jeans were so soiled they were better suited for a trashcan than a washing machine. He threw his backpack over his shoulder and inspected the wallet.

"Here for the festivities?" a guy leaning against a tent post greeted Kage. Tents resembling Fourth-of-July firework stands dotted the town, and from the closest one, a banner hung that read *Ridgewood Treasure Festival.*

"No, looking for work, though." The wallet offered only three dollars. Kage tossed the wallet into the large trash barrel as he approached.

"That a billfold you just threw in there?" The guy eyed Kage and then the barrel.

"Ain't got nothing in it."

"Name's Barrrneee," drawled the young man as he reached out to shake Kage's hand but didn't follow through. A pony-tailed teenager in a *Treasure Festival* T-shirt walking by caught his attention. Barney's eyes followed her, and he winked, striking an arrogant pose similar to that of the late James Dean, his red hair and freckled face, no match to the movie star. Sliding into his dinged-up Pontiac coup as if it were Dean's Porsche 550 Spyder, Barney rolled down his window and revved his engine. "Climb in." He motioned for Kage to open the passenger's door. Kage sank into the bucket seat.

Barney cranked the car radio until the vibration of the dashboard drowned out the song's lyrics. He turned sharply onto a dirt road and without warning slammed on the brakes, spinning the car. Dust smothered the coup. As it came to rest, dirt and gravel showered in through the open windows. He lit a cigarette, ground another gear and blared Billy Holiday's "When Your Lover Has Gone". Singing off key, he hollered out the window on impulse, nodding his head and slapping the steering wheel.

They pulled in front of what looked like an old tobacco barn. Barney turned off the engine, and though Billy Holiday was silenced with the ignition, Barney continued singing.

"This it?" Kage asked. He took in the modestly converted barn, assessing the carpentry work which made it livable.

"Yeeip," Barney acknowledged Kage's question only to revert back to song, butchering the melody. Once inside, Barney waved him toward a ladder. "This way."

Kage dropped his backpack next to one of the cots in the cramped loft. "So, this is where we sleep?"

"Yep. There's some water for you to clean yourself up," he pointed to a bucket of water. Outhouse is 'round back. No fancy flushing toilets here."

Kage had no complaints. Even a barn was better than the orphanage that had been his home.

*   *   *

Gracie frantically turned circles hearing her mother's cry, "Gracie, where are you?" Her voice was unmistakable, "Gracie! My baby ... where are you?" The clear sound of her mother's voice was the only thing recognizable in the foggy, smoke-filled room. A thick gray whirl encompassed her. She could no longer

6

see her bed, dresser, or the rocking chair that held her life-sized Raggedy Ann doll, just inches shorter than her eleven-year-old frame.

Gasping, then coughing, she wrapped her fingers around her throat and prayed for untainted, fresh air. She tasted the smoke on her tongue, thick like molasses, and her eyes stung, only relieved by flowing tears. She pressed the heels of her palms deep into her eyes, moisture pooling their rims. She stepped backward, tripping. Flashes of fire mounted, as if the sun had fallen from the sky, right into the hallway outside her bedroom.

Reaching desperately in every direction, Gracie inched forward searching for the window ledge. Instead, she bumped into her bureau drawers, causing the porcelain knickknacks on her dresser to rock, clank together, and tumble to the floor. She slid down the edge of the dresser to the floor and welcomed its smooth, cool surface against her back. She wrapped her arms around her knees and curled into a ball as she heard her mother scream again, "Gracie!" She covered her ears, and another large beam fell. For a mere second, she saw a small piece of the serene, sapphire sky. Then, like a devouring pack of wolves, the flames rose high again consuming everything above her.

Gracie collapsed, shaking, against the floor. She took shallow breaths, one and another. Then she felt a hand on her back. Could it be her mother? *How?* She tried fiercely to open her eyes. She stretched her brows and strained to no avail—all was endless, empty, ashen. *Are my eyes open and all there is to see*

7

is darkness? The moment of tranquility she experienced when she believed her mother touched her gave way to panic again.

Gracie jolted upright in bed, thrashing, sweat on her face. Though safe in her grandfather's home, Gracie gasped for the unsullied air, taking it in so violently she choked. Reaching out with her arms, she swatted and swirled like a windmill out of control. Her heart raced like the fire in her dream. Her eyes adjusted to the moonlight seeping in through her bedroom curtains. She glanced to the bedroom door and then to the window. She had heard it so clearly. Her mother had said her name—called for her. She'd been there beside her—touched her. Gracie stretched to place her hand on her back where she had felt her mother's touch just seconds before. Aching to relive the comforting sensation, she wanted to hold onto the feeling as long as she could. However, there was no smoke in the room, nor was her mother there with her. As always, the sweet vision faded, along with the nightmare.

Gracie listened for her grandfather. Had she screamed out like last time? The last dream was worse. She had felt the fire consuming her. She had dashed to the bathroom, vomiting in the cup of her hand. Her screams that night had disturbed her grandfather, and he sat with her until she was able to sleep again. He kissed her on the temple, his arms snug around her, as they both rocked to a silent rhythm. He whispered, "You are strong, Gracie; such a strong girl." His encouraging words played through her mind once more.

8

It had been this way since the fire took her father, mother, sister—and her hand—seven years ago. The nightmares were not always a room of fire. There were other dreams—dreams of losing her teeth, each falling out as she desperately gathered them—dreams of falling from the sky, praying for someone to catch her.

Tucking the quilted duvet tightly under her chin, Gracie let her head sink into her pillow. In the warmth and protection of the covers she held onto the feeling of her mother's touch. It was so real that she pretended for a minute that maybe it was.

Gracie moved her lips, but no sound came out, "Mama ..."

Chapter 2

Kage forced himself not to stare at the girl serving Chocolate Swirl to Gene, owner of the sorely renovated barn he now called home. She was without a right hand, yet she managed, with some help from the older man working behind the counter. Her hair flowed with loose curls and shimmered rich tones similar to fresh coffee beans in the sunlight, but it was her dark eyes that he found most curious. Her face was pretty, but her eyes nearly spoke. Though brown, at some angles they looked intensely black. Whatever their color, he liked them.

"Here you go, Mrs. Laurel." She handed a cup with a scoop of ice cream to the feeble lady who took the cup and held it near her eyeball examining its contents.

"Give me another one," she requested and handed the cup of ice cream back.

"Now, Mom," the woman with her chastised.

"Evelyn, you know we always take care of Mrs. Laurel," the older man Kage assumed was the shop owner responded with a wink.

He took the cup, leaned in the ice cream case and appeared to make an additional scoop, but when he presented the cup again, Kage could tell no ice cream had been added.

Evelyn nodded her head in what looked like an appreciative gesture to the owner.

"Mr. Laurel always likes a bite you know," the older lady said turning to Gene.

Gene nodded. Taking Mrs. Laurel's arm, Gene helped the daughter walk the frail lady out the door.

"And for you?" the shop owner asked Kage.

"No, thank you."

"What's your favorite flavor?" the girl behind the counter asked.

Kage shrugged, "Not today."

"Not even a taste?" she suggested.

"No." Kage stuffed his hand in his pocket, digging for change. "I'll pass."

Kage watched as Willy eagerly licked the ice cream balanced on top of what he called the 'soggy-less miracle cone'. Though tempted to get a scoop, Kage knew he couldn't afford to take the twenty cents from his earnings.

"He's savin' up for one of those rocks painted gold," Willy quipped, nudging Kage with his elbow and pointing out the window to one of the eager *Treasure Festival* vendors.

"Bunch of nonsense ..." Gene muttered beneath his breath as he returned to the counter to pay.

11

"Naw," Willy cut in, "I ain't lookin' for no painted kind. Lookin' to find the real stuff." He licked his ice cream cone attempting to catch a drip of Strawberry Swirl with his tongue, but instead the ice cream landed on his chin. He wiped his mouth with the back of his coat sleeve.

Kage had no problem passing on the painted stones, unlike the ice cream. "Who'd buy a painted rock anyway?"

"Ahh," Gene scolded. "Folks ain't got nothin' better to do than track people's business like the weather 'round here! Rumors they's tellin', that's all!"

From behind the counter, the shop owner scooped Kage a sample of Peppermint Pretty and insisted he try it. "Name's Thomas," he introduced himself. "This is my granddaughter, Gracie."

Kage nodded, appreciative.

Thomas, baited by the opportunity to share the tale with a newcomer, continued, "The story of treasure hit the national press in 1945—two years before Gracie was born," he nodded toward his granddaughter. "Two decades later, it's got its own festival around here."

Willy's continuous battle with his ice cream didn't deter him from listening to Thomas tell the story. "They say some greedy businessmen started the rumor to bring in tourists, an attempt to start somethin' like the California's gold rush. But I believe that treasure's somewhere, buried right here under our feet for all we know."

12

Thomas passed Willy a couple of napkins and continued, "Just days after the published article, strangers flocked like blackbirds to Ridgewood. Some stayed for a few days poking around, while others purchased cave land to explore."

"Really?" Kage posed, more interested in watching Thomas' granddaughter behind the counter maneuver around the shop without assistance.

Gene muttered, "Land that wasn't worth nothing and never would've sold went for thousands ... crazy!"

"Well, locals keep the rumor alive, often telling the story like they discovered the handwritten note," Thomas elaborated, reciting it by memory. "*I am writing because in Ridgewood there's lost treasure. We got riches yet to find. Come seek them with me.* T'was all it said."

"You believe that?" Kage asked Willy.

Willy nodded with confidence, crunching on the edge of his cone, ice cream dripping on his Cartwright jacket.

Thomas, seemingly tickled by Willy's faith, persisted, "Someone found that note in an abandoned room at the Hartington Hotel, about forty-five minutes north, as they say it happened. Then from there, who knows what's true? Once the note was published in the local paper, the national press reprinted it with the headline 'Ridgewood Said to Have Buried Treasure'. The treasure hunt was on."

"I bet it was hilarious," his granddaughter spoke up. Her eyes sparkling with amusement, she continued, "Families searched in their basements and cellars, dug up their backyards. Can you imagine?"

"Yep," her grandfather continued as if he'd shared the story hundreds of times. "People that no one had seen inside a church showed up, praying to be led to the treasure."

"All that because of a mysterious unsigned, handwritten note," Gracie added, scooping Gene's Chocolate Swirl.

Willy, eager to put in his two cents, piped, "Because there's treasure here!"

"Willy ain't alone. Many speculate where it might be hidden," Thomas encouraged.

Gracie handed Gene a cone with two scoops of Chocolate Swirl. "Now visitors stop by, especially during the annual *Treasure Festival* every October, to purchase a stone dipped in gold paint with the black letters 'Ridgewood, KY' hand-painted on it."

"Those stones ain't nothin' special, just picked up on an afternoon stroll," Gene scoffed.

"But with a little gold paint and a few black letters," Thomas mused, "they're worth at least a dime or sometimes a quarter depending on the stone's size and the local's eagerness to make a buck."

"Lucky for Granddaddy, tourists enjoy homemade ice cream as much as gold painted rocks." The edges of Gracie's lips curled affectionately as she looked toward her grandfather, who realized she was struggling to remove the lid on a new canister of

14

Chocolate Swirl. He extended his hand, and she willingly passed the container. Her grandfather steadied it with one hand and pulled off the lid with the other, all in one easy motion.

Kage left the ice cream shop feeling less sorry for himself. Where would he be without his hands? Every dollar he earned depended on them.

*   *   *

Gracie neatly arranged the peppermint sticks in the shape of a pinwheel on waxed paper in the backroom of Swirly's Ice Cream parlor. Then without warning, she pounded them relentlessly with a 10-ounce Eagle Brand milk can. Tiny slivers of candy shot across the room like glass spears. Her grandfather was the better peppermint cracker. He put a piece in one hand, and with the back side of a spoon he tapped it until the candy crumbled to his liking—calm and simple. Even though for Gracie the two-handed process was not an option, she preferred her method, though messier. She continued until the candy resembled flakes of coarse white sand.

She touched her index finger to her tongue, then to the peppermint dust on the counter. Tasting it, she thought of her sister and Pixy Stixs. They preferred to eat the flavored sugar from the palm of their hands, not drizzled on their tongues. They stuck their tongues out, licking their palms like bathing cats.

How many Pixy Stixs does it take to make a person's tongue raw and cause a stomach ache? Gracie knew the answer—forty-

15

eight. She had discovered this the Halloween Sarah was four. Their mother had sewn white angel gowns and wrapped twisted clothes hanger halos with silver Christmas garland.

"What beautiful angels you are!" They received compliments at every "trick-or-treat" stop. They'd heard it a dozen times that night, "A blonde one and a dark headed one—precious!"

Gracie glanced at one of the pictures tacked to the bulletin board on the wall. It was of Sarah and herself, posing side-by-side on a sunny afternoon in front of Swirly's. Five years apart in age and a foot apart in height, they looked more like friends than siblings. Sarah's square jaw contrasted with Gracie's oval features. Gracie, like her father, had almond-toned skin that tanned easily. Brunette with brown eyes and long noticeable lashes, Gracie's features resembled a young lady's more than a second grader's. Sarah had taken after their mother with powder-soft, fine, blonde hair and fair skin. She'd burn and freckle at the mere sight of the sun. Gracie remembered wishing she had freckles, like her mother and sister, and once she'd dotted her arms using their dad's ballpoint pen. She ran her finger over the picture spattered with crusted milk and wished now for so much more than freckles.

Gracie had recently recognized her mother's cheekbones in pictures of herself and wondered if she could ever be as beautiful as her mother. Another picture captured the girls, in their frilly dresses, clinging tightly to their parents, along with Thomas and her grandmother, Marilee, on an Easter Sunday.

16

Her mother's high cheekbones made her look like Grace Kelly, especially with the breeze blowing her hair away from her face. Gracie touched her own cheeks and tried to smile as largely as her mother in the picture.

"Gracie, come here," Thomas' voice broke into her thoughts.

She shook peppermint flakes from her hand and headed toward her grandfather's voice. She found him on the front porch, sweat beaded on his forehead, as he leaned over the ice cream maker, trying to fix it.

"Gonna have to take it to town to get it looked at," Thomas admitted in defeat.

Gracie nodded her head in response. She glanced at the broken ice cream maker, looked at her grandfather bent over it, and then peered at a late blooming Stargazer among the flowers peeping through the weed-ridden flower garden that Marilee had once tended so meticulously. Petunias no longer sprouted from the window boxes that now hung forward on loose nails. The buttercups, tulips, and zinnias she'd sniffed as a girl remained only in her memory. She ventured toward the remnant of the flowerbed.

Thomas hadn't painted recently either. Along the trim of the door-facing, the words 'Benny's Barber Shop' showed through the thinning white paint. Thankfully, fresh paint or not, the ice cream sold.

"I've been thinking," Gracie said. She'd stepped down into the flowerbed to pull weeds. Tossing them aside, she followed

17

her grandfather into the shop. "What if we hire someone part-time to help around here, just two or three days a week. To help you ... us?"

Thomas picked up several ice cream scoopers. "No."

"You just ..." Gracie paused, "look tired."

"No, ma'am. I can still do a good two-step if you'd like," Thomas challenged, shuffling his feet.

"I knew you wouldn't listen to me." Gracie smiled, drying one of the ice cream scoopers and placing it in the drawer. "You're the boss."

"No, my sweet girl." Thomas looked up at a bulletin board hanging beneath the clock. "She was the boss." He pointed an ice cream scooper toward Marilee's photo.

Still, years after her passing, Thomas left the notes Marilee had written posted to the backroom wall. Though yellowed, the papers with Marilee's handwriting listed each ingredient and measurement of Peach Popular, Strawberry Sweet, and Chocolate Cream. She'd kept him organized—his master of the details.

"*She* would have hired someone," Gracie pressed, bending to wipe up the drops of water on the floor under Thomas' feet.

He scoffed at the mess he made. "She'd probably fire me for this," Thomas snorted. He looked over at Gracie's peppermint flakes on the counter, and added, "And you for that."

The door chimes clanked, and Thomas motioned for Gracie to go to the front room and help the customer. It was

Gene. He was alone. Without Willy there for a tasting spree, he was out the door in a matter of minutes. With his Chocolate Swirl in one hand, he nodded a 'thank you' with a wink, and made a clicking noise extending his pointer finger as if to say, 'see you later'. Gracie chuckled to herself, reminded of funny stories her grandfather had told her about Gene when she was little. They still made her smile. It was hard for her to image Gene as a boy full of life and with tadpoles in his pockets.

"When I was sixteen," Thomas once shared, "and ol' Gene Carter was maybe seven, I guess, I'd run into him while he was playing at the creek."

Gracie had interrupted, "Seven years old, like me?"

"Yep, just like you. Gene would be up to his nose in mucky water trying to catch fish by hand." Gracie giggled at the picture created in her mind. Thomas admitted he'd been baited by the challenge and tossed aside his pole too. "A tadpole or two t'was all he went home with most days."

"Another time Gene ran up and down the creek bank building a slippery mud path from the highest end of the bank right down into the creek. He slid on his bottom for hours until the mud caked to his jeans looked like bare skin," Thomas relayed.

Her giggles encouraged him. "But Gene was a thinker," Thomas continued, "always doing his own thing, while the other kids played. He once planted a buckeye hoping to grow his own tree. Every day Gene visited that buckeye sunk in the ground

19

and studied it, leaning his eye to the dirt. The most expression I ever saw from Gene was the day that something resembling a small tree branch emerged from the buried buckeye."

"What'd he do?" Gracie squealed.

Thomas spun to the left, then to the right as he mimicked Gene's childlike enthusiasm. "Gene turned, slapping his hands on his thighs and jumping. His heels tapped his own hind end, and he looked like a bucking horse."

Gracie had nearly choked on her laughter—her eyes large and cheeks flushed.

"When he discovered it was the older boys playing a trick on him, Gene dug up the buckeye, stuffed it in his pocket and headed home without a word."

Gracie's favorite part of that story had been about Willy. "Willy, Gene's younger brother, snickered over that one for days, but the worst part was the sound of snot rattling in Willy's nose every time he laughed," Thomas concluded. Gracie had giggled and snorted so hard that Thomas began laughing at her. They had laughed until neither could breathe, and then they had wheezed until their breath steadied.

Gracie remembered when she had asked how he could be friends with the stinky man, he had responded kindly, "Gracie, some people are just different. For example, some talk a bunch ..."

Feeling compelled to give examples, Gracie had responded, "Like Erma Franklin."

An innocent smirk escaped as Thomas concluded, "And then there're folks like Gene, who don't have much to say. Some people are just different. It's okay not to be like everyone else."

A lesson—unknown to Gracie at that moment—that she'd spend a life time learning after the tragic night of the fire.

Chapter 3

Kicking a pebble along the dirt road, Kage mentally marked Ridgewood off his list of places to revisit.

Night's beckoning seeped through the clouds as a breeze picked up, hinting at coming rain, yet Kage didn't alter his pace. His steps were firm, although his shoulders slumped, and his brow furrowed. The dusky skyline collided with the tinted treetops, and the sun—a brilliant orange—faded. Everything around him was so peaceful that he wanted to scream just to disturb its serenity.

He didn't care for Ridgewood, Kentucky, or its rolling hills everyone referred to as "their mountains." Kage knew mountains. He'd seen mountains. These were no mountains. Although the hills were covered with sycamore trees that looked as if they pierced the sky, the mountains he had hiked bowed to the clouds. Stuffing his hands in his pockets, Kage didn't increase his step even when the first drop of rain fell.

At nineteen, Kage had seen enough to last him a lifetime. The hills in Thistle Creek, Kentucky where he'd grown up had enclosed him in the orphanage. These hills trapped him just the same. At the thought of the orphanage, he could smell its hallways, and he winced trying to break free of the unwelcome sensation. He had vowed never to return to Thistle Creek. Maureen's voice still lived in his head. The cruel caregiver's tone rang in his ears as intensely as the rain now beat against his face. He shook his head, willing the memories forever buried. The only hint that she was a woman was her uniform's white, knee-length skirt. Her voice echoed deep and course, harsh like a man's, and her words were profane and indecent.

Once, a construction supervisor asked him why he didn't use the colorful language of the other crew members. "I've worked with priests who curse and swear more than you," the supervisor had joked. Kage didn't remember how he had responded, but he did know the true reason he would not speak those words. Those words were Maureen's, and no one, no matter how deserving, would ever hear them come from his mouth. Kage wanted to be nothing like that woman. Again, Kage shook his head, unconscious of its motion—his mind unrelenting. Maureen's hands were large, much larger than his even now. She hit him across the face with the back of her hand when he didn't speak up. He received the same reward when he did talk, and when he didn't eat quickly enough, and again when he ate too quickly.

Because of Maureen, he even hated the sound of his own name. It was the way she said it—Kaaaedge. She would hold out the "a" as long as she could in one breath, setting the "K" apart from the rest of his name. She would grit her teeth together, moving only her lips. "Kaaedge, sit down." "Kaaedge, get up." "Kaaedge, you're heart's too tender, boy!" His name was printed on the inside tag of his shirts, pants, and even his stained underwear. They had stamped K A G E on its waistband, which served as yet another reminder of his prison.

Because he'd survived worse, Kage tolerated the Carters. Upon his arrival to Ridgewood, Willy, Gene's brother, had been full of questions. He first asked Kage, "Bouts what brangs you hier?"

"Traveling through, I suppose." Kage wondered if Willy realized he was living in the twentieth century. He watched as Willy pulled a leaf of tobacco from his pocket, popped it into his mouth and began chewing. Willy elbowed Barney who was sitting beside him in the wood-splinted rocker. Barney swatted back at Willy without opening his eyes. He'd nodded off. Willy snickered.

"Where's to?" Willy quizzed Kage.

"Louisville, I guess," and the conversation went on, not so much interesting as it was time filling for Willy, who evidently had nothing better to do.

"You got family?" Willy meddled further.

"No."

When Kage was born, his parents already had seven children—Rupert, Adam, Carl, Cecil, Pearl, Beth Ann and Ruby.

His mother discovered at fifty-two that she was pregnant again. She had a difficult pregnancy. With no means to pay a midwife, a nearby neighbor did her best to save Kage and his mother. Samuel Kage, age fifty-three, with eight kids, held a baby in his arms—and no wife. He allowed the neighbor to take the two youngest daughters and his newly born son to an orphanage, a day's drive from the Kage's home in Carriage Hill. Kage, of course, did not remember his father or his promise to return for them, but his two older sisters did. Every day Beth Ann and Ruby walked to the front window, and as long as the caregivers would allow, they stared down the road, watching ... hoping.

"So, what's your plan there, Cowboy?" Willy asked, bringing Kage back to the one-sided conversation Willy had been having. Barney slumped in the chair next to them, snoozing.

"Don't know really. Just keep doing what I've been doing, I guess," Kage responded, trying to figure out why Willy, his front teeth decayed, had such a large smile on his face.

"How's you determine that?" Willy asked as if the conversation had turned intellectual. He looked eager to take notes.

Kage was finding satisfaction in humoring Willy, since he hung on Kage's every word. Willy scooted to the edge of his chair, leaning his elbows on both knees. His ear twisted unnecessarily toward Kage, and a single stalk of straw rested between his lips as he chewed it.

Kage leaned forward and met Willy's gaze. "I've got three rules in life that keep me alive. It's as simple as that."

Willy shifted in his seat and took a few exaggerated chews to his straw. "Oh yeah, tell me 'um?"

"One ..." Kage paused dramatically. He was having fun now. "Never trust anyone."

Willy responded, "Oh yeah, that there is a good 'un. Number two?"

"Always be kind to good folks," Kage said, settling back in his chair.

"Yep, that's a 'nutter good 'un." Willy mimicked Kage's relaxed posture, sitting back in his chair as he pondered that one.

Kage raised his finger and shook it. "One more, and this is a biggie, the one that counts." He paused and scooted to the edge of his chair, again Willy did the same. "Never, never trust anyone."

Willy looked puzzled as if trying to gather something he couldn't get his arms around. Just as Kage thought he was going to have to point out the obvious, Willy slapped his leg and said, "Oh yeah, now that there is the most important of all three. I agree with yous on that!"

Barney kicked Willy's chair, nearly knocking Willy off its edge. "You idiot. Even half asleep, I know that's only two."

Kage hoped Willy never ran into the kind of men that he'd dealt with living on the road. Willy wouldn't have made it home

26

with a penny in his pocket or remembered his own name after they were done with him.

But those were Kage's rules, and he had learned them fast and hard. Even sitting with Willy now and staying under the same roof with the Carters and Barney, he trusted no one. After a few misjudgments and a slight scar over his right eyebrow as a reminder, he had learned to read people well.

When someone was truly kind to him, he remembered it. At that thought, the Lamberts came to mind. His best living arrangement was with the Lamberts, an elderly couple. They took him right into their home. He cut wood for them, and he tore down an old building on their farm, all in exchange for a warm place to sleep and what was the best country cooking he'd found in Georgia. They wouldn't accept drinking or promiscuous women brought in their home, and since Kage didn't have the money to take up either vice, the arrangement worked well. Mrs. Lambert even cut the bread crust off his sandwiches. That was where he'd planned to stay, until that evening the phone rang, and it was for him. His sister Pearl was on the other end of the line, and so began his venture back to Kentucky.

*   *   *

Once again, Gracie awakened screaming. Her grandfather darted to her doorway so quickly she wondered at first if she was imagining him. She hadn't seen her grandfather move that fast in years, not since two kids had reached around the counter and grabbed several dollar bills from his register. He'd had their wrists in his grasp before they turned to run.

Thomas sat on the corner of Gracie's bed, holding her. She intertwined her fingers with his and felt the security that his arms offered. They both sobbed. Gracie wished she could stop the nightmares, if only so she would not upset her grandfather.

"Tell me about when I was a little girl." This was something they did in the wee hours of the night to move past the nightmares.

Her grandfather thought and then spoke, "I remember when you were six and started helping us at the shop on Saturdays. You'd skip up the sidewalk holding my hand, and as soon as you saw your grandmother, your steps would grow bigger and you'd tug me along. Marilee would reach out toward you—her smile a match to yours."

"I remember hugging her so tight that I could almost clasp my hands together around her," Gracie reminisced, "and you always gave me peppermint candy."

"Yep. You were my little Peppermint back then and still are." He nudged her with his elbow.

"I like it when you call me Peppermint. 'Hey, Peppermint ...'" Gracie repeated, just to hear the comforting sound of his nickname for her.

"For a little thing, you were a big help. You'd pull up a Coca-Cola crate next to the counter and stand on it—still having to tippy-toe to reach the register."

"Running the cash register made me feel so grown-up."

"Even at six you were smart, especially for your age. We worked together on how to add up the coins. You'd get confused, not understanding why the smaller dime was worth more than a nickel, but you could match up money in the register just fine though."

"People were honest—thankfully," Gracie acknowledged.

"Yep, you'd just ask how many dollars, quarters, dimes, nickels or pennies they needed. I can see you standing there, your hair falling around your face and those dusty bare feet on the Coca-Cola crate. I'm thinking of a particular Saturday when you wore a little white and blue daisy print sundress, the one that tied with bows on the shoulders. The skirt ruffle came to your knees—your right one skinned from a tumble off your bicycle in the backyard."

"I remember that too! The blue sandals mom bought rubbed a raw spot on my pinky toe. You let me walk around without shoes, and Grandma didn't like that," Gracie mused.

"Oh, yes," Thomas recalled. "And that same morning, your mother tied your hair into pigtails at each ear with blue ribbons. One ribbon dangled more loosely than the other, and I tried to fix it, but Grandma swatted me away. 'Here now, let me do that,'" Thomas said in his best Marilee voice.

"And Gene ..." Gracie interrupted.

"Yep, ol' Gene. Hasn't changed a bit, has he? I remember the time you got into an argument with him about how to say your last name."

"I don't remember that ..."

"He'd ask, 'How's the Hireds today?' You just learned to spell your last name and told him, 'It's Howard, spelled h-o-W-a-r-d.' He got a hoot out of that."

"And his teeth! The first time he wore them I remember him askin' me, 'How's Gracie?' I wouldn't have recognized him except that he smelled just like a stinky pig. And you were so good at holding your breath. How'd you do it again?"

"Well, when I'd see Gene drive up, I'd take a deep breath and nod, 'hello'. Then I'd wave my hand over the ice cream case, keeping a tight smile. Gene back then always took his time looking over the flavors, reading aloud all their names."

"Yeah, and you opened your eyes larger and nodded as if to say, 'That's a good one. How about it?'"

"He'd piddle until I thought I'd explode." Thomas puffed out his cheeks.

Gracie piped in with a deep voice, "Then he'd finally say, 'Just give me two scoops of the Chocolate Swirl.'"

"And I'd lean down toward the ice cream case, a little lower than usual, and release my breath. Just as the cool air flowed from the case, I'd breathe in the clean air before scooping his ice cream order."

Gracie remembered watching her grandfather's chest rise to hold his breath as he stood from the case and handed Gene his ice cream cone. "Thankfully, Gene always had his money ready," Gracie added.

"Yep, so again, no words exchanged," Thomas concluded, "and you'd place the money in the register, while I waved goodbye."

"Gene always smiled back, teeth or no teeth," Gracie recalled. "I was never good at holding my breath."

"You'd pinch your nose," Thomas reminded her.

"How embarrassing! Everybody thought it was *so* funny ..."

"Only because you were *so* cute."

Gracie nudged her grandfather. "Gene would smile so big I could even see how his teeth fit in his mouth."

"Now that's funny!" Thomas laughed pointing at Gracie's imitation of Gene's smile.

"He'd sometimes leave me an extra nickel. Thanks to Gene's nickels I earned enough to buy Sarah Sue, my favorite doll."

"Even back then Gene would point his finger with his thumb extended upward making that clicking sound and wink his right eye." Thomas tried to mimic Gene. "Then he was off."

"Yet the squalid odor remained." Gracie pinched her nose.

"People really enjoyed it when they saw you behind the counter." He gave Gracie another squeeze. "Mrs. Laurel's tired eyes would shine at the sight of you. For a few seconds, the tiny wrinkles washed right off her face."

"Oh, yeah, and remember when Evelyn insisted that Mrs. Laurel only have a sample, because she was diabetic? That didn't go over well." Gracie rolled her eyes.

"I remember, and then we started charging her half price for an extra small scoop. Then she started asking for double scoops," Thomas smirked.

Gracie found comfort when they laughed together. "Love you, Granddaddy," she whispered. Gracie remembered skipping barefooted around the ice cream shop that Saturday that she had worn the sundress and pigtails. She counted the days each week just as if the approaching Saturday were Christmas Day, until that awful night when she was eleven, and everything changed.

*   *   *

Thomas crawled back into bed, his head awhirl though his body was spent. When Gracie was smaller, it had been easier. He'd pull her out of bed onto his knee and cradle her, leaning his head against her shoulder—sometimes crying, too. After their cry, Gracie would wipe his tears.

He wondered sometimes how he'd made it through those years without their son and his precious family and then without Marilee.

Gracie's screams in the night had crippled Marilee. Thomas would rush to Gracie, and then return to his bed to find Marilee trembling, her fists twisted and tangled in the sheets, fighting the tears as if another frightful cry would break her.

He'd struggled too, angry at everything, even God. He shuddered—terrified by the memory of that sunken point in his life. He'd quickly discovered though that if he missed church on Sunday, Pastor Ted, along with a troop from church, visited the next morning to check on him. Or if he didn't open Swirly's for its scheduled hours, he'd find Gene on his doorstep with something freshly slaughtered. So, he kept up the act for everyone, but especially for Gracie.

Now looking back, along with the Lord's hand, he realized the concern and support of others had carried him through. On his worst days, it helped to talk about his feelings. Pastor Ted prayed with him, and Gene listened as long as he needed to ramble. Marilee hadn't been able to talk about the loss, and he worried that Gracie was more like Marilee.

Chapter 4

"See anything down there?" Kage asked Willy who stood over the sunken well behind Swirly's looking for more than his reflection.

"I knows it's down there. It's gotta be. I's looked everywhere. Dug nearly 'til my hands bled." Willy lifted his dirt-creviced palms to Kage as if still scabbed and blistered.

Kage humored him. "Wish we could find a way to get it out."

"How you think we'd do it?"

"I'm not smart enough to figure that one out." Kage stepped toward the ice cream shop, leaving Willy standing over the well with his arms across his podgy frame, lips puckered, and eyes squinted in concentration.

Kage opened Swirly's front door as Thomas asked Gene, "One or two scoops?"

Gene held up two fingers and nudged his elbow toward Kage. "You gettin' any?"

"No," Kage answered.

"No ice cream!" A lady decorated in flashy colors that matched the Sherbet Swirl reacted as if he'd turned down something as essential as oxygen.

"No, ma'am." Kage stepped back from the counter glancing toward the backroom. No sign of the dark-haired girl working today.

"Gene, did you see *I Dream of Jeannie* this week?" The flamboyant woman went on about the episode and her plans to buy a color television. Gene ignored her. He didn't have a television.

"Someday I'll find it," Willy declared, Swirly's door slammed behind him as he stepped inside. "Erma," Willy acknowledged, getting out of the way as the lady finished raving about the possibilities of a color television and waved "tootles" to everyone.

Gene cut his eyes toward Willy and pronounced, "Ain't no treasure. Should be more concerned about protecting the land around here than diggin' for treasure." Gene stepped closer to Willy. "And if I see you diggin' on this here land for that treasure, you gonna clean the stable yourself next time, you understand?"

Willy slapped his hand down on the counter. "They's have to come through me before they get our land!"

Gene scoffed, "I say those politicians is the devil. Some is as crazy about it as the gold painted rocks. I ain't sellin' my land to none of 'em. Ain't no need for some kind of big roads goin' through here and across the whole county."

"Guess if they build those roads, all kinds of people will be traveling this way to buy the gold painted rocks," Kage interjected. He glanced at Willy curious to see if he believed it.

The crease in Gene's forehead relaxed and a chuckle, kin to a hiccup, escaped.

*   *   *

Laughter carried in the crisp fall breeze as Gracie walked past the school yard headed to Swirly's to help her grandfather. Two snickering boys pushed one another as they toppled off the end of the slide. When they ran around to climb the ladder again, they bumped into another friend, frozen, mid-step on the ladder. They followed his eyes to Gracie.

The stares didn't pierce Gracie's heart today. Instead she was inspired by the strong pin oaks bursting deep scarlet, vivid gold and then brown. She watched a gold leaf float from the biggest oak. It glided lazily and settled in front of her path. She stepped over it as another breeze grabbed it into a whirl. Gracie loved autumn leaves. She remembered burying herself up to her neck in her backyard along with her sister Sarah and then rolling all over the yard until she itched from head to toe.

Gracie smiled at the boy who'd first spotted her as he edged up to the top step. The other two boys were lined up like dominoes at his heels. One said, "Ain't you ever seen that girl with no hand? Ain't you seen her at Swirly's?"

The other domino responded, "That's Gracie. She always lets me taste as many flavors as I want!"

Then the last domino pushed the two boys ahead of him still staring. "Go, would you ... or are you two in love with the girl without a hand. Bobby, do you looove her?"

From the top rung, Bobby kicked his foot backward to their surprise. The taunter on the lowest rung fell to the ground, landing on his bottom, while the little guy in the middle managed to keep his balance. Bobby took off down the slide. Gracie's lips curled into a smirk. The boys' laughter became distant.

Gracie heard Erma Franklin call to her as she passed Franklin's Grocery, "The apple pies Thomas loves are fresh this morning." Erma extended her arm flamboyantly waving its entire length.

Gracie nodded. "Thanks. I'll let him know," she called back loudly enough for Erma, standing on the grocery porch, to hear her.

"Tell him to stop by today. They go fast!" Erma pressed.

Erma Franklin, owner of the town's grocery store, was a single lady who had, without question, never met a stranger in her life. Erma, though already blessed with a full head of hair, teased it from all angles and then attempted to tame it with a clasp in back. Her effort to mimic Jaqueline Kennedy's popular hairstyle failed miserably.

Erma, now perched on the edge of the porch bench, pumped her makeshift folded paper fan, though it wasn't a hot day. When one of the town's men passed and exchanged a wave, she flicked her hair off her shoulder with her free hand and exposed the gaudy baubles dangling from her ears. She particularly perked up when Pastor Ted appeared outside the church to work on the grounds, as he did this morning. She stood and steadied herself against the porch bench which was painted bright red with a Pall Mall cigarette promotion.

"How are you this morning, Pastor Ted?" Gracie called out as she passed Mt. Pleasant Church. He was a simple looking man, and his graying hair suited him. He wore thin, round wire-rimmed glasses. Although a preacher, he had the look of a doctor.

Pastor Ted was bent over pulling weeds around the welcome sign. He rose, resting his forearms on his knees in a crunched stance. "All is well, all is well ..." he sang out like the familiar hymn. He waved and leaned forward again pulling the weeds and pitching them out into the street. As he bent over, his pants rose well above his ankles showing not only his dingy white socks but also his bare legs.

"Gracie, need a ride?" Aaron, Erma Franklin's nephew, called from the driver's seat of the family's newly-purchased, 1965, smoke-gray Ford Mustang, which perfectly matched the thick rims of his eyeglasses. Gracie, less than a few yards from Swirly's, pointed ahead indicating her destination.

Chippy Martin, owner of the wood mill, chugged by so slowly the sawdust on the hood of his truck barely moved. He lifted his chin when he passed, and Gracie did the same. Gracie's father had worked at the wood mill. She thought of how she and Sarah used to call him Mr. Wood Chippy, giggling until their heads felt dizzy or they got the hiccups—sometimes both.

Gene Carter backed his truck from Swirly's. Passing Gracie, he smiled, no teeth today. Cone in hand, he made a clicking noise and pointed his finger in Gracie's direction.

*   *   *

"Want in?" Barney called out to Kage.

"Are you talking treasure again?" Kage quipped, not interested until he noticed the cards spread on the table.

"Naw, cards!" Willy held his hand of playing cards fanned nearly touching his nose.

"Okay. What's the game?" Kage took a seat at the table.

"Seven Card Stud, Five Card Draw or Texas Hold 'em ... you call it. Willy's getting the hang of 'em all." Barney nodded toward Willy who grinned as if the five-dollar bills at his elbow equaled the pile of cash stacked in front of Barney.

"Let's go with Five Card Draw. Deal me in." Kage swatted the table ready for the challenge.

"Alright then, your deal, Willy." Barney slid the cards toward Willy.

"Deuces wild. Those are twos," Willy announced, proud to think he might teach Kage something. "One ... for you. One ... for you. One ... for me." He dealt in no hurry.

"Where's Gene?" Kage wondered aloud.

"Ah, he doesn't like cards. Says it's the devil's game," Willy scoffed. "Cards and moonshine."

"Didn't know the devil played," Kage jested, rearranging the cards in his hand. He had learned poker the hard way, with no introductory lesson. The construction men he had worked with were always pleased to take him for everything in his pockets.

"I just won the last three hands. Barney says I'm showin' *him* hows'ta play now!" Willy blurted out.

"Well, I'm just getting warmed up," Kage teased, though planning to bail if he didn't win the first few hands.

"I'll take a card," Willy piped, tossing a seven of hearts down to exchange.

"Dealer goes last," Barney scolded, and Willy picked up his card and lifted the bottle in front of him for a drink. Barney motioned for Willy to share it, and he handed it over to Barney who took more than a sip.

"Two for me," Kage sneezed the words out.

"You allergic to this place?" Barney asked, as Willy passed Kage his cards.

"Allergic to this whole town, I think."

Willy interrupted, "So which ace did you say always beats my hand, no matter what I got?"

"The trump card," Barney said and winked at Kage.

"Now which black 'un is that?"

Barney flipped through the deck and pulled out a spade. "This's a spade," Barney snarked.

"Ah, thought you said before it was the other one. So, it ain't the one that looks like doggie tracks?"

"Those are clubs." Barney held up a club.

"Yeah, doggie tracks," Willy said with a nod, then tossed down his seven of hearts once more and picked up a new card from the top of the deck. He took another pull from the liquor bottle. "Want some 'shine?" Willy offered the bottle to Kage.

Kage glanced at Barney and then Willy, confused. He shook his head passing on the offer. "We're playing Five Card Draw, right?"

Barney nodded his head, and Willy muttered, "So spades is the card, huh?" Willy nudged Kage. "If you can't remember they's called spades, you can call 'em shovels. That's what I call 'em."

"What 'cha got?" Barney asked.

"A'right," Willy proudly placed his cards on the table.

Barney elbowed Kage, before displaying his cards.

"Ah, how'd you do that? You got that winning card again," Willy whined, taking another sip of moonshine.

"I'm out! You two have fun ..." Kage pushed his chair from the table, leaving Willy to be Barney's prey.

*   *   *

41

Gracie pulled the sheet over her head to muffle her sobbing. How many more nights could she bear these nightmares? She relived it all over again, just as it had happened.

Sarah's scream and the stench of thick smoke awakened Gracie. Eyes wide with fear, she ran from her room into the hallway almost straight into the hurling flames. She screamed for Sarah, "Where are you?" She heard her sister cry, first for their mother and then for their father. Gracie alternated between screaming her sister's name at the top of her lungs and screaming out to God.

The flames shot several feet taller than her head and traveled down the hallway, blocking her sister's bedroom door. Gracie called for Sarah and grabbed her Cinderella blanket. She remembered her father once throwing an old tarp over a small fire in the horse barn.

She took only a moment to look over her shoulder down the banister to see if the stairs were still intact. Edging closer to the flames, she felt the heat from the blaze sting her face and squinted. With all her strength, holding the corners of the blanket, she whipped it high into the air. The lavender blanket landed flat on top of the flames, smothering them for mere, critical seconds. The air that the whip of the blanket generated blew the flames toward Sarah, and Gracie saw her jump backwards, almost losing her balance. Then she saw her sister's face, fearful beyond description, darkly stained by ashes but for two clean trails from her eyes to her chin. She held her stuffed rabbit tucked against her chest with both arms.

Gracie reached across through the broken flames for her hand, stepping so close she could smell the singed threads. She screamed for Sarah to take her hand. Sarah edged forward, dropped one arm's grasp from the rabbit so that it dangled to her side. She reached toward Gracie's hand and their fingers touched. Gracie grabbed her wrist and pulled her with all her might, encouraging her sister to jump over the flames that seconds later had consumed the blanket.

Sarah fought her sister, tugging with all her will in the opposite direction. Gracie nearly lost her footing and stumbled forward into the flames which rose, encompassing their arms. Sarah's cry was now so loud that her words were inaudible.

Gracie, desperate to find help, released her sister. Grabbing the sheet off her bed, she wrapped it around her shoulders, and it instantly stuck to the skin of her right arm. Squalling as loudly as Sarah, she ran down the stairs. Her feet tangled in the sheet and she fell to her knees. Scrambling back to her feet, she ran out the front door yelling, "HELP!"

Firefighters scurried like a colony of ants under attack. Fountains of fire leapt into the heavens. Bright flames and Gracie's screams pierced the darkness. A sobbing fireman sat her under the oak tree by the horse barn, away from the house. She screamed, "Daddy!" She whispered, "Mama ..." Then, she choked on her sister's name through her tears.

Chapter 5

Rain emptied from the sky all day Friday. Saturday morning was no different. Each drop on the barn's tin roof pounded louder than the one before. The smell of bacon filled the barn. "It's here if you want it," Gene called as Kage climbed down from the loft. Willy was at the table, gravy flooding the edges of his plate. Not waiting to talk after each bite, Willy called to Kage, "We's gonna do it. Me and Barney—we's got a plan."

"Shhh," Barney quieted Willy.

Gene went about his business, ignoring Willy. He flipped the bacon strip-by-strip with a fork in the cast iron pan—each strip slaughtered, cured and thickly cut. Kage wondered if Gene was a drunk who stayed on the wagon during warm months, working until winter set in. He learned working construction that many men lived like that—sober when there was work and drunk otherwise.

Willy, the more heftily built of the two, sat shirtless with his belly exposed. The bib of his overalls rested in his lap. His hair looked to have been cut by his own hand—jagged and untamed.

44

Gene, passing up six-feet and lanky, stood center of the kitchen floor with his overalls buckled over his bare shoulders—yet the buttons at each hip unfastened exposing the waistband of his underwear. His hair, considerably thinner than Willy's, was neatly combed to the side, though questionable as to the last time it was washed.

Although a first assessment revealed the differences between the two brothers, they had one thing in common—each was in his own isolated world. He once asked Gene if it had always been just the two of them. Gene had answered, "No." That was it—no explanation. He went on about his work as if Kage hadn't even tried to make conversation.

"I got the shovels in the back of my car." Barney shared Willy's ardent enthusiasm, winking at him as if they were plotting some covert operation.

Kage took a slice of bacon from the table, mumbled "thanks" to Gene and reached for his jean jacket hanging from a nail near the door. It was damp from the moisture that seeped through the cracks of the barn.

"You want in? We got it all figured out!" Barney offered.

Lifting his jacket above his head to shield the rain, Kage left without a word to them. He'd be soaked by the time he got from Gene's to Franklin's Grocery. Eager for the money so that Ridgewood would be no more than another unpleasant memory, he'd picked up several shifts at the store.

*　　*　　*

The rain tapping Gracie's bedroom window reminded her of Erma Franklin's nails on the ice cream shop counter as she waited for Willy Carter to decide between Chocolate or Strawberry Swirl. Gracie used to enjoy easy, rainy mornings, appreciating the slowing of the world around her. When her father was not able to farm outside, he sat in his recliner working his way through stacks of unread newspapers. Her mother fixed country ham, eggs, biscuits and sausage gravy for breakfast, and the family was napping by noon. Gracie's mother rested on the couch, arms tucked under a pillow and legs pulled to her chest, leaving just enough room for both girls to curl up at her feet. Gracie's mom wiggled her toes, and the girls giggled as they grabbed her toes with theirs. This lasted until Gracie's dad, half asleep said, "Here now," in a deep, gruff voice. Silence instantly absorbed the room, and it sounded as if God turned up the volume on each rain pellet. Gracie slept deeply and sweetly.

But this morning Gracie awakened as tired as she had gone to sleep. After the nightmare, miserable images swarmed her mind: the shattered look on her grandfather's face as he gathered her from under the oak tree, her grandmother face-down on the front lawn where she'd collapsed as neighbors pulled her back from running into the flames, and Pastor Ted's desperate pleas to God and then his silence—crippled by a complete loss of consoling words.

Gracie recalled the low voices murmuring at the funeral home, muffled like never-ending whistles caught in a shrill breeze. She experienced again the panic she suffered after the surgery, when she saw her right arm—with no hand or fingers. These panic attacks felt as she imagined the last seconds of life would be. Her chest aching beyond words and her mind racing, she pleaded for life's sustaining fuel, one deep breath. She calmed herself with words, the words of her grandfather, "You are strong, Gracie. Hold on, my sweet girl. Breathe ..."

A clap of thunder startled Gracie from her unrelenting memories. She finished making her bed, though fighting the urge to slide back under the covers and disappear.

Sitting at the kitchen table, Gracie's grandfather looked through the screened back door, concentrating so intensely he jumped when she spoke. He chuckled aloud at himself. Usually Gracie would have laughed too but laughing took too much effort today. Still in her long, flannel nightgown, Gracie took baby steps toward the refrigerator.

Her grandfather wore a gray suit—the same one he had worn to church for years—alternating between two ties. Today the blue striped tie had its turn. Thomas was the typical grandfather—gray hair with facial features that looked as if he was meant to be that particular age his entire life. Today was Saturday Revival Celebration at Mt. Pleasant, and she'd forgotten.

"You sick?" Thomas asked, trying to see her face under her disheveled hair.

"No. Maybe. I don't know," she answered in one muddled sentence. She didn't want her grandfather to worry, but she

47

didn't feel okay. Gracie wondered if there was a medical term for just being in a rotten mood. Several terms came to mind, none medical and none appropriate.

"Maybe some spiced apple cider would help?" Thomas offered.

Gracie ignored him and leaned into the refrigerator. No juice. Only a taste of milk left in the jar. She drank it and absentmindedly put the empty jar back in the refrigerator. That left water or the stiff coffee her grandfather made. "Figures," Gracie mumbled.

"You going to church?" she asked her grandfather.

"You not? Everybody will be asking about you."

"Remember? I don't feel good," she returned with a pout, hoping for a grandfather-sized portion of sympathy.

And she got it. "Curl up on the couch." He rummaged through the refrigerator with no luck. "Gotta get you some spiced cider."

Marilee had believed spiced cider fixed all ailments: headache, sore throat, back pain, you name it. Gracie suspected they were both thinking the same thing but neither saying it. *If Marilee had still been with them, there would have been spiced cider in the house.*

"Some coffee make you feel better?" He reached for the pot and poured a cup before she could say no.

Gracie was sure that later she would regret not going to the revival. Pastor Ted's messages always spoke straight to her, so

48

often giving her strength through another week, but she wasn't in the mood for idle chitchat about the weather, as if it really mattered. They didn't know how it felt to have the memories—the joyful ones battling against the frightful ones, each replaying in snippets, and both resulting in equal pain. Her mind was never at peace, not when she was awake—or asleep.

After Thomas left, Gracie rested in a hot bath until it turned cool and was no longer soothing. She pulled on a pair of faded overalls and an old T-shirt. Her grandmother's voice played in her mind, "Ladies wear dresses." For a moment she considered her grandmother's disapproval, but she continued tugging and clasping her overall straps and reached for her sneakers. She combed through her wet hair and stepped outside meeting the drizzling rain without hesitation.

*   *   *

Cars wrapped around the parking lot of the grocery store the same way a load of busheled ripe peaches drew a crowd, yet as Kage scurried inside, there were no customers. The sound of the congregation singing *Amazing Grace* filled Franklin Grocery's parking lot, along with the vehicles. Kage's washed-out jeans suctioned to his legs and his scuffed boots sang a consistent squish-squash rhythm. Though soaked, Kage was pleased to be working, as the majority of businesses were closed.

"You couldn't catch a ride in with Gene?" Aaron called as Kage stepped through the door. Erma Franklin's nephew, Aaron, sat behind the register working a crossword puzzle.

49

"Naw, he's tied up with a new born calf." Kage shook like a wet dog.

"He's missing the revival?"

"Yeah, so?"

"Ain't like Gene to miss the revival."

"Why do they schedule it on a Saturday anyway? If you ask me, he wastes too many Sundays just sitting around reading, and then he's out of bed before daylight Monday morning like we've got more than we can get done," Kage ranted.

"Gene likes the Word." Aaron adjusted his glasses and made conversation as if he knew something about everything.

"Yep, guess so," Kage agreed. "Once Gene sat at the table with his eyes closed and his head bowed so long I thought he'd expired."

One Sunday Gene asked if Kage believed in God. He had shrugged; he never read the Bible at the orphanage—the print too small, the words too big. Thinking of Gene reading his Bible reminded him of the orphanage lady who read Bible stories to him—not Maureen, the mean one with the big hands, but the one who was full of hugs. Kage couldn't remember her face or her name, but he could remember feeling his arms wrapped around her tiny frame. She was the one who taught him right from wrong as she rocked him, whispering in his ear that he was a good boy until he could no longer hold his eyes open. Then her name came to him—Lady. Kage realized now that it was probably spelled Lattie, but as a boy she'd been his

50

"Lady." She made rounds each night and said prayers with the children.

Prayer hadn't worked for him. He prayed as a little boy for his father to come back and later he prayed for a new family—any family to love him. He'd struck out on both accounts. *So why bother?*

Just then the bell on the door clanked as the first customer entered. She walked across the front of the aisles reading the handwritten signs hanging from the ceiling.

"Hi," Aaron called out and waved. The girl returned a strained smile and brushed away the raindrops from her cheeks.

"Can I help you, Gracie?" Aaron called from the stool behind the register.

She replied, "No, just grabbing a few things."

Aaron went on, "So how about this year's revival? It looks like a full house."

Gracie acknowledged Aaron but remained focused on her shopping list.

He persisted, "I know most of the businesses in town close for the annual Saturday Revival Celebration, but Aunt Erma expects it to be one of our busiest days when service lets out."

Walking down the condiment aisle, she didn't respond. Aaron, not getting the hint or just eager to have a customer, continued, "Before you know it, you'll have Swirly's open on Celebration Saturday."

She kept her distance, yet spoke over her shoulder. "Nope, not us."

As if he did not get it, Aaron leaned forward and elevated his voice so she could still hear him as she picked up a jug of apple cider at the other end of the store. "Yep, heard your grandfather was quite vocal on the subject last year when the gas station didn't close. Aunt Erma heard how much they made though, and here we are!" Aaron extended his hands presenting the result.

"We got a threat when we first announced we'd be open," he added. "Can't remember who Aunt Erma said it was from, but the note said the devil was going to close this place down. It said the only businesses that would stay open on Celebration Saturday had to be dealing in 'illegal infringements' of some kind. Whoever it was called the sheriff on us. The sheriff came in apologizing, but he still looked this place up and down," Aaron paused. Gracie didn't respond.

"Aunt Erma hollered him right outta here. I'd suspected she was sweet on him, but she surely ain't no more. Mention that man's name, and Aunt Erma goes into a fit," Aaron chuckled. "You need help finding anything?"

"Nope," she answered.

Aaron went on, "Aunt Erma's at church. She's started going real regular you know. She bought a new Bible and everything. Mom's excited she's taken interest after all these years. And she swears it ain't just because someone left that note saying Aunt

Erma was a devil worshiper. That's crazy! Who in this town would do that? Aunt Erma knows everyone, and they are all as friendly to her as a cat that rubs on your leg every time you come near."

Kage knew what Erma had interest in, and he was pretty sure that if Pastor Ted weren't a holy man, she'd be rubbing on his leg like a friendly cat. He'd witnessed Erma scurry about the store to dust near him.

As Gracie rounded the first aisle, carrying a grocery basket, Kage hadn't moved quickly enough, and he was caught—caught staring at her. He felt his face redden as he turned away and awkwardly began rearranging the canned vegetables.

He'd wanted a glimpse of her face. He wanted to know if what he saw in her eyes was what he heard in her voice. He couldn't put his finger on it, but it was familiar to him. Those pretty eyes he had seen at the ice cream shop were angry. Not particularly at Aaron's one-sided conversation but at the world; the kind of anger he had felt more than once—a hostile anger that consumes.

Then all of a sudden Kage felt sick; his stomach burned. It occurred to him that she assumed he was staring because of her arm. He supposed many people stared, especially strangers. Kage, angry with himself, tried to make eye contact with her just to share a smile. But she didn't look up, not once.

*   *   *

"How was Celebration Saturday?" Gracie asked her grandfather as he poured two cups of hot cider.

"Everyone asked about you," he answered, blowing on the steam rising from his mug. "Ben was there, in his dress blues. Hardly recognized him."

Ben Franklin, Erma's younger brother, joined the military the day after high school graduation. It had been John F. Kennedy's words that convinced him: *Ask not what your country can do for you, but what you can do for your country.*

Gracie had predicted that with a name like Ben Franklin he'd do great things.

"Do you think you'll feel like going to church service in the morning?"

Gracie nodded. "The cider helps."

"Glad you're feeling better. If I'd been here, I wouldn't have let you walk in the rain to the store when you aren't feeling good."

"Just tired, I guess."

Thomas topped off her cup of cider. "Maybe more warm cider will help you sleep."

Gracie, though tired, didn't want to sleep. She remembered telling her grandmother once that when her eyes closed the monsters came out.

Chapter 6

Kage picked up his pace when he saw Gracie lock Swirly's and place the keys in her overcoat pocket. She tightened its hood around her face and wrapped a lavender scarf around her neck, covering her mouth and nose, so only her eyes escaped. The trees were no longer full of color. With the flip of the calendar to November, the leaves had disappeared with the winds, and the evening air felt brisk.

"You closing early tonight?" Kage asked.

Gracie jumped. "Oh, sorry."

"Didn't mean to scare you."

"That's okay. Did you want some ice cream?"

"Kind of." He shrugged his shoulders. Then he couldn't think of another thing to say. Even though the evening had turned cold, he felt his hands sweating. He shoved them deeper into his pockets.

Drawing her shop keys out of her pocket, Gracie started to open Swirly's front door. "When it's slow, we sometimes close early."

Kage stepped forward. "No, no ... I'll be fine." He shifted his weight from one foot to the other. He remembered how he'd been caught staring at her at Franklin's Grocery.

Gracie confirmed his fear. "You look familiar. How do I know you?"

Deciding to go with a roundabout answer, he hedged, "I'm working for Gene, you know the Carters? I'm trying to make a little money to get to Louisville and see my sister soon, hopefully." Kage felt odd mentioning his oldest sister Pearl as if they were family when he had never even met her.

Gracie stared at him for a second. "Maybe," she said irresolutely as if trying to remember. "You were the one who didn't get any ice cream?"

Kage pulled his hands from his jeans pockets, wrenched them twice and then stuffed them into his coat pockets. "Yes, but I'm sure it's good ice cream. In fact, Gene has convinced me I have to try the Chocolate Swirl before I head off." Kage straightened his back, rising an inch in height and edged a step back, not sure how to read Gracie's reception.

She took a step away from Kage. "Chocolate Swirl is our most popular flavor." Her disengaged tone made him feel unwelcomed.

"No problem. I can always stop in with Gene sometime and try it. Sorry to be a bother." He waved from his wrist and turned in the opposite direction, toward town where he had no purpose but to flee.

He was about three steps in the other direction when Gracie called, "I remember. I saw you at the grocery Saturday."

Kage stopped in his tracks, not sure if he should try to convince her she was confused and that it couldn't have been him or just say he was sorry. He paused, waiting to see if she would say anything else. She did.

"You must think I'm a real grouch. I really shouldn't have been so mean to Aaron. He just always talks to me the entire time I'm in the store. Once when he was stocking the shelves, he followed me around every aisle talking about ... oh, I can't remember." She pulled her scarf down past her chin exposing her face.

Kage, still three steps away, didn't move to close the gap between them.

Gracie continued, "Aaron's a nice guy, and I know he means no harm. His mother and his Aunt Erma are the same way, you know. The 'Friendly Franklins', they are referred to in kind-like humor. But I just wasn't in the mood to go along with all the talk."

Kage nodded his head, still not sure what she might be thinking of him, but at least he didn't drive her crazy with a bunch of idle chitchat. He was having more of a problem just making conversation.

"I didn't think you were a grouch. You just looked a little angry," Kage said, still tentative.

"Oh, I wasn't angry," she insisted, then paused and grimaced.

57

Kage felt his blood pressure rise. Had he offended her?

"Humm, I guess I was, but ... well, I mean I wasn't angry at anyone. I feel better today." She smiled and extended her left hand, "I'm Gracie." She stepped toward him.

Kage's broad shoulders eased, and he closed the distance between them and took her hand, "I'm Kage."

"Nice to meet you." Gracie's words came out in a shiver.

"You don't have to walk home every day, do you?"

"No, my grandfather has the car for a doctor's appointment in Hartington," Gracie shuddered. "Are you headed to town on foot at this hour?" Gracie tipped her head in the direction Kage had headed earlier.

Caught off guard, he tried to come up with another answer besides the fact that he just walked forty-five minutes for ice cream in forty-degree weather. He replied, "Just sightseeing. Maybe I'll stumble on some gold, or treasure, or whatever."

"You believe that silliness?" Gracie squinted her eyes. "Do you? You know no one from around here believes it. Sure, they talk about it, but only a few out-of-towners ever thought it could be true. It's just a silly rumor ..."

Kage interrupted, appreciating Gracie's lighthearted conversation, "I never figured there to be treasure. If there was treasure, with my luck I'd never find it, if it was right under my feet." Kage felt the muscles in his face relax, hoping she was welcoming the company. "But Willy is ready to dig for it. He thinks it might be in that old well." He pointed past Swirly's toward the railroad.

"I can't tell you how many people have said that. You'd think someone would've torn that thing apart, if it was true."

"Well, Willy might be your man." Kage was now by her side, and he began walking with her in the direction Gracie led.

"I don't think Willy's anybody's man. Why are you staying with those two? I mean, I know they are nice and all, but well ..." Gracie didn't finish.

"It works for me, I guess. I just need a place to stay while I make money for the road. They aren't so bad. Gene speaks rarely, though Willy's only quiet when required. Willy's conversations alternate from treasure to moonshine and then back again."

"That sounds like Willy."

"Gene has good taste when it comes to ice cream, though I've only had a sample of the peppermint flavor. I'm sure it's all good," Kage contributed, pleased to see her return his smile before she pulled her scarf over her mouth and nose again.

"Folks don't take too kindly to strangers around here, do they?" Kage inquired.

"That's because a lot of people came for selfish reasons and caused trouble. My granddaddy remembers going to bed one night and waking up to strangers everywhere, poking around. Even now, visitors come to the *Treasure Festival* most wanting nothing more than cotton candy and a couple of painted rocks. They just aren't trusted by lots of folks around here."

"So, do I look like the treasure hunting type?"

"No, you look like the 'pass on ice cream on a hot day but come to buy a scoop on a cold evening' kind of guy."

"Whew. That's better than looking like a Willy-wanna-be."

Gracie smirked, and Kage relaxed into their even, easy stride.

*   *   *

As Gracie walked next to Kage and listened to him talk about Willy and his recent treasure antics, she watched him closely. She didn't remember his face from the grocery the other day, but she had noticed that his arms looked strong. As dusk set in, the thought crossed her mind once more, and this time she wondered what it would be like to be held in those arms.

In the escaping twilight, she concluded that he was handsome. It was not just one thing. It was the slight dimple that flared, even when his lips were closed. It was the tranquil sound in his voice, mixed with the way his eyes shifted when he spoke. Thanks to a full moon, there was just enough light that she could see his lashes when he blinked and the slightest shadow of a scar above one eyebrow.

As she listened to Kage talk, awkwardly moving his hands from the pockets of his jeans to his jacket pockets and back again, Gracie felt her countenance transform. She pursed her lips, as she recognized an unsuspecting smile on her face.

*   *   *

When her grandfather returned home, Gracie could tell he was behaving peculiarly. She wondered if someone told him that a boy had walked her home. He carried in a grocery bag from Franklin's. Aaron might have seen her with Kage as they passed the grocery, and it was in Aaron's genes to gossip. *Would her grandfather ask her about it? Would he be upset if she kept a secret from him? Could he read it all over her face? And why did she want to keep it a secret? Because he was a stranger to Ridgewood? Because it was a boy?* All kinds of thoughts raced through her mind, but none of her thoughts were to ask about her grandfather's doctor appointment.

*   *   *

"Need a ride?" The man in the truck slowed as Kage walked past the gas station headed toward Gene's.

"Sure, that'd be great." Kage opened the passenger's door and got in. Sawdust covered the seats and dashboard. Kage coughed and leaned toward the open window for a fresh breath of air.

"Name's Chippy." The man reached over to shake Kage's hand.

"Kage."

"You're the boy working for Gene, right? You can roll up that window if you're cold."

"Yeah. I don't mind the breeze. Thanks for the ride."

"Gene told me he had another hand. I saw you with him the other day when I was passing Swirly's. You here to stay for a while?"

"No, don't plan on it."

"Where you off to next?"

"Louisville."

"Nice city. Took my wife, Geraldine, to the Kentucky Derby last year. First time I'd ever been to Churchill Downs. You ever been?

"No."

"Well, we had a big time. She grew up in Cincinnati and went a lot with her family. You got family?"

"Nope."

"Well, her family was quite well off. I am a lucky man to have turned her head. After the war, I was determined I wasn't going back to millin'. We own the wood mill over there," Chippy pointed as he passed. "I grew up with splinters in my fingers and sawdust flakes in my ears. I thought since I'd survived the Battle of Midway, I could do anything. I headed to Louisville. You been to Louisville before?"

"Uh uh."

"Met my wife there at a dance hall. I didn't know how to dance and had no business being there but that's where everyone seemed to go on the weekends. She showed me a couple steps, and I picked it up purdy fast. You do any dancing?"

"Never have."

"We won a few contests. If I hadn't been able to shake a leg, doubt I would've had a chance with her. Won big at the Kentucky Derby last year too. I bet Northern Dancer to win because my wife grew up in Ohio and she loves to dance. That horse won the Derby and then went on to win the Preakness. Did you know that?"

"Didn't know that."

"Enough about me. Tell me about you, son."

"My story isn't much to tell."

"Oh, everyone's got something. Where you from?"

"Thistle Creek. Carriage Hill. Doesn't matter."

"Why don't it matter?"

"I left at twelve and been on my own since."

"Ain't easy, is it?"

Kage didn't answer.

"I spent my money like there was no tomorrow. I was young and running, to tell you the truth. I was running from what I'd seen and done in that war and running from Ridgewood which didn't seem to fit anymore. That lifestyle broke me, and I ended up desperate for work and took a job at Louisville Lumber. You look strong. What kinda work have you done?"

"Anything I can find."

"Ever worked with wood?"

"Chopped a bunch."

"My wife tells me the reason I think she's so purdy is because I ain't seen nothing in my childhood because I was always walkin' behind the butt of a mule pulling timber."

Kage chuckled, "How'd you get back here?"

"My father got sick. My mother called and said to come home. I did. Geraldine came with me. Don't know what I'd done if she hadn't said yes. A man stuck between doing what his mama says and his love for a girl doesn't always end up paintin' a good picture."

"Wouldn't know."

"You ain't said much."

"Not a lot to share."

"Character, in my opinion, comes from livin' not talkin'. My bet is you've done some living." Chippy pulled up in front of Gene's barn. "Tell Gene and Willy 'hello' for me. I've gotta get home."

Chapter 7

Thomas was sure Gracie suspected his bad news. She kept watching him and was too helpful when he got up from his chair. Once she grabbed his drink and refilled it without him asking. She hardly sat still long enough to take two bites of supper. Nothing she said made sense to him, but nothing going through his mind made sense either.

He knew that Dr. Laben had been watching him closely, but all indications had been good—until yesterday. He had been so worried about Gracie the past couple of days that he hadn't thought about his doctor appointment. He hadn't been prepared for this kind of news. Though he understood better than most that death was a part of life, even at sixty-nine, he never thought of himself when he heard the word—not until Dr. Laben told him to start planning.

The conversation sounded too familiar. Only six years ago, he had sat in the same doctor's office and learned his wife had cancer—not the same cancer, but still that haunting word. They thought Marilee might have six months. She held on for two.

After Gracie turned in for the night, Thomas went to his room. Balancing himself with his hand, he knelt slowly beside his bed, closed his eyes and began to speak in a low voice. His conversation was not with God this time.

"What do I do?" he murmured. "Marilee, what do I do?" He felt weaker than he ever had before—his body drained of energy, drained of hope. "I don't want to tell her." He wiped a tear from his cheek and willed no more to follow, then cradled his face in calloused hands. "Marilee, I've tried so hard. How can I do this to her? How can I leave her?"

His years with Gracie ran through his mind. It had not been easy for them after Marilee's passing. They'd both grown accustomed to Marilee being in charge. Once, Marilee rearranged all the ice cream flavors without consulting Thomas, and he'd playfully moved one of the containers back to its original location mumbling lightheartedly, "Marilee, Marilee, Marilee, Marilee, life with you is but a dream." Marilee, without hesitation, lifted the ice cream tubs and placed them back in the order she had determined. Thomas had encircled her in his arms and leaned toward her ear jovially. "What will I ever do without you?" When the day came that it was just Thomas and Gracie managing Swirly's, they gradually made it work. Not just as Marilee would have done it, and certainly not as well as she had, but they made it.

Without Marilee, Gracie started doing more things independently, yet Thomas didn't know when to offer help.

Once Gracie spent half an hour getting dressed in her room with the door closed. Finally, Thomas knocked softly, and when she didn't respond he cracked the door. Gracie sat on the edge of her bed. She managed to tuck her knee against her chest, leaning forward with one shoe string in her mouth and another shoe string in her left hand. She successfully made the first bunny ear, as Marilee called it, but she struggled after that step. When she saw him, she dropped the shoestring from her mouth, released the bunny ear and slapped at her shoe in frustration.

When she leaned forward taking the shoestring in her mouth again, Thomas stepped forward and grabbed the other string. Kneeling down beside her bed, he looped it into a bunny ear. Gracie dropped the shoestring from her teeth and took the string in her left hand encircling the ear. Then together they tied her shoe.

*   *   *

"Am I too late?" Kage asked out of breath from the jog to Swirly's. He'd cut it close trying to clean up, thankful for the power of lye soap.

"Just in time!" Gracie looked up to see Kage.

"Guess I'll try the Chocolate Swirl," Kage announced.

"Hate to disappoint you, but our ice cream maker broke again. Granddaddy took it to get it fixed. No Chocolate Swirl left, sorry."

"I can live with that, but beware: Gene has the cattle trailer ready to load in the morning, and I'm not sure he'll like that news."

"Well, Granddaddy hopes it's something easy to fix. So, what flavor would you like to taste?"

"You pick for me," Kage said.

"Okay, this is Peppermint Pretty. It's almost gone," Gracie lifted the ice cream container from the case and set it on the counter. Placing pressure against it with her right arm and chest, she tried to steady it as she scraped the spoon along the bottom of the container with her left hand.

"Here ..." Kage reached across the counter and held it firm for her.

"Thanks," Gracie offered him the taste.

"That is good! I think that's the one your grandfather offered me when I first come to town." Kage licked the spoon. "How much is a taste of every flavor?"

"Hmm ..." Gracie tilted her head to one side. "I've got an idea. If you'll help me with the closing chores, then you can have a taste of every flavor."

"Deal!"

Gracie took out two bowls. "I have to look at this stuff all day. You'd think I wouldn't like it anymore. Oh, but I do!"

"I don't see how you do it."

"We're usually busy and by the time the shop closes, I'm ready to get home,"

68

"Hard work, huh?"

"Kind of, for me," Gracie said and looked away. "Opening chores are a lot easier than closing." She moved her right arm and blushed.

Kage wanted to ask what happened but was afraid. She offered no explanation.

"Where's home for you?" Gracie asked.

Kage thought for a second and almost said he didn't have a home, but instead he simply answered, "Thistle Creek."

"Bet it's nice there."

"It's okay," Kage lied.

"Tell me about your sister." Gracie began closing duties, wiping down the counters.

Between bites of ice cream, Kage followed Gracie, helping her with whatever she asked. He told her all he knew about his sister. "She moved to Louisville to get a job at a fancy hotel there. She cleans rooms, and it pays good."

He might have asked Gracie if she had sisters or brothers, but he had noticed she stumbled at the word "sister" as if it were hard for her to say.

Instead he asked, "Do you like Ridgewood?"

Gracie shrugged. "I was born here. It's all I've ever known. I've traveled very little." She paused and added, "I like it well enough I guess."

Gracie asked lots of questions, and Kage shared with her how he'd worked in Alabama on road construction and most recently in Georgia for the Lamberts. The closing duties moved quickly, and before he knew it, she was turning out the lights and locking the door.

"I was thinking of heading to Florida for work until I decided to visit my sister." Kage walked with Gracie.

"So, you want to live in Louisville? Are you going to work at the hotel too?" She looked up at him innocently, as if he had some great, exciting life. And Kage thought, if you left out all the details, it almost sounded exciting.

"Well, it's called The Brown and isn't exactly a resort. I think you have to get closer to the ocean to call anything a resort, maybe. I still haven't been to the ocean, but I plan to someday." Hearing Gracie's interest in his life made him look at it differently.

"Oh, I want to go," Gracie chimed in, speaking over his words with girlish excitement.

And before he thought—as if he were five years old and had just found his first friend—he said, "Maybe we can go someday." He paused in shock, wondering why the portion of his brain that was crafting and censoring his every word had stopped working.

Even in the dusk as they walked, he could see Gracie's undaunted smile. She shrugged her shoulders, and simply replied, "Who knows," reacting as if he had invited her somewhere as off limits as the moon. "I'd like to go somewhere someday. Anywhere, I'm not picky."

"To see the sights?"

"Yeah." Gracie looked off in the distance. "I want to go somewhere where people don't know me. Not forever, but just a couple weeks. Where I can pretend that I'm somebody else. Live someone else's life just to see what else is out there."

"Paris?"

"Kentucky?"

"No, France ..."

"Oh, not that far. Wait, maybe ... do they wear big, frilly dresses there?

"I don't know."

"Doesn't matter. Granddaddy would have a fit! I'd never have the guts to go anyway. Do your parents worry about you?"

She asked the question he'd been asked so many times, in so many different ways. He usually answered, "Never knew my parents—orphaned at birth." From there the conversation would go in the direction it always did. He wanted Gracie to see him as a man, not as the orphan boy he felt like. Once, a guy on a construction crew in Alabama said that his orphan story would be a great line to pick up women. Kage, trying to fit in, laughed along with him. But Kage knew that careless comments came from a person looking in from the outside. It crossed his mind to avoid the subject and take the conversation in a safer direction. However, he paused too long, long enough for Gracie to take a close look at his face. They stopped walking, she waited patiently for his answer.

He stumbled over his words. "Well, I'm," he paused, "I'm ..."

"Sorry," Gracie apologized, though it was obvious she wasn't sure why.

"My parents are dead," Kage answered honestly in a quiet voice, looking at nothing but the ground. His concentration was so intense that when he closed his eyes, he pictured every pebble and twig's position resting in the road. "I never knew them. I grew up in an orphanage."

The words flipped a switch inside him. He felt reticent and dreaded the course of the conversation, sure the wistful tone of their conversation was doomed. Gracie did not respond as he had expected. It was the most peculiar thing he had ever seen from anyone.

*   *   *

In the small town of Ridgewood, Gracie had always been the only kid whose parents died tragically. If she had a dime for every time she had heard a kid say, "What happened to her?" she wouldn't need to dig for treasure. Once a boy said to her, "My mom told me that your mommy and daddy are in heaven. They died and God took them to heaven to live. I hope God doesn't take my mommy and daddy to heaven."

Gracie rarely talked about her family. Ridgewood folks were as uncomfortable with the conversation as she was, and just about everyone knew about the fire. She typically sensed if a

72

person knew her story by the expression on his face. Did Kage know?

Kage's voice had softened and become weaker as he mentioned the orphanage. Taking her hand from her pocket, she loosely grasped his elbow. She didn't think about it, she just reached out and held his arm, until he lifted his eyes. As the sunset dimmed her view, Gracie studied his face. He didn't know.

"What?" He shifted his eyes away from Gracie. She realized her intense gaze made him nervous. She kept searching his eyes.

Running his hand through his hair apprehensively, an uneasy grin appeared, and he repeated, "What?" This time he chuckled. "What are you looking at?"

"Nothing," she replied as she looped her elbow around his and placed her hand back in her coat pocket—locking their arms. Then she took a step forward with him, and in a slow, steady voice that surprised her, she said, "My parents are too."

"Are what?" Kage paused in step.

"Dead."

Linked with Kage's arm, Gracie felt that everything that had weighed on her heart, every day since she was eleven, was somehow—maybe—okay.

Chapter 8

Thomas poured the ice cream mix into a bowl behind Swirly's, hoping that birds or a stray cat might like it. The vanilla extract bottle had slipped out of his hand and emptied into the mix. He was having trouble concentrating since the news from his doctor, and his hands seemed less steady. As he wiped the counters, he tripped over the corner of the rug causing him to knock over a ten-pound bag of sugar; the grains flowed like a crystal waterfall onto the linoleum. Though his morning wasn't going well, he was glad to see Gracie smiling again.

When she saw his mess, she didn't give him a hard time about being clumsy. Instead, she grabbed the broom, humming, as she swept the sugar into a mound. He stood against the door-facing and listened, hoping to hold on to that sound forever.

*　　*　　*

Gracie found herself doing what she had never imagined she would ever do. She was stretched on her tippy-toes to see out Swirly's front window, hoping that Gene Carter was craving Chocolate Swirl so that she might see Kage again. Their goodbye had been short at her front door. He'd walked her all the way home, neither of them acknowledging when they passed his turnoff toward Gene's.

She wondered what Kage thought about her arm, yet she had been relieved when he didn't ask. In all the years, no adult had ever asked her. It was only children, whose parents quickly reprimanded them.

Gene did stop by for ice cream, but he was alone. Gracie wanted to ask him about Kage but didn't, because her grandfather was there and because she was finding these new feelings confusing. She worried that if she admitted they existed, the feelings might disappear as suddenly as they had come.

As Gracie scooped his Chocolate Swirl, she made the scoop larger than usual. Maybe as a thank you for giving Kage a home, or whatever. Strange thoughts were tumbling in her head. Though Gene hadn't left her a tip in years, he pulled a tightly rolled dollar bill from his pocket and tossed it on the counter. Gracie gasped and reached out to hand it back, sure that he wasn't serious. Ignoring her gesture, Gene clicked and smiled his way out the door.

She caught a glimpse of her reflection in the tarnished mirror hanging on the wall. She felt different. Did she look different? She tilted her head in one direction and softly touched the ends of her hair with her left hand. Then she tilted her head in the other direction.

"You're beautiful, Gracie," her grandfather whispered as he passed. Color flooded Gracie's cheeks; she felt embarrassed she'd been caught starring at herself, yet she wondered if she'd ever hear someone else, maybe Kage, say words like those to her.

*   *   *

"Can I borrow the truck?" Kage asked Gene.

Gene didn't say a word at first, which was common. He wasn't hard of hearing, just slow to respond.

"Why you need it?" Gene finally answered, paying more attention to dicing sweet potatoes for a pie than to Kage.

"To run a few errands."

"Right now?" Gene quizzed.

"Yes, sir. I'll be careful with it, promise."

"Hum?"

"I'll pay for the gas."

"Hum?"

"I'm not headed far."

"Barney say you couldn't use his vehicle?"

"Didn't ask. It's fine if you say no. I'm gonna run the errands, either way."

"You be back in a couple of hours?"

"Yes, back in a few minutes and then running out again for a while—if that's okay?"

"Well ... it better be important."

"It is." Kage grabbed his jacket and dashed out, leaving the barn door standing open behind him.

A few minutes later he was at Franklin's Grocery with a bottle of Breck shampoo and a bar of Zest soap. He remembered the commercial on the radio at the orphanage years ago say, "For the first time in your life, feel really clean." Like a rite of passage, he picked up a second bar. He'd contemplated buying new clothes, but considering his limited funds, decided instead to borrow a clean shirt and pair of jeans from Barney. If Barney tried to refuse, he'd threaten to tell Gene about Barney sipping on Willy's shine in the middle of the night.

Back at Gene's, he unrolled the water hose and pulled it to the back corner of the barn. Stripping down, he poured a handful of shampoo on his hair and sudsed his body from head to toe with the Zest soap bar. Bubbles floated in the air like a swarm of bees.

*   *   *

The knock on the Howard's door startled Gracie. She couldn't remember the last time someone had visited during the evening. Thomas opened the door. "Can I help you?"

"Yes, sir. Is Gracie home?"

Gracie recognized the voice right away, even from the kitchen where she was drying her grandfather's favorite coffee cup. She jumped, and it almost slipped from her fingers.

"She is," Thomas answered, and he moved forward to block the doorway with his frail frame.

"Sir, my name is Kage. Ben ..." Kage stammered. "Benjamin Kage. I am staying with Gene and Willy Carter helping them on the farm. I'd like to see Gracie this evening if that's possible."

Gracie stepped closer, and her grandfather turned to see her. "Do you know this boy?" he asked, using a tone she'd heard only a few times before when Thomas had been disappointed with her.

"Granddaddy, he's a friend," she answered, trying to contain the smile that got loose.

He turned to look back at Kage. "Tell me about yourself, boy," Thomas required, oblivious to the cold air that flowed into the room.

"Mr. Howard, I am from Thistle Creek, and I'm working at the Carter place. I'm not sure what else you are interested in knowing, but I'll be glad to answer your questions. My intentions with Gracie are just to sit with her this evening in your home, if I may. I'd like to get to know her better."

Gracie could tell Kage was nervous, and she was concerned her grandfather would turn him away. She'd never seen him give anyone the third degree before.

Thomas reluctantly stepped aside. She instinctively placed her arms behind her back. She turned her lips in, pressing them together to stifle the emerging smile. "Thanks, granddaddy," she said as Thomas headed toward the kitchen.

His eyes still very serious, he gave her a little wink. "I'll finish up in the kitchen. Stay in the house."

Kage sat on the couch and Gracie settled in her grandfather's recliner. She would have liked to sit beside him, but she could see that her grandfather was watching.

"What did you do today?" Gracie asked.

"Cleaned out the stalls for Gene, the ones in the barn, not in his house," Kage said looking around the room. His eyes come to rest on a family picture above the fireplace. Gracie's glance followed to the portrait of Thomas, Marilee, Walton, Rebecca, and Gracie when she had just turned five years old and Sarah was a newborn.

"There are stalls in their house?" Gracie repeated.

"Yep, you know it was once a barn. Well, it still is a barn. They just added a few things that make it fit for humans, I guess. I'm surprised they wired it for lights. They still cook on a black cast iron stove, the same one they use to keep the place warm."

"Really?"

"Yep, they make their own lye soap too, which smells about as bad as the south wind from the hog barn. You ever smelled that stuff?"

Gracie pinched her nose and nodded, adding in a nasal voice, "I'm not sure I've ever seen them go into Franklin's Grocery before. Guess they drink milk straight from the cow, huh?"

"From what I can tell they got it all, all but ice cream," Kage smirked.

"Do you like it there?" Gracie asked. She could hear the clanks her grandfather made, putting away dishes.

"I work twice as hard for half the money I made in Georgia and without the luxury of a warm bath."

"What's it like at Gene and Willy's place?"

"Gene, he don't say a lot, but Willy's kind of crazy and says stuff that Gene just ignores most of the time. Gene is a good cook. I've been eating good. And this other guy, Barney, is living there too, helping out around the place. I'd rather hit him sometimes than look at him."

Gracie chuckled, "He seems sneaky."

"Yep, I don't know his story and really don't wanna," Kage concluded.

"So, your destination is Louisville?" Gracie continued thinking of questions.

"Just as soon as I make enough money to head that way."

"What's your sister's name?"

"Pearl."

"What's she like? Does she act like the big city type?"

"Don't know. Never met her."

"You've never met your sister?" Gracie blurted out, then remembered the orphanage. Thankfully, he didn't seem to mind.

"She's older than me. Well, all my brothers and sisters are older than me. But I only know two of them, Beth Ann and Ruby. We grew up at the orphanage together. I finally heard

80

from Pearl by phone after trying to find her for several months. A message I left at the hotel must have found its way to her. I hated to leave the Lamberts, the family I was staying with, but once I made contact with Pearl, I was up at dawn the next morning."

Gracie leaned forward in her chair. "What did she say when you first talked?"

"She didn't speak for a few seconds and then the next few words made no sense, until she started with so many questions I couldn't keep up."

"That's exciting," Gracie paused, listening to her grandfather fumbling around in the kitchen. "What was it like living at an orphanage? Were there a bunch of kids? Were they nice?"

"For the most part, but I didn't care for it. My sisters left when they were old enough. I was eleven, so I was ready to get out of there as soon as I could. I ran away at twelve."

"Where did you go?" Gracie was fascinated.

"Everywhere. Hitched rides a lot. I started working the day after I left for a man needing wood cut who offered me a place to stay. Can't say everyone I've run across was as nice, but it was a good start."

Gracie's grandfather sat down at the kitchen table and snapped the newspaper open. Gracie could tell from the angle he sat that he was listening.

Kage adjusted on the couch, continuing, "I don't think I'm cut out for a life like the Carter's. Not to say I couldn't do it, but it just seems like there'd be a better way."

"Granddaddy used to own a farm ..."

"Really? How much farm land?"

Gracie leaned over the arm of her chair. "Granddaddy, how much?"

Visibly startled to have been included in the conversation, Thomas picked up his cider and took a sip, acting distracted by Gracie's call for him. He held the cup in midair. "What?"

"How much farm land?" Gracie asked again and shot a glance in Kage's direction as if to say, "He is all worked up over this."

Thomas rattled the newspaper, folded it, and stood from the table. "What did you say?"

"I asked ..." Gracie drug out her sentence, as if talking slower might help. "How much farm land did we have?"

"Awh, awh," Thomas responded as if just hearing the question. "'Bout three hundred acres or so. You wanna hear the story?"

Gracie's eyes shot open curious. "Which story?"

"How you was born. That story," Thomas said, and motioned for Kage to scoot to the other end of the couch; then he took Kage's seat as if the question had been a full invitation to join them.

"Sure," Kage welcomed Thomas, shuffling over on the couch.

"Well, Walton, my son," Thomas pointed to the photo, "and Rebecca, Gracie's mother, were excited when they learned soon after they married that they'd be having a baby. But they weren't the only ones happy about the news. Me and Marilee were excited out of sorts. Especially when the little girl was born. We were crazy over the pretty thing."

Gracie blushed but was pleased her grandfather had let up on Kage a bit. He continued, "Rebecca took several years off from teaching as she was a passionate mother. Walton was doing good with the farm and had also gotten into horse breeding. That's when Marilee and I decided to leave the farming to him and open Swirly's.

"Then when Gracie's little sister was announced, they talked about adding on to the old farm house, but Rebecca convinced Walton to build a new house. When Gracie was eight, they moved into their new home just atop the hill overlooking the big valley." Thomas pointed north. "Walton had done well with the horse breeding. It *shore* was a big house too. It was a beautiful place. You could see it up on that hill from a mile away—two-story with black shutters, three window dormers upstairs, each bedroom with an incredible view of the valley. I was proud of them," Thomas reminisced.

Gracie enjoyed listening to her grandfather talk, and joined in with her own memories. "But the best part wasn't just the house, it was the backyard. The poplar trees were enormous. Sarah and me, we'd lay under them, planning how to get to the top. We played for hours running around, hiding behind and attempting to climb them until Mom called to us from the kitchen window to get down before we broke something."

Kage's eyes went back and forth between them. Thomas added, "Finally, Walton got around to hanging two swings off a couple of sturdy branches, and the girls swung as high as they could, screaming at the top of their lungs. Gracie would say, 'Granddaddy, look, I'm a bird!', 'I'm a plane!' and Sarah screamed, 'I'm flying!' Their long hair flowed behind them as they stretched out their legs and kicked back harder, making the swings go even higher.

"But as soon as they saw Walton coming ..." Thomas broke into a cough. His upper body jolted with each raspy breath that followed.

He cleared his throat and continued, "When they saw him coming, they'd stop their swings by dragging their feet and run to him, tackling him before he got to the back door. One would grab his leg tugging and the other his arm. Once he was down, they'd crawl on top of him, wrapping their arms around his neck. He'd lay on his back, facing the sky with two beautiful little girls nearly choking him with hugs. 'Me first, me first!' they'd scream, which meant it was time for him to roll over onto his hands and knees so the girls could crawl onto his back to ride the horsey. 'Go, horsey. Go.' Squeals could be heard half way down the hill.

"Each one got a turn as the horse trotted around the backyard. After several minutes the Daddy-horse started bucking and hee-hawing, until they rolled off his back onto the grass. They were sweethearts."

He slapped his knees and stood up, looking Kage straight in the eye. "Son, I might be an old man, but I ain't never been a fool." He peered at Kage and raised his eyebrows, looking over the rims of his glasses and saying nothing for several seconds.

Kage nodded his head appearing to acknowledge Thomas' unspoken message.

"This girl means more to me than anything in this world. I don't want you coming around here again without calling first."

"Yes, sir." Kage straightened his posture in response.

Thomas bent to hug Gracie as he passed, and she stood making it easier for him. He whispered to her, "Not much longer. I'm getting tired, and this boy needs to leave before I turn in tonight."

"Okay, Granddaddy." Gracie kissed him on the cheek. Thomas stepped to the front window and opened the curtains. Waddling in rhythm with a limp she hadn't noticed before, he went out onto the front porch with his paper in hand, where he could keep an eye on them.

"Enough about me," Gracie whispered, embarrassed by her grandfather's frankness. She pointed for Kage to move back to his original spot on the couch closer to her chair.

Kage scooted to where she pointed. "That's so amazing," Kage admired.

"What?"

He nodded toward the front window where Thomas sat on the porch swing in clear view. "How much he loves you," Kage paused. "Your family and that story about your dad and sister ..." he trailed off.

She watched Kage as he looked around the room—the family portrait, the coloring-crayon, cardboard-framed artwork—and when his glance returned to Gracie's his eyes were moist.

"No one ever came back." His eyes dropped.

Kage pulled out his wallet from his back pocket and reached to hand Gracie a picture. Gracie stood and glanced out the front window at her grandfather's profile. Taking the picture, she sat on the couch with Kage. The picture was of two little girls in loose cotton dresses.

"After the youngest, Ruby, turned of age, Beth Ann and Ruby left the orphanage. They didn't promise to come back. Maybe because they knew what it was like to wait." Kage made excuses for them.

"Where are they now? Do you know?"

Kage turned toward Gracie. "Don't know."

Gracie leaned slightly closer to whisper, and Kage did the same. "Tell me something else about you," Gracie encouraged not wanting him to go.

"What?" Kage asked as their eyes met.

"Something else, I don't care." She held his gaze.

"Well, my parents' home was in Carriage Hill and about a year ago I went to look it up. On one of the rides I hitched, a man told me that my father had passed away and that no one lived in the house anymore. I asked him about my older brothers and Pearl. He couldn't tell me much but that they were no longer in Carriage Hill. He said he'd heard that my oldest brother, Rupert, was killed in a logging accident."

"I'm sorry," Gracie interjected.

"I never knew him." Kage shrugged. "I spent several days sleeping in the back room of the dilapidated old house that I was born in. I imagined what it would've looked like before I was born. The weeds stood past my head. The roof had caved in on one side. Other than a few rusted chairs and a broken table, it was empty, the wallpaper blackened with mold," Kage paused, "Do you really want to hear this?"

Gracie nodded.

Kage continued, seeming to share whatever came to his mind. "The floor was weak in spots, so I took careful steps. Spider webs linked door facings to torn out light fixtures and extended across the room to an old mattress leaned up against the wall. When I touched the mattress to pull it to the floor, mice scurried out. The entire lower end of the mattress was eaten out and several mice ..."

"Oooh," Gracie grimaced and looked away.

"You don't really want to hear all this, do you?"

"Yes, but less the mice detail."

Kage chuckled. "Okay, no more mice. Are snakes okay?"

Gracie glared and shook her head.

"Got it. No, mice or snakes. How about ..."

"Finish the story!"

"Okay, okay but it's just not the same when I leave out the part about the black widow spiders."

"Definitely leave out that part, would you?"

"Boring ... okay, where was I?"

"Skip mice, snakes, spiders ... pick up at the word people. Try that."

"Okay, that works—people. I asked a few people if they knew my brothers and sister or their whereabouts. One suspected they'd gone north somewhere near the Ohio River for work. Another suggested they went south toward Alabama for logging or Florida for road construction.

"The best tip I got was from Pearl's friend at the diner. They worked the morning shift together. She said Pearl went up to Louisville to work in that large hotel with a bunch of meeting rooms for business folk. I traveled first toward Alabama and along the way I'd ask if anyone knew Adam, Cecil, or Carl. It's strange. They're just names to me. I have no idea what they look like. I imagine Adam and Carl as strong, stocky guys, maybe because of the stories my sisters told me, but I see Cecil differently. My sisters described Cecil as more like my mother. They said he was gentle and much kinder."

"Like you," Gracie suggested.

Kage shrugged. "I don't know if that's me." He then told Gracie about the man on the bus and his unplanned stay in Ridgewood.

"So that's why you're here? You jumped off a bus passing through?" Gracie was amused by his story and how he flexed his muscle as he talked about his run in. "I'll be careful not to make you mad." Gracie flexed the muscle on her left arm. "I don't think I'd have much of a chance."

"That's why you need a strong man around." Kage sat taller.

"To scare off mice?"

"Snakes and spiders ..."

Gracie smiled, yet a thought carried it away. "You know, I think a lot about what it would be like to see my family again." Gracie's voice faltered.

Keeping his voice low, he scooted a bit closer to hear her. "What happened?" Kage asked.

Gracie struggled; shaking her head, tears formed in the corners of her eyes. "I don't know why this happens." Gracie blinked several times. "I want to talk about it, but I can't."

Kage lifted his hand as if he wanted to take hers to comfort her, but instead he hesitated, after a glance toward the front window. "It's okay ..."

"Sometimes I feel much older than eighteen," Gracie confessed, keeping her voice low and slightly wavering with emotion.

"Really?" Kage listened.

"Yeah, for example, the other day I said that to an elderly lady at church; she always pinches the kid's cheeks." Gracie rolled her eyes. "The kids measure their maturity not by who takes communion but who escapes her pinches." Thinking of the lady at church, crunched over, scooting her feet toward the little ones who were running with all their might made her smile though.

"I bet Aaron got his cheeks pinched all the time."

"Funny you say that. When we were kids, he'd actually walk straight up to her with his hands clasped behind his back and turn each cheek toward her."

"I can believe that." Kage got a kick out of the image. "So, what did the lady say when you said that to her, about feeling old?"

"'Oh Gracie, you're so young,'" Gracie mocked her feeble voice. "'You have such a long life ahead of you.' Then she got distracted by a four-year-old boy trotting past and forgot all about our conversation."

"That wasn't nice."

"I was relieved the conversation ended. People act like their advice from their cozy, secure life holds the secret to moving on. When I was smaller, words and hugs built a safe haven, but it seems harder now."

"I understand. The lady at the orphanage who made rounds at night was the closest thing to a mother I guess I ever had. She'd cuddle me in her arms and say, 'God's got you, dear boy. You'll be fine.' She'd wake me in the morning and put me to bed. I got a total of five minutes a day with her. I had to share her with twenty-five other kids. She'd read to us. I liked that story about Joseph in the Bible—Old Testament I think, you know it?"

Gracie nodded, and Kage continued, "It's silly but ..." Kage paused. "Sometimes when I was a boy, I imagined I was Joseph. You know how the story goes of him and his brothers? How they sell him off? Then years later the brothers come asking him for food, but they don't know it's him. He makes them go back and get their father. Joseph's father is delighted when he learns that his boy is still alive. Then Joseph moves them all to his town where everyone respects him and holds him in high regard. I want that."

"You would be the hero."

"Yeah, I guess. I'd ask her to read me that story over and over. She'd be so pleased that I was interested in hearing the Bible story, but to me it wasn't a story. It was much more like a dream, I suppose."

"It's possible!"

Ignoring her encouragement, he shook his head and continued, "After several years I quit asking if anyone knew my family or where they might be. I was tired of the same orphan boy conversation."

Gracie slid a strand of hair behind her ear and placed her right arm in her lap, laying her hand over it, covering the scars. As she moved, Kage's eyes followed, and she tucked her arm tighter to her.

Changing the subject, he backtracked and asked, "Your grandfather always that protective of you?"

"No, he's just not used to strangers showing up on our doorstep."

"I shouldn't have stopped by?" Kage asked penitently.

"I'm glad you did," Gracie reassured him.

"Nice house." Kage commented, his finger following the pattern of the couch upholstery.

He had a way of saying things that caught her off guard—that made her life sound normal. "It is," she answered simply.

Gracie missed her sister and parents, but she didn't feel like an orphan. She had always been loved. Kage had never lived in a home like hers or with a family who loved him. Who had ever loved him?

Chapter 9

Thomas hoped for a miracle, and he prayed harder than he had in years. How was he going to tell her?

"Goodnight," Thomas called to Gracie, hearing the board creek in the floor outside his door.

Gracie leaned into her grandfather's room. "Did you like him?"

Thomas looked up. For years, even with pangs of arthritis, he'd stooped beside his bed on his knees. He now sat on its edge, head bowed. "I did."

She rubbed her hand over her arm. "We have a lot in common."

"I could tell," he said kindly. "You know, I just worry about you. I don't know anything about this boy. He's a traveler from what it sounds like."

"It's not like that exactly. He's never had the chance to have a real home," Gracie rebutted.

"I'm just saying to be careful, really careful. You're precious to me and whether his intent is pure or," he paused, trying to think of an appropriate word, "or otherwise, we know nothing about him. He could be here today and gone tomorrow, and I'd hate to see you get hurt."

Gracie nodded, "Sorry to interrupt you ..."

"Just making plans for the 'big reunion.'" He winked before dropping his head. He'd said those words to her so many times before, when she'd stepped in his room to say goodnight ... but never had they been as real as now.

*   *   *

Kage had shared more with Gracie in that visit than he'd ever shared with anyone, and he hadn't left feeling sorry for himself. Kage remembered his rules for survival and wondered about love and if it could trump them. He mumbled "Gracie Howard" under his breath just to hear the sound of her name. Had he found a friend—someone he could trust?

Kage wondered if Gracie would like him if she really knew him. He thought about telling her about the places he'd been and the things he'd seen that young eyes shouldn't know, but he didn't.

He remembered asking Lady, "What does it mean to have a tender heart? Is that a disease?"

She responded, "Oh, a tender heart means you'll be a great daddy someday and a good husband when you grow up. God loves tender hearts."

Unlike many of the lawless drifters he'd met, he battled with his conscience. He felt bad about food he'd stolen from backyard gardens during the night—Lady's voice in his head as he snuck away with his pockets stuffed and arms full. More than once, living on his own and embracing the dull anger within, he had wondered if there was anything tender left about him.

When Kage got back to Gene and Willy's place, he was surprised to see Gene awake. He had tea brewing.

"Where you been?" Gene asked.

"Just out," Kage replied.

"You ain't been causing no mischief, have ya? I don't want to go findin' out that you been causin' trouble."

"No sir, just been to see Thomas and Gracie Howard. Thanks for letting me use the truck."

"They're nice people. How you 'come acquainted with them?" He laid down the newspaper he was reading.

"I ran into Gracie a couple times, and we talked. She have any other family than her grandpa?"

He looked Kage over, pondering something. Again, Kage was reminded of the differences between Gene and Willy and wondered which he preferred. Willy put it all out there, so you knew everything about him. Gene was different. One minute there seemed to be nothing going on with him, and the next he was like this.

"What you want with her?" he asked, ignoring Kage's question.

"I like something about her. I don't know. She's pretty and I know ... well, you know ... it really doesn't bother me." Kage thought for a second before asking, "Was she born that way?"

Again, Gene ignored his question and just stared at him before speaking. "You passin' through, ain't 'cha?"

"Yes, sir. I suppose."

"Then leave the Howard girl alone. She don't need some young travelin' boy poppin' in and out of her life," Gene said, his voice sterner than Gracie's grandfather. "Don't care if you like her. You ain't no good for her. Gracie deserves a stable man, one who can offer her something." Gene took his glasses off without breaking eye contact.

"Sir, I mean no disrespect, but I don't much appreciate you suggesting that I'm not good enough for her, or anyone for that matter." Kage stiffened.

Gene continued to eye Kage closely. "You are a hard worker and that's enough for me, but you ain't got nothin' to offer a woman. You ain't got but those clothes you a wearin'.

Though Gene's point was further made by the fact that Kage couldn't even claim the clothes on his own back, he resented Gene's remark. "You don't know anything about me."

Gene continued as if Kage hadn't spoken. "You travel light, boy, because you ain't stickin' around. You ain't plannin' to stay in Ridgewood. Until a few years ago, everybody was looking to get out of Ridgewood. Now we got crazies movin' in here thinkin' theys can get rich in this town. Let me tell you

96

something. There is only one way to get rich off this land and that's to work it. And then, you still ain't gonna be any kind of rich. That's all it is, somethin' made out of nothin'. Nothin' a'tall. You oughta leave here and go 'bout your business somewheres else." Gene picked up his newspaper and turned away from Kage.

"Sir, if you think I came here as one of those crazies looking for some stupid treasure, you're wrong. I have family I'm trying to find. I might be just passin' through, but it don't mean I'd never come back. I just got a few things I have to take care of." Kage hoped Gene heard though the newspaper that separated them.

"Then go do the things you gotta do. Just don't you go hurtin' Miss Gracie," Gene said through the newspaper.

"Can you just tell me one thing? What happened to Gracie's arm? I'd just like to know."

"Did you ask her?" He put the paper down only half way so that he saw Kage over its corner.

"She's not comfortable talking about it. Gets upset easy ..."

"You think maybe that is her business to tell?"

"Yes, sir. I'd say you're right."

"Okay then." The paper rose, blocking them again.

Kage grabbed his jacket and climbed the ladder into the loft.

"I heard you talkin' to Gene downstairs," Barney said from under his covers.

"Yeah, so?" He didn't care much for Barney.

"I know what happened to that girl—the girl you's askin' 'bout." Barney sat up.

Kage narrowed his eyes. "How's it that you know?"

"I asked."

"Who'd you ask?" And without even a half second pause, Kage added, "and why?" He peered at Barney.

"I noticed it, that's all. I asked Willy, and he told me. He said she got burnt—her whole family got burnt up in a fire. All 'em dead—her mama, her papa, and her sister. She's the only one that made it outta that house alive. That's what happened." Barney looked pleased with himself.

Kage turned away and kicked his cot as far as he could to the other side of the room. Barney's voice running through his head, "burnt up ..." Kage resisted hitting him square in the eyes and knocking him from the loft with one punch. Barney's incessant mouth, showing no respect, degrading women, and using colorful language, wore on him like grain in his shoe.

Glaring at the cracks in the walls, Kage observed the bits of moonlight they cast across the room. Gene's words reverberated in his mind, and he wondered if Gene was right on all accounts. *Was he just the traveling sort? Would he always be a vagrant? Did he have anything to really offer someone?*

Kage closed his eyes and could still see the family portrait over the mantel at Gracie's house that Thomas had pointed out. He imagined the house Gracie's grandfather had described. Images played through his mind of the family he craved and had imagined so many times in the orphanage. He wondered which would be more painful, never to have had a family or to have had something so special that was taken away.

*   *   *

Gene folded the newspaper and began to unroll a dollar bill on the table. It was carefully rolled, mimicking the look of a cigarette. He'd dropped off some late season vegetables to Mrs. Laurel a few days earlier. Few people visited her because she thought her late husband was still alive. He'd just call out "bye" to Mr. Laurel, and she'd smile so pleasantly, blinking her eyes in appreciation. She'd insisted on paying him, though he tried to refuse. He'd done well to give away a couple of the rolled dollar bills she handed him at the stops he'd made that afternoon, spreading Mrs. Laurel's generosity—or more accurately not taking advantage of an overpayment from an old lady who was losing her mind. He recalled Gracie's surprise when he left her the rolled dollar bill. It had made his day to see her smile.

Gene Carter was the first to admit he didn't know much about love or anything else near the subject for that matter. His wife left him years ago. He was Kage's age when he fell in love with Olivia. She was tall, slender, and full of spunk. She could skip a rock farther across the steam than most men, yet in his arms she was as yielding as a baby rabbit. She was beautiful. Too "purdy" for him, everyone had said—and he knew it.

He remembered well the day that Olivia had left. It was late into the night before he'd accepted something was wrong. That

99

morning he'd gotten up before the sun and set out for the corn field. When he stopped in for lunch, she wasn't there, but she'd left ham and turnip greens for him on the table. He assumed she went into town with Willy's wife, Vera, as they did once a week. When supper came, they weren't home. His concern wasn't for them but instead for the time lost from the field. He made a couple of sandwiches and pointed out the ladies' evening chores for Willy to do before sundown. Gene headed back to the field. When dark came and he saw Willy walking toward the light beams of his combine in the field, he knew something was wrong.

Once inside the barn, he saw the ring. He'd missed it earlier. He hadn't been looking for it. His mind was focused on the corn in the field. Olivia's wedding ring lay beside the trash can, where she must have tossed it. When he stepped closer, he saw Vera's lying on top of the trash, resting in a broken egg shell. Willy had cried like a baby. He slobbered and mumbled all sorts of stuff. Gene cried inside. He hoped Oliva would come back. He had a phone installed and waited for it to ring. She'd always wanted one. He knew she didn't know that he had it or its number, but somehow in his mind it increased the possibilities of hearing from her again. She was in his prayers every night—still some nights even now, but she never returned.

*   *   *

"Help!" Gracie wailed, her lips pressed against the cool, cast iron door. Blood splattered the door in a pattern that resembled the dusty paw prints of the rats scurrying over her feet.

"Let me out," she pleaded. The rats multiplied and she could feel the prickles of their toes dancing across her belly and tickling her thighs.

She whimpered. "Please, please ... please, open the door."

"I hear you ..."

Gracie buried her ear against the door's frame, as if it had spoken. "What? Who's there?" She knocked and banged. "Talk to me!"

But there was nothing.

Gracie sniffed in feathers and swatted them off her face as fiercely as she'd slapped at the rats. She'd ripped her down pillow at the seams, its stuffing stuck to her skin and coasted in the air.

"Kage ..." she whispered. It had been his voice in her dream. He'd heard her cry for help. She prayed again for the nightmares to stop.

*   *   *

Thomas' mind raced, though his body stalled. Although his heart wanted to get up and go to Gracie, his body begged him not to move. Painful memories passed through his head—the picture ever-burned in his mind of the fire reaching for the heavens, the stench that remained the next day as he sifted through what was left of his son's home, and the last night he had sat by his wife's side. His thoughts tumbled and flowed, crashing into one another.

After the fire, Marilee had let him organize the ice cream flavors with no opposition. Where she used to awaken before the sun, she instead conjured excuses to stay home. On occasion Gracie and Thomas had managed to coax her out of the house but soon she would complain and insist that Thomas take her home. As soon as they got home, she'd crawl back under the covers. In that bed, Thomas had held her in his arms as she slipped away while he sang quietly, "Marilee, Marilee, Marilee, Marilee—life is but a dream." She softly mumbled along with him until her lips stilled.

Now it was just Thomas and Gracie. Years had carved Marilee's words into his mind: *Are you watching the time? Don't forget the grocery list. You've got to plan ahead, Thomas.* More than once, Thomas had thought to himself that Marilee would have been proud. He had been thinking ahead, but not thinking ahead far enough to plan for what Gracie would do after he was gone.

Chapter 10

Gene Carter didn't expect visitors at that time of night or ever. So, when he heard the car engine turn off outside the barn, he looked out the front door to see Thomas Howard walking toward him.

"Just made a pot of hot tea," Gene welcomed Thomas.

Willy, at the dinner table sharpening his pocket knife, nodded hello to Thomas who tipped his hat in return. Barney and Kage were stacking a load of maple wood logs next to the stove.

"You mind if I have a few words with you?" Thomas asked as he looked around.

"Boys, take a walk," Gene ordered.

Kage nodded "hello" at Thomas who ignored him.

"Willy, you too," Gene added.

"No," Thomas insisted, "I'm interrupting. Stay right where you are, Willy. I just need a few minutes to talk with Gene."

Gene and Thomas walked to the far side of the barn outside of Willy's earshot. "Gene, I really don't know what to say,"

Thomas started. "I hadn't planned what I was going to say. I just ..."

"Thomas, you need a favor. I'll be glad to help," Gene offered.

"I'm not sure about any favors, Gene. You got all you can handle with this here farm. You're busy, and I don't mean to take up your time. I just figure you know this Kage boy better than anyone around here. And I'm real worried about Gracie."

"He done something?" Gene asked. "Cause if he has ..."

"No, nothing but come courtin' Gracie all unannounced." Thomas fidgeted.

"I's afraid of that. He came in the other night askin' questions 'bout her. I didn't tell him none. As I see it, ain't none of his business."

"Gene, I've been to the doctor this week, and they ain't telling me good news," Thomas' words rushed out.

"Oh Thomas, I hate hearin' that."

"Well, I still ain't let it all set in yet. I haven't even talked with Gracie. Just don't know how." Thomas kept his voice low.

"Well, you got some time, don't 'cha?"

"They never really know."

"What can I do?" Gene took his glasses off and rubbed his forehead with the heel of his hand.

"Nothing, really I just always figured Gracie would be courted by someone that I knew and knew what kind of family he was from—not some stranger. That, on top of this news about my health—it just makes things tougher."

"You wanting me to send him away? I can do without him."

"No, I'm not asking you to do that. I don't know what I'm asking. Do you trust the boy? I mean, you trusting him working for you and me trusting him with Gracie are two different things. But I need to know what you know about him, and if he's done you right so far."

"Well, he's been workin' good. He follows direction and from what I can tell hasn't spent hardly a penny of what he's earned. He says he's leavin' as soon as he gets enough money to make his way to Louisville. Shouldn't be much longer."

Thomas released a long, shallow breath. "Gene, it ain't good. I know Gracie, and she's not going to take his attention lightly. She's bound to get hurt when he leaves. That's what I want, him to leave." Thomas chuckled lightly. "Crazy how timing works, ya know? I said a prayer for Gracie's future, you know, without me. I asked for someone to take care of her, but I didn't have some stranger in mind!" Thomas shook his head, peering at the floor, then lifted his eyes. "Gene, I know you believe in God ..."

"Why, yes, sir," Gene spoke up. "Just ain't in church because I got nothing better to do." He smiled, his gums shinning. "Relies on God for everything."

Thomas repeated, "Praying just felt like the right thing to do. I don't want her to be alone." Thomas paled as he spoke. "But then, come knockin' on my door was this boy. Now I know God knows best, but Gene, I didn't have a boy in mind." Thomas tilted his eyes toward Gene.

"I can make it rough on him. You know, where he wants to get out of town," Gene offered.

Thomas considered Gene's offer. "Maybe a good idea, or maybe she'd consider moving to live with my sister, Elaine, in Bellmont. It's a nice place," Thomas thought aloud.

"It is," Gene agreed. "Saw you put Elaine on the prayer list at church. She okay?"

"Yes. She's recovering from surgery on her hip after a fall. Arthritis taking its toll. Well, I really just wanted to hear what you had to say about that boy. I hate to have interrupted your evening. Gracie might get worried if she finds I've run off."

"Pleased you stopped by. Really sorry to hear about your health, Thomas. Maybe those doctors are wrong, you know."

"Not sure I'd be that lucky, but thanks, Gene. If you do find out anything on that boy, good or bad, I'd sure like to know."

"You bet I'll let you know, and me and Willy, you can bet we's gonna keep a close eye on him. He may just have to work a couple fifteen-hour days this next week or I might take him to the old creek and make him catch his supper bare-handed." Gene winked at Thomas as he let him out the front door.

*   *   *

Barney had not shut up the entire time, talking craziness about a plan to dig up gold. A "theory" he called it. Kage was pretty sure Barney didn't even know what the word theory meant, because each time he repeated it twice, stammering on the word.

Then Barney had asked about Gracie. He didn't remember her name and called her the "girl who was missin' part of her arm."

Kage cringed at the crass remark. "She's got a name. It's Gracie."

"You seein' that girl?" Barney asked.

"Maybe, we talk some."

"You think she's pretty?" Barney pressed on.

"I do," Kage answered, aggravation evident.

"Alright then."

"Alright then, what?"

"Alright then, I won't go callin' on her."

Had he not been on edge because of Gracie's grandfather's visit, Kage might have taken Barney's ignorance more lightly. "You best not say a word to Gracie. She's a nice girl, not the sort I've seen you with."

"You don't know my sort. I've been known to take up with some mighty fine women, much finer than a one-armed girl," Barney called back, just as Gene opened the front door to let Thomas out.

Barney, at least smart enough to know he'd been caught, blushed so that his face matched his hair.

Kage, on impulse, stepped forward. "Mr. Howard, can I have a word with you? I'll walk your way so as not to hold you up."

Kage didn't wait for an answer and fell in step beside him. "I know you don't know anything about me, and I'm sure you have lots of questions about what would bring me to this town and why I'd want to get to know your granddaughter."

Thomas didn't look at Kage. "Yes, those are a few among the questions I have."

"Well, ask me any questions, sir. Anything, and I'll answer you honest, promise," Kage said, eager to have any chance to sway Thomas' opinion of him.

"Why Gracie? You got to be older than her. How old are you, boy?"

"I'm nineteen, just turned it. Ask me the question you're really thinking. Go ahead, ask me again, 'why Gracie?'" Kage pressed, surprised at his boldness.

"Ok, why Gracie?"

"Because there's something about her. I don't know what it means, not like you do. I don't know all her pain. But I know about disappointment. I think we understand something about each other." Kage's words rushed out so fast he found himself out of breath.

"Disappointment?" Keeping his step, Thomas turned to look at Kage for the first time. "'Disappointment' is when you don't get the Christmas present you wanted. That's disappointment. Try devastation! Do you have any idea what that girl has lived through? Do you have any idea what she and I have endured together? You think you see hurt and pain in her eyes. You bet, and there is nothing you or I can do to make it better. You think you're going to waltz into this town and fix all her pain, like some kind of miracle man who hasn't any idea where he's going to be living two weeks from now." Thomas grabbed the car door handle.

Kage opened his mouth to rebut but no words came out. Thomas jerked open the car door, crunched into the driver's seat, started the engine and left Kage in a swirl of dust.

*   *   *

Gracie pulled the curtain back when she heard the old Chevy pull up. She'd gotten out of bed when she heard the car start up earlier and watched as he drove away. Thomas took a minute to get out of the car and several more to get to the door. She noticed that he moved more slowly than he had a year ago, or yesterday for that matter. His face looked pallid. Even the cool air hadn't added the usual color to his cheeks.

"Are you okay, Granddaddy?"

Her grandfather looked up. His creased forehead and troubled eyes scared her.

"What's wrong?" Gracie became anxious. "What's happened?"

He reached both arms out to her. "Peppermint ..."

"Please tell me what's wrong," Gracie pleaded, falling into his embrace.

"I'm sick, Gracie. The doctor ..." Thomas stammered. He dropped his head.

"You're sick?" Gracie repeated, her voice trembling.

"Gracie, we're going to do all we can, but I'm an old man." Thomas made a weak attempt to encourage her.

"Granddaddy ..." Gracie's voice broke. She pulled away and wrapped her arms around her waist, rocking and pressing against her stomach.

"Gracie," Thomas reached out and pulled her close again. He seemed to be searching for his words.

Gracie kept rocking, now in his arms, a dull moan escaped.

*   *   *

Gracie tiptoed past her grandfather's door. Every few steps the floor creaked and she paused to listen, checking to see if her grandfather stirred. There were no nightmares. Gracie couldn't sleep. Her swollen eyes felt like anchors. She was thankful for the full moon outside showing through the windows, giving enough light to make her way to the front door. She pulled on her coat and stepped outside. She knew if she started the car her grandfather would waken, so she began walking.

*   *   *

Barney slowed his vehicle edging toward the lady walking on the side of the road. He knew it was a woman because her long hair flowed from under the toboggan. As he slowed, she kept a solid pace, her head down and her arms folded. He rolled down his window. "You okay, miss?"

Barney recognized Gracie as she nodded. "Where you goin' at this hour? You headed to see Kage?" Barney asked.

"Just out for a walk."

Barney ignored the unwelcoming shift of her eyes. "You want a ride?"

"No, thanks."

"It ain't smart to be walkin' at this hour. Only drunks and crazies out, you know."

Gracie didn't answer.

"So, you drunk or crazy?" Barney asked still slowly cruising beside Gracie.

"You both?" Gracie snapped only looking at him for a second.

Barney laughed, "A little of both, but ain't gonna hurt 'cha. Kage is stronger than me."

"Well I'm fine walking, if you don't mind." She wrapped her arms tighter around herself.

"I can sneak Kage out if ya want. You know, without Gene or Willy knowin'."

For the first time since Barney pulled up, Gracie looked interested in what he had to say. "You'd do that?"

"Yep, I do what I can for love." Barney let out a howl like a coyote. Somewhere from the distance, a coyote answered.

Gracie was not amused by Barney as he revved his engine and sped off toward the Carter's.

*   *   *

Kage pounded his fist against the cot and groaned as Barney's car backfired outside the barn. Thoughts of Thomas had kept

111

him awake for the first few hours, and thoughts of Gracie had bombarded his mind since midnight.

Barney made his way up the stairs, walking with a light step, unlike his usual careless stomping and shuffling. Kage pulled his pillow over his head.

"Kage," Barney hissed a whisper.

Kage pressed the pillow tighter against his ear.

"Kage!" Barney tugged on the pillow.

"You drunk, Barney? Go to sleep," Kage huffed, although muffled by the pillow.

Barney jiggled Kage's shoulder.

Kage jerked the pillow from his face. "What ... do you want?" Kage screeched through clenched teeth.

Stepping back, Barney almost lost his balance as he tripped over one of Kage's boots. "I's just tellin' you that girl you seein' is on her way here. I's saw her when I was driven' here."

Kage sat up. "Gracie's? Coming here? Outside the barn?"

"Yep." Kage could make out the big, silly smile on Barney's face thanks to the moonlight seeping in through the wooden plank above his cot. "Outside to see you."

Kage was on his feet in seconds. He pulled a T-shirt over his head and stuffed his feet in his boots. "She okay?" He stepped around Barney.

"Guess so. Found her walking this way," Barney said keeping his voice unusually quiet.

Not remembering where he left his jacket, Kage threw on a flannel shirt and scurried down the ladder from the loft. For the first time he was thankful for the moonlight seeping through the cracks of the barn so he could move so quickly. "Gracie," he whispered as he stepped around the corner of the barn and walked toward the shed. He saw her all bundled up, next to the wood pile.

Gracie ran to him and threw herself against him. "My granddaddy ..." she muttered, muffled against Kage's flannel shirt, "he's sick."

Kage didn't know what to say to stop her tears, so he wrapped her more tightly in his arms as she sobbed. Rubbing his hand through the back of her hair, he closed his fingers at the nape of her neck caressing the soft strands. She was delicate in his arms, fragile. "I've got you," he heard himself say. "I've got you." Gracie needed him; he was needed.

He lifted her chin and brushed the tears from her cheeks in the moonlight. Drawn in by her dark eyes, Kage leaned forward and hesitated. Then their lips met softly.

Chapter 11

Gene worked Kage all day and into the late hours each night for the next five days. Kage was suspicious the first night but was sure Gene had ulterior motives the second night when Gene sent him out after dinner to clean the cobwebs from the ceilings of two barns that were barely standing—waiting for the wind to blow them down.

"You missed that web and that one." Gene pointed to spider webs that Kage thought had to be older than Gene and were out of the reach of his ladder.

Kage challenged, "Why does it much matter to the hogs if they got spider webs around them? They ain't particular."

Gene didn't respond. He just pointed to several more spider webs and walked out.

Working with a fading lantern and numb fingers, Kage balanced on the top step of the 5-foot ladder and stretched, swatting the cobwebs with a broom. With only ill-fated spiders to keep him company, he reflected on the past few weeks, on meeting Gracie, and on what it felt like to hold her. "So, this is what good memories are like," Kage thought.

*   *   *

"Good to see you." Gracie greeted Kage as he stepped through the front door. He leaned toward her, hesitated and touched his nose to hers but pulled away when he caught a glimpse of Thomas in the kitchen. Thomas' spoon clanked in the coffee cup like a timer clicking.

Earlier that day, when Gene stopped at Swirly's, Kage asked Thomas if he could stop by to see Gracie. Thomas had reluctantly agreed.

"It's okay," she encouraged wanting Kage to feel comfortable in their home, despite her grandfather's antics.

"I'm not sure it is. I think Gene's working me overtime so I can't see you," he said, lowering his voice. "I had to convince him I had hours at the grocery tonight to get away," Kage whispered.

"Really?" She heard the clanking fade into the distance, indicating her grandfather may have stepped into a back room of the house for a minute.

"Listen, I'll have enough money by the end of the week to go to Louisville to see my sister."

Gracie's eyes sombered instantly. "Oh."

"But you could come with me?"

"No," she answered automatically. She hadn't lived like he had, chasing after something. Instead, she lived to hold on to all she had.

"I thought you'd say that. I mean, I didn't expect you to leave your grandfather."

She took his hand and pulled him toward the couch to sit. "I don't know you well enough to follow you around the world."

"Around the world? It's Louisville!" Kage exclaimed.

Gracie pulled back from him.

"Sorry," he apologized, scooting closer to her.

Gracie took a deep breath. "Well, what I meant was," she held her voice firm, "is that, I can't just leave my grandfather who's always been here for me. I can't run off—" she glanced over her shoulder then lowered her voice, "with you. I haven't lived a life like you, heading off whenever I get the urge and staying with strangers. I can't do that."

Kage pressed on, "Not even for a week?"

"No," Gracie repeated, shocked that he thought such a request was of any possibility.

"I understand ..."

"Will you come back?" Gracie asked, afraid to hear the answer.

"I might. I mean, look around. There ain't much here for me. I don't plan on living with Gene and Willy Carter forever."

Gracie blinked several times. She nodded, "You're right, I guess."

*   *   *

Gracie made hot cider for Thomas each morning, tip-toed into his room and set it on his nightstand. Most mornings she'd returned to find it untouched, but this morning Gracie was relieved to hear her grandfather stirring around in his room.

The hardwood floor stung her bare feet as she groped for her slippers under the bed. Frigid morning air always made her feel lazy. Returning to the kitchen, she added an extra pinch of cinnamon to her hot cider. She considered not opening the shop again today. Word spread about Thomas' illness since Swirly's hadn't kept regular hours.

"Want a fresh cup?" she asked her grandfather as he hobbled into the kitchen, the hairs on his head fuller of life than his dragging feet.

He nodded and reached out for the steaming mug she'd just made for herself. She poured herself another. As he sipped, he spilled the warm cider down his sleeve. His arm jerked to life, as he growled.

Gracie handed him a dishtowel and led him to the table.

"You remind me of Marilee," he scoffed.

"Good," Gracie teased, "then I'm doing something right."

"I'm ready to go back to work." Thomas took a second stab at sipping his cider.

"Let's stay home. Another day's rest would be good for you— and me."

"Nah. Gotta get busy."

"Nope. I'm staying right here with you." Gracie pulled a chair up beside him at the kitchen table, and she laid her head on his shoulder.

Thomas kicked his feet under the table, his right house shoe shooting out to the center of the kitchen floor. "I'm going. I feel better today. In fact, I'm pretty sure I look good too," Thomas said, raising his chin assertively.

Gracie chuckled at her grandfather, glad to see some spirit. He hurried to his room. She heard clothes hangers clanking in his closet.

"Almost ready," Thomas finally called out. Gracie stood from the kitchen table, sliding her chair under and also straightening the other chairs around the table, just as her grandmother would've done.

Entering Thomas' room, Gracie frowned. "Will you let me do that?" she insisted as he bent over to put on his work shoes.

He had managed to get on his clothes and socks, but all the blood had rushed to his head and several beads of sweat ran down his cheek.

"Let me do that." She wrestled with him to hand over his shoe.

"I can put on my own shoe," Thomas wheezed.

Slipping the shoe on his foot, Gracie pulled one string with her teeth and the other with her hand, tightening it on his foot. Thomas shook his foot, and Gracie's head bounced with each tug. Through her clenched teeth, she mumbled, "Would you stop?"

Thomas jerked his foot away from Gracie, and she watched as his feeble hands took hold of the strings and, twice, he failed at securing the knot.

"Dag blasted!" Thomas sat staring at his shoe—defeated.

Gracie's heart broke. Standing up, she put her arms around her grandfather.

"I'd rather not argue right now, if you don't mind," he glared at her resisting defeat.

She knew his stubborn side, but she was too much like her grandmother to let him win.

Thomas grabbed the shoe strings again. Gracie cautiously took his hand and squeezed it. She looped the string and made a bunny ear. He meekly smiled, nodding, and took the other string to loop it around. Together they tied his shoe.

Thomas kept his shoes on but stayed home after all.

"Okay, but promise me you'll go in tomorrow." Thomas insisted. And Gracie agreed.

*　　　*　　　*

Kage worked from daylight until dark for Gene until he didn't remember what it felt like to eat a full meal anymore. He climbed the rickety ladder and swatted at another set of cobwebs with his broom as Gene opened the door and looked in to check on him.

"You got the trailer cleaned yet?" Gene cracked the barn door open, stepped in and turned a circle counting the remaining spider webs.

"Trailer? No!" Kage turned so quickly on the ladder that he almost lost his balance.

"Yeah, I told you to clean out the trailer. We's loadin' cattle for auction in the morning."

"No, sir, you didn't. Willy and Barney always do that. What do you have them doing?"

"I don't care for your tone, boy. When I ask you to do somethin', I expect it to be done."

"Sir, you told me to do no such thing. I've been doing the work of three people the last week and a half, and I'm tired of it." Kage stepped down from the ladder and threw the broom down. "I think that you ought to have Barney get up extra early in the morning and do it. He ain't had to work nearly as hard since you've been working me to death."

"Boy, you best pick up that broom and go back to workin', or you ain't going to have a job here no more." Gene took several swift steps toward Kage.

"I don't think I will," Kage challenged, moving closer to Gene.

"You will if you want to work here any longer." Gene's jawbone tightened.

"That's it. I'm done with this!" Kage stomped passed Gene and kicked the bottom edge of the door with a force that ripped it loose at the hinge.

Chapter 12

Before leaving for work, Gracie kissed her grandfather on the cheek and glanced at the thermometer near the door. Thirty-nine degrees wasn't unusual for November. Gracie closed the air vents on the car, so they'd stop shooting in more cold air. Her teeth chattered, and her shivering complicated the already difficult task of driving. She could drive only because her grandfather had traded in their old car for one with an automatic transmission. Pressing her knee to the bottom of the steering wheel to guide it, she shifted the car into drive. The uneven pressure of her foot on the gas pedal caused the car to jerk and jolt forward. She grabbed the steering wheel, wishing she hadn't promised her grandfather she'd go in today.

Gracie arrived early, planning to defrost the spare freezer in the back room, but instead, out of habit, she started the opening process. The sound of someone's fist pounding on the front door startled her.

"Kage!" she called out, nearly dropping a bucket of Peach Popular. "What on earth?"

Kage motioned for her to open the door.

"Are you okay?" she exclaimed, touching his crimson cheeks. When she took his hand, she jumped back. "You're ice cold!"

His voice shook along with his shoulders as the shiver worked its way down his body. "I-I-I slept over th-th-there l-l-last night." Kage pointed to the bus station. "T-They k-k-kicked me out this m-m-morning once they realized I wasn't b-b-booked for the six a.m. bus, so I've been s-s-sitting next door under those s-s-stairs waiting for you to come to w-w-work."

"Really?"

"Yeah."

"Why were you sleeping at the bus station?"

"Looks like I'm done at the Carter's. I kept thinking about you though." Kage's hand steadied as he reached toward her. "You are the only reason I'd stay in this town. I hate it here, Gracie. I hate working for Gene. I hate Barney's ignorant conversations. I hate the way this town thinks it's got some kind of treasure. There's nothing here worth even my time, besides you."

"You gotta be the best worker Gene's ever had in years."

"I doubt that, by his opinion." Kage doubled his fists.

"Sorry," Gracie said, regretful that Gene hadn't been kinder.

"I ain't sorry. I hate this place. I don't want to spend another day in this town. No offense. I want to get out of here. But I'm not leaving you. I got a ticket for the late afternoon bus out. Come with me, Gracie?"

123

This time Gracie didn't answer as quickly, but she knew in her heart she wouldn't go.

*   *   *

Pearl dug through her purse for spare change and tossed a broken lipstick tube in the trash. Finding a couple coins in her purse after digging for a minute, she headed out the door with the tablet she'd scribbled Kage's phone number on, planning to call him as they'd discussed late the night before.

She had tried to clean her place, tossing the pillows back on the couch and carrying a garbage bag through each room, picking up trash she'd neglected for over a week. She wiped the coffee grounds from the counter, ignoring the stains left behind. The place was not fit for company. Kage would have to sleep on the couch. When she talked to him, he hadn't seemed bothered by the arrangement.

She wondered what her baby brother might look like. When their father died a couple of years ago, she looked for Kage. Granted she hadn't looked very hard, just a phone call to the orphanage only to find it had been shut down.

She'd always pictured him in her mind as a little boy, and since she'd never met him, her vision had remained that way. How had that baby she held only once become a man? Pearl wasn't much for emotions. When she felt a twinge of any sort, she would just wash the thought away with a drink—bourbon— her favorite choice of cure-all. But she had to be at work in a few

124

hours, and she'd used all the logical excuses to miss—some twice.

*   *   *

"You know I can't leave ..." she paused, "my grandfather."

"Then spend the day with me," Kage whispered.

"What?" she exclaimed, his breath tickling her ear.

"We can do anything you want. Just spend today with me," Kage persisted, lifting Gracie and twirling her around. She was tempted.

"Kage, I've got to open the store," Gracie insisted, though contemplating the possibility in her mind.

"Who'd know? You've had odd hours with it anyway, between it already feeling like winter and your grandfather. Oh, I'm sorry, is he doing okay?"

Gracie's countenance changed. "He isn't himself. When I'm around I think he tries hard to act like he feels good, but I stayed with him all day yesterday, and he didn't act right." Gracie walked over to the freezer and took the top off an ice cream container and then struggled to remove the next one. Kage put the lid back on the open container and took the container she had pressed against her chest wrestling to open it.

"What are you doing?" Gracie giggled.

"Helping you," Kage replied, almost pulling off a serious face.

"I don't think so." Gracie pulled the lids off again, eyeing Kage not to replace them.

125

"Come on, Gracie. You've got your grandfather's car. Let's go somewhere. I've got some extra money from working so many hours. Let's go to Whitehorn for lunch! It's a short ride. I need to buy a few things, at least something presentable to wear if I'm going to interview for a job in Louisville. Never know, maybe I can work for the hotel."

Lifting her from the ground, holding her against his body, her feet inches from the floor, Kage wrapped one arm around her waist as he took his other hand and replaced the lids on the ice cream containers. She kicked his shins, pretending to struggle.

"Let me down," Gracie squealed. "You can't just kidnap me. People will come looking for me."

"Seriously, you think so? You honestly think that they are going to be so outraged that Swirly's is closed that they'll come looking for you, especially when you didn't open yesterday?" Kage put Gracie on her feet. Keeping his arm around her waist, he pulled her away from the ice cream freezers and grabbed her coat.

"Maybe." Gracie pushed away from him and stumbled over her own feet.

Kage cornered her with his palms flat against the wall at both sides of her shoulders, their faces inches apart. "Please?" his wide eyes begged.

Gracie, lightheaded from the playful struggle with Kage as he had replaced the lids on the ice cream containers, whispered, "Okay, you win."

126

Kage reached over and flipped off the store lights, his hand coming to rest on her cheek. Only sunlight dimly lit the room as their lips met.

*   *   *

Gracie turned in a circle, swinging her arms out wide taking in the sun's rays breaking the chill. Earlier they had stopped in a few shops. Kage tried on a pair of khaki trousers that he didn't buy. Gracie soon realized that he hadn't really planned to spend his money on new clothes. It was a hoax, and she'd fallen for it.

Kage splurged and bought lunch at the Whistlestop. Gracie was careful to order the least expensive thing on the menu. The portions were large though, and Kage finished hers when she couldn't take another bite. Now sitting on a park bench, Gracie found the fountain in its center relaxing and hours passed as they talked about nothing important—nothing that mattered.

They'd teased each other, acting lighthearted all day, as if time weren't running out, but she couldn't pretend any longer. "You're still leaving today?" Gracie asked hesitantly.

"Yes." Kage took Gracie's hand. "I know I'm crazy to ever think you'd come with me, but if I get everything settled in Louisville, will you at least visit me? I can save up and buy you a ticket."

Gracie loved the feeling of his face so close to hers. No one else was at the park, and it felt as if they owned it. "You don't need to pay for my ticket. You know my grandfather needs me. I've got to stay," Gracie countered, realizing that this was the first day since her grandfather had told her that he was sick, that she hadn't thought of him the whole day through.

"I understand, but I really think you're just scared to leave that little sad town," Kage challenged, placing his arm playfully around her shoulders and leaning back against the bench.

"Don't you tell me what I'm scared of." She pulled away from Kage. Gracie wasn't sure why his words sat so wrong with her, but they did.

"What's wrong?"

"Stop saying it—that Ridgewood is so bad. You don't know. You don't really know anything about it!" Gracie pushed her fist into his chest pushing him away. "I like it. It's my home. I know I haven't traveled like you have, but Ridgewood has good people. If you gave it a chance, you'd like it." Gracie hadn't raised her voice like this before.

Kage appeared taken aback. "I'm sorry. I guess I've never had a place I felt that way about. Nothing much is special anywhere I've been. I wasn't meaning to make you feel bad. So, say you live in Ridgewood for the rest of your life, what are your plans? Are you going to run Swirly's by yourself forever? Who's going to take care of you when your grandfather is gone?"

Kage kept his tone gentle and contained, causing Gracie's harsh edge to ring out in even greater contrast. "Take care of me? I can take care of myself!" Gracie wasn't sure why she was so upset. She knew he was only saying what she had thought too, even just yesterday.

"I didn't mean it like that, I ... I just meant ... well," Kage paused, aware he wasn't finding the right words. He continued to stumble. "I just imagined, someday falling in love with somebody and taking care of her—protecting her," Kage said almost apologetically.

Gracie turned her back to Kage and stared over the bushes, seeing another young couple walking in the distance, holding hands and laughing. Jealousy shot through her. "I don't have any choice here, do I?" Gracie said between clenched teeth.

"What do you mean?" Kage asked, reaching his hand out to rest it on her shoulder but swiftly withdrawing it when she flinched.

Gracie could keep saying that she was fine, but it was not working. All the emotions were still there. She turned toward Kage. "I didn't even know you a month ago, and now you're leaving, and it feels like I'm losing my best friend! My grandfather is all I've had, and he is dying! I can't even sleep through the night without waking up screaming!" Gracie exploded in tears, doing everything she could to suck them back. She held her breath and hit her fist against the bench. When Kage reached for her hand, she knocked him away.

"Why?" Kage asked puzzled. "Why don't you sleep?"

"Because I keep having bad dreams about everything!" Gracie screamed out, causing the couple across the park to look their way. Neither Gracie nor Kage moved or said anything for several seconds.

Then Kage put his arms around her, though Gracie's gaze was still coldly affixed on the shrubbery in the distance. He took her hand and brought her fingers to his chin, intertwining his fingers with hers. He kissed each knuckle and said nothing else. He'd done just the right thing. Kage had stopped talking and just held her.

Gracie, slowly giving in to his embrace, sank against Kage's chest. When she finally spoke, pulling slightly away from his embrace to look into his eyes, her voice was faint and cracked as she spoke. "Okay, now you can say more of that nice stuff you were saying, about the one you love and your plans. I wasn't listening then."

Kage's smile was one of subtle triumph. "As I was just saying," Kage paused, playing up the fact that he had been rudely interrupted, "I have these pictures in my mind. To me, well, if I could have anything on this earth, it's a simple question for me to answer. I want a family. I want to take care of a beautiful woman and keep her safe and make her happy. That's all."

"So, you *want* to take care of me?" Gracie asked, with the edge noticeably absent.

"Honestly, Gracie, I think about it every day. I want to know that you are okay. It bothers me what you're going to do when—" and he stopped.

"When my grandfather dies," Gracie finished his sentence.

"Yes, he loves you, Gracie. But I know what it feels like to be alone, and I hate it," Kage said, looking straight into Gracie's eyes.

Her eyes dampened once more. "I'm scared. I don't know what I'll do when he goes. I just can't imagine it. There is a part of me that thinks I might go crazy. Did anybody ever tell you about Mrs. Laurel? She went crazy all alone in that big house. She thinks her husband still lives with her. If you ever see her now, she's talking out of her head," Gracie shared. "That could be me someday," she added, her eyes playfully wide as she tried to lighten the mood.

"You aren't going to go crazy. Look at everything you've been through, and you're not crazy, Gracie Howard. I've met some crazy people. *You* are not!" Kage said, as he placed her hand between both of his and brought it to his chest. "What you are is beautiful!" Kage leaned forward. Gracie leaned hard into Kage. She returned his kiss more fervently than ever before.

When she was with him, she felt like someone she didn't know—someone new, someone special. Gracie broke away and whispered, "I'm going to miss you so much. I don't have lots of people I can run to in the middle of the night, you know." Gracie tried to force a laugh.

"Not many people I'd get out of bed in the middle of the night to see." Kage drew her close. Gracie wondered what she could say to make him stay.

PART TWO

Chapter 13

As the bus loaded, Kage contemplated getting off. *Would that make Gracie happy? Would that make him happy?* The bus doors closing settled his dilemma.

The gentle vibration of the bus's motor eased Kage into a light slumber. Outside the bus window, in a matter of a few hours, homes grew and multiplied. The buildings flaunted extravagant gold letters, large with business names. People on the streets sported scarves and hats for flair.

"Final stop!" the bus driver called out. Kage awakened to sounds of the city. From his pocket, Kage pulled the paper with Pearl's address scratched on it, stepped off the bus and headed in the direction he thought was the way toward Pearl's place.

He picked up his pace when he spotted the Old School Apartments—once a boarding school. Someone had roughly painted over the S and L on the sign and added another 'choo', now reading 'choo choo Apartments'. With the L&N rattling through its backyard, the compromised name fit. Climbing the first set of stairs led him directly to Apartment A21. He double-checked the number on the wrinkled piece of paper and knocked. Locks fumbled and clicked, then the door swung open.

"Ben!" Pearl exclaimed, nearly tackling him. "Let me look at you!" She pushed him back an arm's length. Then she placed her hands on his cheeks. "You're a handsome man. You got Daddy's eyes, and I can't believe it, Mama's dimple on your left cheek. Oh, look at you, little brother!" Pearl exclaimed, "You're a man. I can't believe it!"

Kage had seen a picture of his mother, and Pearl looked nothing like her. Pearl's hair was blonde and didn't match her dark eyebrows. Her long red fingernails grasped his chin. Wrinkles edged her eyes. With the dark eye shadow, she looked older than her mid-thirties.

"So, this is your place?" Kage glanced around the modest room permeated by Pearl's floral scented perfume.

"It is as long as I pay the rent." Pearl lit a cigarette and with the first puff its tip reddened to match her fingernails. "Go ahead," she insisted, tossing the cigarette pack to him.

He placed the unfiltered Pall Mall to his lips instantly tasting its bitter tobacco tang against his tongue, lit it and took a series of weak puffs.

"You look like you're giving it kisses. You ain't a smoker?"

She took another deep puff, and he noticed the wrinkles around her lips.

"Here, watch." Pearl sucked in, held it for several seconds and then released, curling her lips to control the ascending smoke.

Kage tried the same, and coughed.

She took the cigarette from his hand and put it out in the ash tray. "You can sleep on that couch," she pointed across the room, "until you find a place." She nodded, "Kitchen there, bathroom that way."

Pearl's phone rang. "Yeah," she answered, releasing another puff from the cigarette wobbling between her lips. "What time?" she snapped, her voice raspy.

Kage picked up a photo of Pearl and a man wearing a Dallas Cowboys hat.

She grabbed it out of his hand and tossed it in the trash. "Been meaning to get rid of that. Gotta go into work. Someone didn't show."

"You really got to go?"

"You're welcome to make yourself at home. We can talk later." Pearl poured out her cup of coffee and stepped into the bedroom.

"You seen our brothers lately?" Kage asked, too curious to wait.

Pearl's toothbrush now dangled from her lips, as she stepped from her room. "Not lately." She squinted. "Guess it's been two years. Before that, I guess it was when daddy died."

"What are they like?" Kage fidgeted with the change in his pocket.

Pearl held the palm of her hand up indicating to pause the conversation and disappeared into the bathroom. Returning with her mascara brush in hand, she said, "Well, they're mean for the most part. Not so much Cecil. He was my buddy growin' up." She pulled on a grease-stained Town Tavern sweatshirt over her T-shirt. "When Mama died, and they took you, Beth Ann, and Ruby away, we'd go to the cellar and cry."

"Beth Ann and Ruby always said nice things about Cecil. Said he was a lot like Mama." Kage had said the word mama so few times that it felt odd.

"Yep, that's it. How are *they*—Beth Ann and Ruby?" Pearl asked, sounding more as if she were asking about *his* family than her own.

"Ain't seen 'em since they were old enough to leave the orphanage. You seen them?"

"Not since Dad's funeral."

"They were there?"

"Yep, sorry Ben. The orphanage had closed up, and no one knew where you'd run off to." She dashed past Kage to grab her purse. "Beth Ann and Ruby told us about you, well what they could remember, and the preacher said a prayer for you. Listen, I gotta run, but we'll talk tonight."

Pearl rushed out the door, then turned back. "Glad you're here."

Before the door fully clicked shut, Kage dialed the phone. Gracie answered on the first ring, her voice sweeter than he'd remembered.

"What's Louisville like?"

"Nothing like Ridgewood ..."

Gracie interrupted, "Anyone on the bus stumble over your foot and meet your right hook this time?"

"You're funny," Kage laughed. He already missed her. He asked questions about her day and anything he could think of just to listen to her talk. Aware of his limited funds and the cost of a long-distance call, Kage promised to call her again soon and reluctantly said goodbye.

Kage overlooked the purple floral embroidered curtains and imagined Pearl's place was his own. He pictured bringing Gracie there and seeing her delight as he promised her a future in their new home. Pearl's simple apartment provided two basic rooms, one a bedroom and bath and the other a small sitting area and kitchen. Yet to make ends meet, she worked two jobs, six days a week at the hotel and five nights a week at a local lounge. Kage wrestled in his mind with the picture he'd painted for Gracie in the park before he left, wondering if he could be that man for her—considering even his own father hadn't been able to care for his family.

Kage flipped through the phonebook, thinking about where he might find a job. He stopped at a name scribbled on the top corner of a page—Cecil Kage. Even though he didn't recognize the area code, he dialed the phone, taking in a long, deep breath, just to hear the number was disconnected.

*   *   *

Wrapped in her grandmother's tattered, hand-quilted blanket, Gracie rested in the porch swing, envisioning how many hours it must have taken her grandmother to sew the detailed stitching. The brisk night air reminded her of when she and Kage had first walked together, getting to know bits and pieces about one another. That had been the Kage she didn't know. The night air also reminded her of when she had met him outside of the Carters' place—the night a connection had been made—the night Gracie knew she would never feel the same about life again. She had found comfort in Kage's arms, a security like none she had ever known before. "Kage ..." she whispered, "will you please come back?" Gracie looked up at the stars, feeling he was as distant.

She imagined being by Kage's side when he met his sister, creating her own fairy tale. She pretended the quilt around her shoulders was an expensive wool coat—Kage's—and the smoke from the chimney belonged instead to the *Belle of Louisville.*

Her thoughts were interrupted by her grandfather coughing, then gagging. She stumbled over the quilt and ran inside. Grabbing his elbow, she led him to his bed.

"Cold," he mumbled, his forehead shimmered with sweat like the condensation on the windows.

137

"You're cold?" Gracie asked, taking his moist hand. He pointed to the quilt she dragged in behind her. Gracie covered him from toe to chin, just as Marilee had done for her when she was little.

*   *   *

"I wouldn't have bothered you, but, the sheets, they're soaked." Gracie's words tumbled out as Dr. Laben rushed through the front door.

Dr. Laben pointed to the car and asked, "Can you get the wheel chair out?"

The wind hit Gracie's face like a slap, as she stepped outside toward Dr. Laben's car for the wheelchair, while Dr. Laben took a look at her grandfather. Gracie opened the car door, knowing that getting the wheelchair out wasn't going to be easy for her. Nothing about this was going to be easy. She'd never seen her grandfather like this before.

"I'm taking him." Dr. Laben said as he forced Thomas to swallow several pills.

"To the hospital?"

"Yes, we've got to get this fever down."

"Can I go?"

"Help me wrap him up in these blankets."

Gracie didn't have a fever, but her hand was damp and shook like her grandfather's.

"How long has he been like this?"

"A couple of hours, maybe."

138

"What has he eaten?"

"Some soup, a few crackers, a sip or two of cider."

"Can you find his house shoes?"

Gracie reached under the bed. "Here. Is he going to be okay?"

For the first time since Dr. Laben rushed into their house, he paused to look at Gracie. "I sure hope so."

"Can I come?" Gracie asked again.

Dr. Laben motioned for her to take hold of Thomas on his other side and help sit him up. "I'm not much help," Gracie admitted. She awkwardly did her best using her left hand and chest to push him up, as they prepared to move him into the wheelchair.

Gracie balanced her body against her grandfather as they pulled him from the bed. "I'm coming," she grunted, releasing him into the chair.

"I didn't think I could talk you out of it." Dr. Laben pointed at a picture of Marilee and shook his finger at it and then at Gracie. "You've got more than just your grandmother's smile."

Chapter 14

Gracie hadn't slept well at the hospital and was glad to see Pastor Ted show up. She gathered her things. She wanted to be out of there. She wanted to be home. She wanted her grandfather to get well, though the doctors didn't share much good news. Dehydrated and fighting pneumonia, Thomas had looked ghost-like, fading to blend with the white hospital sheets. Only her first wish was granted. Pastor Ted had come to pick her up and take her home for a couple of days and then return to the hospital to stay with Thomas.

Gracie's head rested against the car window as its vibration kept her awake. The desolate blur of bare trees and stark brush hypnotized her. The image of her grandfather in the hospital, the needles and the tubes, haunted her. *I should have made him drink more cider.*

Pastor Ted slowed in front of Gracie's house. "There's nothing there you can do," he tried to reassure her.

Gracie nodded.

"He's going to be okay."

Gracie nodded again.

"It's not your fault ..."

It seemed he had read her mind. Gracie turned to him and exclaimed, "It is!"

"No, Gracie. Don't do this to yourself."

"What if—" she stopped.

"It's out of our hands, Gracie." Pastor Ted stopped the car and reached for Gracie's bag.

Gracie didn't get out of the car when he opened her door.

"You not ready to go in yet?" he asked.

Gracie shook her head.

Through her misty eyes, she saw him get down on one knee on the ground beside where she sat in the car and bow his head. He began to pray. *"Dear God, today we pray for Thomas. Please make him strong, again. Help the doctors and guide them. Take care of our sweet Gracie. She needs you. Rest Gracie's mind. Give her peace."*

"Peace." Gracie reached out and grabbed onto the word. Pastor Ted, unaware of the powerful memories his prayer had ignited, continued though Gracie's mind drifted elsewhere. She had once found peace—in Kage's arms.

*   *   *

Willy and Barney tugged their overalls on in the dark. Willy, with his on backwards, grunted as he tried to stumble out of them. They tiptoed in large, exaggerated steps. Willy leaned toward Barney in the dark placing his finger in front of his lips.

"Shush!" he mouthed as he put on his coat trying not to wake Gene.

When they got to the barn door, they gave one another the thumbs-up sign. They were counting on the moon to light their way to the treasure. Earlier that day they'd heard two men they'd never seen before at the stockyard talking about Lost Cave. They said their sons had played in the cave and found a message scratched on the rock wall that said "THIS WAY" with an arrow beneath. At those words Willy's eyes widened and his soiled straw hat nearly shot off his head as he turned toward Barney to see if he'd heard the same thing. Barney nodded, and they both leaned in, listening as the men speculated that the treasure might be in the cave. One man continued, "Then the boys found another etched wall that said "HERE" in big letters." With that piece of information, Barney and Willy had revised their theory and put a new plan into action.

Gene threatened that if he found out that any treasure nonsense was going on, he'd dock their pay for every daylight hour that either of them wasted hunting treasure. So, they determined a new angle for their covert operation. Treasure hunting would begin at midnight.

Grabbing a five-gallon bucket, flashlight, shovel, and large pick, they trotted swiftly, not because it was cold, but because they wanted to beat anyone else who might have word about the treasure's location.

When they reached the entrance of the cave, Barney headed in first, flipping on the flashlight. Barney shrieked and jumped backwards into Willy, proving that, without the incentive of treasure, spelunking wasn't Barney's forte as he had bragged. Their first steps revealed a possible companion.

"Lookie there. We ain't the first ones here." Willy picked up the snake skin and it crumbled. "Yep, one of those live ones got around my leg when I was a boy. The black snakes won't hurt'cha, but the colored ones I don't mess with anymore." Willy emphasized, as if there were more to that story than he'd shared.

"I don't like no snake a-tall, especially when the only light I got to spot one is a flashlight," Barney confessed, as their pace slowed.

"'T'ain't no snake you gotta worry about. It's the bats!" Willy flapped his arms.

"There it is! Right there!" Barney called out, and Willy's eyes shot in the direction Barney pointed.

"Well, do you believe that? Those men was tellin' the truth. Right there in front of us." Willy looked upon the words 'THIS WAY' scraped into the cave wall with the delight of a child catching Santa beneath his Christmas tree.

Barney, hopping, sputtered, "Okay, okay, what did the men say next? Didn't they say the arrow points to it? Right?"

"Yep! They says the arrow points in the direction of the treasure, and you knows you found it when you come to the word 'HERE' scratched on the wall," Willy recapped, rubbing sweat from his brow, although the cave air was cool.

For whatever reason, they both began tip-toeing, as if sneaking up on the fortune were a strategic part of treasure hunting. Minutes later the ray of light landed on the word. Willy walked up to the letters as if they were the jewels sought and brushed his hand over the word. The *H* was large, and the *E* was followed by a lowercase *r,* and then the final *E* was faded but still could be made out if you touched your nose to the rock wall, which Willy did.

Barney turned in circles ready to begin digging. "Do you take the pick straight to the wall there, Willy? Knock it down and pull that treasure straight out, you think?"

Willy looked at Barney like he was stupid. "Naw, you don't do that. This is t-r-e-s-u-r, boy." He spelled out the word slowly as if that was the only way Barney would understand. "We hunt for hidden treasure *where it's buried.*" He placed the shovel dead center of the ground floor parallel to the scratched stone wall.

Barney smiled and shook his finger at Willy. "You's a smart one. Right there, huh? Okay, I'll give it the first lick."

"Fifty-fifty remember," Willy reaffirmed their deal to split whatever they found.

Throwing the pick back above his head and shoulders, Barney gave the unadulterated red clay floor a whack, chipping a piece of it about the size of the pick's tip. "Hum, that stuff's harder than I thought."

"Here, let me do that." Willy took the pick and mimicked Barney's motion, adding intense facial expressions resembling constipation as he used all of his arm strength. Willy's efforts were even less successful.

Barney guffawed, his laughter bouncing off the walls of the cave.

Not easily deterred, they both took turns pecking and shoveling the clay. Willy removed his jacket and tugged his shirt away from his neck.

"Should've brought a water jug." Barney listened as his voice echoed.

"You can get you some water over there." Willy pointed to the water trickling down the cave wall.

"You really suggestin' that I stick my tongue to that rock wall and lap up that water like a dog?" Barney mocked sarcastically.

"Yes, sir. That there's some good water, as fine as any you'll drink. I promise." Willy walked over to the cave rock and stuck his tongue out letting the drips fall from the ceiling to his extended tongue.

Barney's pick struck the ground this time with an unmistakable ding. Their eyes shot to one another. Barney threw his pick again and the clank echoed once more. Willy jigged, leaping toward Barney. "We's done it, Barney. We's found the treasure!"

Pushing Barney aside, Willy started digging with the shovel breaking away at the ground. A dirty, silver edge peeked from the red clay.

"Is it a chest full of the treasure, you think?"

"Uh-huh," Willy said and placed his foot on the upper edge of the shovel. He grunted as he pushed the shovel's blade into the ground.

Barney propped the flashlight on a rock and started singing and dancing, hollering, "Yippy, yippy, yea. We found us some treasure today."

Amid Barney's whooping and leaping, something swooped down and fluttered in front of his face. Barney slapped madly at it. Instead of song, curse words poured out in high pitched squeals. Willy leapt up, to see the commotion, and the fluttering creature swooped next toward him. Both Barney and Willy jumped and twirled like wild cavemen ingesting magic mushrooms and took off running in a fierce scurry, leaving everything but the flashlight behind. Neither slowed as they exited the cave. Their careful navigation lost in the frantic exit, they ran directly into a wild patch of blackberry bushes, and hundreds of tiny thorns scraped their exposed hands and faces.

*   *   *

"Who is it?" Gracie yelled, jerking from the porch swing and backing against the house in one full step. The cool night air helped after the nightmares—this time she'd been walking in circles, desperate, lost, and alone. Yet now, realizing that she

146

wasn't alone, she eased toward the door, the shingles on the side of the house tickling her back. She didn't take her eyes from the path where she heard the voices.

"Go away! I have a gun," she called to the trees. Gracie now wished she had paid better attention when her grandfather taught her how to shoot his gun. She thought he was simply trying to do something special with her, since he knew more about guns than fingernail polish. But now she wondered if he had been concerned for a night like this, concerned for her safety.

"Don't you come near here!" She screamed and reached for the screen door handle. Even her empty home didn't feel safe any longer. She tried to remember if she had locked the back door.

Just then two men emerged from the forest, running and squalling. They immediately turned down the gravel road, away from Gracie, swatting their heads and leaping insanely. The thinner, taller man took to the gravel like a jackrabbit, quickly gaining distance on the plumper one. Gracie, not sure if there were more people in the thicket, ran inside and locked all her doors.

*   *   *

Pearl came home after midnight, stumbled and dropped her keys just inside the door. She was not alone. "Harold, I dropped my keys," she giggled.

They both bent to pick them up and bumped heads. Pearl squealed.

Harold embraced her from behind and tried to walk forward—their feet tangled. Pearl tripped, and Harold pulled her up.

"Shhh, you'll wake my little brother, Beenjaammiin," she sounded out his name, slurring each syllable.

Kage pretended to sleep.

He had tried earlier to call Gracie but couldn't get through. Pearl's phone was dead—no dial tone. He had unplugged it and plugged it back into the wall and still nothing.

Chapter 15

"Thanks for taking these to Gracie." Pastor Ted helped load the donated goods into Aaron's car along with the groceries Aaron had packed for her.

"Glad to," Aaron answered, distracted by Barney strutting across the street at Charlie's Gas Station, flirting with the girls in the car behind his.

Pastor Ted's eyes followed. "How do you think Gracie is doing?"

"Holding on."

"I can tell she doesn't seem herself, and it breaks my heart to see Thomas like that, too."

"I know," Aaron agreed, listening to the girls' giggles as Barney leaned in their open window.

"He's an interesting one." Pastor Ted nodded warily toward Barney. "You have any idea where he came from before he started working for Gene?"

"Oh, Barney Cartwell? No, but he's trouble." Aaron stepped into his vehicle and adjusted his black rimmed lenses over his eyes as if taking a closer look at the scene.

Across the street, windows rolled down and music blaring, Barney peeled out of Charlie's Gas Station leaving a trail of rubber.

*   *   *

"Gracie? You home?" Aaron called through the screen door.

Gracie stood from the couch more slowly than her grandfather would have and opened the door. After seeing the men in the middle of the night, she hadn't slept.

"You look tired." Aaron pushed his way past her and headed toward the kitchen to unload the bags of groceries in his arms. "Think I got everything you need."

"Thanks for the groceries, but you didn't have to ..."

"Glad to." Aaron moved around the kitchen, putting away the bread and eggs. He held up the sugar, and Gracie pointed to the pantry.

Gracie took a jar of cinnamon from the grocery bag and placed it in the spice rack.

Aaron grabbed it. "I make a tasty cinnamon roll," he announced, turning the oven to 350. "You have flour, don't 'cha?"

When the phone rang, Aaron whirled toward Gracie and asked, "Can you get that?"

Sure, it's my phone.

"Hello?" she answered, nodding to Aaron who pointed to the flour canister.

"Gracie, just wanted to say I was sorry to hear your grandfather's sick," the gruff voice came across the line.

"Who is this?"

"Barney. I was wonderin' if you'd like to go out some time. I know you's there all alone and everything."

"Barney, I'm not really in the mood for anything like that." Gracie wished she hadn't answered the phone.

"You heard from Kage?"

"Yes."

"Welp, I figure he won't ever be back this way. He didn't much fit in 'round here. Gene didn't care none for him." Barney snorted, spitting his snuff without regard.

"Guess he didn't." Gracie's grasp tightened on the phone.

"Well, if you change your mind, let me know. There's a good chance I'll be coming into some big money soon."

Gracie ended the call, made faces into the phone and slammed it down. Then she dialed Kage's number. The call didn't go through. She steadied her hand, pressing her neck tighter against the phone receiver nestled against her shoulder, and dialed again, but his line now played a disconnect recording.

*   *   *

Gene had been contemplating it for months, but Thomas' visit convinced him. He wasn't getting any younger either. He propped his heels against the baseboard and pushed the dresser

151

toward his bed. Then bracing his palm against the wall, one knee at a time, he bent to the floor—further convinced by the aches in his bones that he was making the right decision. Lifting the plank from the floor, he pulled out a cigar box and wiped the dust from its lid. Benjamin Franklin's face on the bills greeted him, sharing Gene's similar solemn expression. His life-long savings were neatly stacked and tied with grass string in bundles. When he had first started saving, it had been to build a house for Olivia. Then when she'd left, he planned to use the money to pay a lawyer in Hartington to find his wife. Gene remembered adding bills to the box, like each was a penny tossed into a wishing well for Olivia to return.

When the lawyer returned with only divorce papers, he hadn't taken Gene's money.

*   *   *

When Pearl realized their phone was not working, she cursed and banged the receiver against the phone. "I swear! I send the bill in a day late, and they cut it off," Pearl squalled.

Although writing wasn't Kage's forte, slim on options, he mailed Gracie a letter on the way to see about a job at a gas station.

Chapter 16

"Two more bites," Gracie encouraged, sitting beside her grandfather. She mixed the warm oatmeal with a spoon. Thomas shook his head. Since he'd been home from the hospital, she'd done better at making sure he was drinking fluids, but now he wouldn't eat. His appetite hadn't returned, nor had the spark in his eyes. Once he called her Marilee, and she acted as if she hadn't noticed.

Waving away the oatmeal, he reached for her hand. "Peppermint," he began.

Gracie leaned in.

"You're growing up."

"I don't want to," Gracie admitted.

"That boy ..."

"Kage?"

"Yes, you know my first thought when I opened the door and saw him standing there, asking to see you?"

Gracie shook her head.

"I thought he can't be here to see my Gracie. She's just a little girl. That is exactly what I thought. Then I turned and saw you standing there, a woman."

"I don't feel like one," Grace confessed, gripping his hand, trying to warm it. "Everything scares me. For you to ..." Gracie paused, "to go scares me. To be a woman—that scares me."

"Me too, Gracie," Thomas said, his voice a whisper. "Gracie, it's a big mountain. Keep climbing my sweet, precious Gracie. Please keep climbing."

*   *   *

Gene couldn't read half the words on the papers that arrived in the mail for his signature. On the phone, the banker he talked with explained the different stocks. It took a minute for Gene to realize the conversation wasn't about cattle. Gene wadded up the papers and tossed them in the trash. He trusted banks about as much as self-serving treasure hunters. He picked up the phone and dialed a faded number taped on its side.

"Sounds like you're doing well?"

"Alright, I guess," Gene unnecessarily moved the phone receiver closer to his mouth when he spoke and then against his ear when the lawyer spoke.

"I gotta ask. Did you ever hear anything from her again?"

"Naw." Gene shook his head.

"Sorry to hear that. How can I help this time?"

"I ain't gonna last forever. I've been talkin' to a banker and need some advice from someone I can trust."

154

Over Aunt Bee's voice on the television, Gracie heard a car pull up outside. Peeking out the window, she didn't recognize the vehicle until it stopped and backfired.

Barney knocked before Gracie could stumble to the backroom to hide.

"Hello there, Gracie. Got a pie for you." Barney extended the box balanced on the palm of his hand. Gracie, with no intention of inviting him in, tried to take the pie through the cracked door, but she couldn't get a good hold on it, so she stepped outside.

Barney sang out, "I got the afternoon off, if you'd like to do something."

Gracie noticed the scabs on his hands, neck and forehead. "I really don't think so. I have lots to do around here, especially for my grandfather. Where'd you get all those scratches?" Gracie asked, curiosity getting to her.

"Ah these little scratches?" Barney looked over his hands. "Got into a tussle with one of the local boys. He don't look near this good." Barney smirked and bobbed his head as if he were proud.

"Thanks for the pie." Gracie turned her back to Barney.

"You got his new number?" Barney asked.

"What?" Gracie stopped and turned toward Barney.

"Kage called Gene today. Heard Gene say he had a different number to be reached at and left his address for Gene to mail him somethin'. Sure did. Thought you might want it." Barney stuck his hands in his back pockets and rocked on his heels.

Where had Kage gone now? Why had he called Gene and not her?

"What?" Gracie asked, trying to collect her thoughts.

"Gene's supposed to mail his remaining pay, since he ran off all the sudden." Barney sounded pleased with himself.

"I've got his number. It doesn't work anymore," Gracie challenged.

"Nope, does too. I know for a fact, 'cause Gene dialed him back and talked to him this afternoon. Told him he would mail the money. I think he said it was his work number maybe if I heard right."

Gracie swallowed. She wanted the number, but she wanted Barney to leave and never come back.

"I'll get it for you," Barney offered.

Gracie hesitated.

"Or not, whatever you want," Barney added nonchalantly and turned away.

"If you hear from him, tell him my grandfather has taken a turn for the worse. I'm worried,"

"Sure will. Can do." Barney trotted toward his vehicle.

Gracie slid inside her house and locked the door behind her.

*   *   *

Kage awoke to the smell of Folgers and cigarette smoke. He rubbed his back where the broken spring on the couch had poked through its cushion and irritated him. Pearl scurried around the apartment.

"Oh good, you're up. Does this stink?" Pearl tossed him her hotel uniform.

"Why?" Kage caught it.

"I ain't washed it."

Kage tossed it back to her. "Stinks like smoke."

"Good, that still works then." Pearl headed toward her bedroom.

"I tried to call Cecil. I found his number scribbled in your phonebook."

Pearl interrupted, "Phone working again?"

"No, I mean the other day."

"Phonebook?" Pearl looked as if she didn't know what he was talking about, but then remembered. "Yep, guess that was his number when he was in Georgia. I think he's in Alabama now. All of them are. I know I've got their numbers 'round here somewhere." She dug for a minute in a dish on her dresser. "Well, I can't find it, Ben. I'll look later, another time." She called to him as she shut her bedroom door.

Through the door she yelled, "Found out I didn't pay the phone bill. That's the problem."

*   *   *

Gene watched as Barney copied down Kage's number and address. "Whatcha doin'?" Gene asked.

157

"Gonna call Kage. Gracie asked me to let him know her grandfather ain't doin' well," Barney answered, trying to read the handwriting scribbled on the paper.

"When did ya run into her?" Gene quizzed.

Since Barney and Willy had come home with a hundred or more scratches, he had watched their every move. Willy had admitted to their botched treasure escapade, and Gene hadn't gone easy on them.

"I never in my life seen anything more ridiculous from two grown men!" Gene had said, his lips curled around his gums indignantly. "You two just earned you both the task of putting up the new fence around the hog barn. Both of yous gonna get all that diggin' out of your systems after you dig all those holes for fence posts."

Gene hiked to the cave, not to look for hidden treasure, but to collect the bucket, shovel and pick they had left behind. While he was there, he checked out the small cavity dented in the cave floor. It didn't take Gene long to discover they'd hit rock. He told them about the rock they discovered not so much to taunt them but to discourage them from returning.

Barney continued rambling on about Gracie, "I took her a pie."

"You went to her place?" Gene asked skeptical of Barney's motives.

"Yep, sure did. And she invited me back again. Tomorrow night, I think she said," Barney rendered.

Looking at Barney with disapproval, Gene didn't respond. He had caught Barney more than once in a lie.

Though Gene hadn't been fond of Kage either, he appreciated his work ethic. Kage completed in a day more than two Willys and a Barney put together.

Gene remembered the night he had awakened to the sound of what he thought was a gun shot. Not sure if he was dreaming or had actually heard something, he had gotten out of bed to check.

He heard Barney come in and head upstairs. Then a minute later, he thought he heard Barney leave again. Getting nervous that Barney might have gotten into trouble and brought it home with him, Gene had pulled his gun from the drawer beside his bed.

Once outside he had expected to see Barney but had seen Kage instead, holding Gracie while she cried. He watched as Kage brushed his hand through her hair, Gracie's face pressed against his chest. Her body was shaking as she wept, and Kage's grip tightened as he laid his head against hers. Then they exchanged a few words and Gracie lifted her face toward Kage's as he leaned in and kissed her.

Gene had stepped quietly back inside.

Chapter 17

Gracie ran outside when it started to rain and grabbed the sheets drying on the clothes line. Even after Thomas had splurged on a washer and dryer, Gracie preferred the fresh smell of line dried sheets. She pulled on the pillow case's corner, causing the clothespins to dart upward like boomerangs. Leaning away, dodging their decent, she didn't notice the car approaching.

When she heard the popping of gravel under the vehicle's tires, she dashed toward the house, bundling the sheets in her arms. Since Barney's visit, she'd been careful to take cover. The rain fell in large pellets, and the edges of the sheets dragged the ground. She recognized the car just before she stepped inside. She'd forgotten to pick up the mail at the post office, something her grandfather had always done.

After tossing the sheets on the back of the armchair, she jogged to unlatch the front yard gate. Mr. Foster insisted on carrying the stack of mail to the house for Gracie. He stuttered as he spoke, a habit he had had as long as she could remember.

He mumbled concerned thoughts for Gracie's grandfather but insisted she not disturb him. He headed back to his vehicle with his hand above his head to shelter his windblown combover from the drizzling rain.

Gracie sifted through the mail and found an assortment of Get-Well cards and a few bills. Then she noticed the return address on one letter. Although smudged, she could make out the words "Louisville, KY". She tore it open, ripping the corner of the letter along with the envelope.

Kage's words rushed in her head as she read quickly.

Gracie,

The phone is out at Pearl's. It's frustrating not being able to call you. How are you? I really wish you'd come see me here. If you don't give me any other choice, then I guess I'll have to come back to that treasure-crazy town of yours and get you. I close my eyes when I sleep at night and I can see you. Are you still as beautiful, Gracie?

I got a job at a gas station. I know you are busy with your grandfather and the ice cream shop. I know you aren't happy that I'm in Louisville. When we talked on the phone, I could hear the sadness in your voice. This may seem strange but knowing the love you and your grandfather have, and hearing him talk about your family, made me even more than ever want to find mine.

Pearl is nothing like what I imagined (don't ever tell her I said that), but she has welcomed me in and I find it surprising that it took me this long to find my own sister. I have to find my family, just like I understand that you can't leave your grandfather. I want things like a family and a place to call my own. Meeting Pearl is a first step.

This may sound strange to you, but I've never trusted anyone in my whole life. But I trust you, and I want to trust Pearl. I was so afraid you wouldn't talk to me that day I stopped by the ice cream shop. I don't think I ever told you how nervous I was.

I know it upsets you when I mention that I don't like Ridgewood, but the farther I am from you the more I seem to think of that place. I miss you and if you can't come here, I'll come back soon if only for a day to see you. I promise. Pearl's phone hopefully will be fixed soon.

Kage

Sitting on the edge of the chair, she nudged the sheets out of her way. She looked at his words again and read them once more, slowly. Tears in her eyes one minute, and a smile that nearly broke her cheekbones the next, Gracie took in every word. She read it a third time, focusing on his handwriting, seeing a part of him he had not shared with her before. He slanted his letters shifting randomly from print to cursive. She ran her finger over the words yet again, imagining Kage writing them to her.

162

Aaron finished washing the dishes after he swept the kitchen floor. Overly comfortable in Gracie's home, Aaron answered her phone when it rang.

"Yes, she is here," he said but didn't extend the phone to Gracie. "And may I ask who's calling?" Aaron pushed his glasses up on his nose. "I see, and can I give her a message for you?" Aaron shot a skeptical gaze toward Gracie.

Gracie realized then who it was. She waved her hand motioning and mouthing, "No, I'm not here."

"She isn't available to come to the phone right now," Aaron said, nodding his head in full confidence that he could take care of Barney.

"No, Barney, we aren't an item, as if it were any of your business. No, I don't believe she is interested in courting anyone right now. No, she hasn't mentioned your name lately."

Aaron stifled a chuckle seeing Gracie wrap her hand around her neck, pretending to choke.

"Kage's?" Aaron raised his eyebrow.

"Kage?" she repeated in a whisper to Aaron.

"You got what for Gracie?"

"What?" Gracie grabbed the phone from Aaron.

"Howdie there!" Barney's voice rang in a high pitch.

"Hi, Barney. Listen, Aaron's here, and we're busy."

"You got any plans tonight?" Barney asked.

Gracie looked at Aaron rolling her eyes. "I just said Aaron's here. Did you say something about Kage?"

"Well, I got that address and phone number for you, if you want it."

"Great, let me get a paper and pencil." Gracie tucked the phone under her chin and shuffled in the drawer for a pad of paper.

"Well, I don't have it with me right now. I was gonna bring it by next time I was out."

Gracie tightened her jaw. She wanted so badly to talk with Kage. "Okay, maybe, tomorrow."

Seeming satisfied, he let her go, snickering, "Have fun with Aaron."

*   *   *

Kage called Gracie's number from a payphone, but it was busy. He then dialed Gene.

"Gene there?"

"Nope," Willy answered. "This here phone rang and nearly caused me to jump right out of my pants."

It had occurred to Kage that it was strange Gene had a phone, since he didn't embrace many other modern-day conveniences. "It's Kage. I think he's got it, but write this number down." Kage rattled off the number to the gas station, though his boss wasn't pleased with him using the number.

Willy spoke as he wrote, "How you spell it?"

Kage began more slowly with the number.

"Nah, your name ..." Willy stopped him.

"K," Kage said and patiently waited for Willy to write as he repeated each letter.

"Okay, now the number," Willy prompted.

Kage heard Barney whispering loudly in the background, "Is that Kage? Hey, let me talk at him."

"Barney wants to speak at 'cha," Willy said after taking down the number. He handed the phone to Barney.

"Kage, it's Barney here. Gracie asked me to call you."

"Is she okay?"

"She is fine, but her grandfather ain't doin' no good," Barney shared. "But I've been watching her."

"Watching her?"

"Yep."

"What do you mean by that?" Kage's temperature rose.

"We're going out tomorrow night."

"You and Gracie?" Kage asked not sure if he heard Barney right.

"Yep, called her up tonight, and she can't wait," Barney added. "Well, she's just fine. Just wanted you to know I'm taking good care of her. You left town, so I thought you wouldn't mind there, buddy. I'll tell Gracie you said hello."

The dull buzz in the phone after Barney hung up rang in Kage's ears, which were still burning from Barney's words.

Chapter 18

"Go," Thomas insisted. "This arguing is making me tired." He'd eaten better today, and she was pleased to see the color returning to his face.

"I don't want to leave you, especially today. A person is supposed to be with family on the holidays."

"The Franklins would enjoy having you for Thanksgiving dinner. You know Roberta is an incredible cook."

"I know. Every time Aaron brings groceries by, he brings something his mom's baked and sometimes I eat it all. Sorry," she apologized, lacking remorse. Thomas smiled and that made her happy. "I imagine Erma will be there?" Gracie said as if she were counting pros and cons.

"Go. I'll be fine." Thomas reached for the paper on the edge of his bed and began reading.

"Okay I'll go, but only if you promise to eat the whole plate of turkey, dressing, and sweet potatoes that I bring back to you."

"I'll try," Thomas promised.

Gracie didn't want to make it obvious to her grandfather, but she wanted to get out of the house, not as much to spend Thanksgiving with the Franklins, but more so she could stop by Mr. Foster's house on the way there. He'd called to tell her he had a bundle of mail for her and hadn't had a chance to run it to her. She'd asked if there was a return address from Louisville, Ky. He'd said, "Yes."

*　　*　　*

On their first Thanksgiving, Gene had cooked for Olivia. He hunted a big turkey and fixed enough sweet potatoes, dressing, and cranberry sauce for a family of six, though it was only the two of them. Watching Willy drown his turkey and dressing with gravy and Barney stuff his face with sugar-and-spice-cooked apples, Gene thought they acted as if they hadn't eaten since the day that he had left for Hartington earlier in the week. He had an appointment with Robert Myers, the lawyer who had handled the divorce. Meyers now had a partner and was located in a fancy building downtown with signage over the door reading *Meyers & Murphy.* Gene's visit consisted of a night's stay in a hotel with a shower and flushing toilets, a spicy steak at a restaurant with a name he couldn't pronounce, and a meeting in an office with chairs cushier than his own bed. Finally, he had driven home to Ridgewood with his cigar box by his side, empty.

*　　*　　*

Roberta Franklin set the mashed potatoes on the table, steam rising to the ceiling from the bowl. Ben Franklin was home from

167

the service for the holiday, and Aaron's mother had prepared a feast in honor of her brother. Ben, in a gold cardigan and slacks, still stood as if he wore his dress blues. Gracie figured that once a person had shaken the hand of President Kennedy it was hard to act like a normal person again.

Erma offered to help her sister with dinner but immediately started telling Pastor Ted a long story about her donation of canned goods to the church for the annual food drive.

"Pastor Ted, I just knew when you were speaking last Sunday that you were talking directly to me," Erma said and leaned forward, dramatically placing her hand over her low-cut white blouse.

Pastor Ted nodded and added making conversation, "It was so kind of you to donate several boxes. We surpassed our goal, doubling what we collected last year." Pastor Ted was dressed more casually than his usual church attire. It was rare that Gracie saw him without a tie.

Erma continued, "I couldn't be more pleased to contribute to such a worthy cause. I think of those children without food on their plates, the little ones starving, and I just want to cry." Erma put two fingers to her forehead and closed her eyes, as if the thought was too much to bear.

"Yes, it is sad," Pastor Ted agreed. His eyes followed Erma as she swayed across the room to perch on the edge of the upholstered wing backed chair.

Picking up her cup of hot tea from the end table, Erma crossed her legs and tugged at her burgundy satin skirt to raise her hem to her knees. She'd overdressed for the occasion. She lifted the cup and blew on it, shifting her eyes from the tea to Pastor Ted and back again. "Were you offered some tea?" Erma asked in a cooing tenor.

"No, but no, thank you," Pastor Ted replied focusing on the elegant décor in the living room. "That's a beautiful vase." He motioned to Gracie for her to look.

Gracie nodded. The home, decked with collectables and antiques, resembled a quaint museum. Where the walls in Gracie's house were dull with only a few, simply-framed photos hanging, Aaron's home was adorned with ornate mirrors the size of the front window of Gracie's house and with large signed portraits.

"Oh yes, it was our mother's," Erma said as Aaron called everyone to the dining room.

Whereas Gracie was accustomed to passing the dishes, Roberta walked each dish around the table allowing the guests to take their portion.

"Ben, when is the big day?" Pastor Ted asked after the blessing.

Ben, thought Gracie, though the conversation continued about his deployment to Vietnam scheduled for the day after Christmas, Gracie thought of only her "Ben". Gracie peeked into her purse to see the letter from Kage. Although she'd already read it, she wanted to make sure it was still there, close to her.

"Gracie, how is your grandfather today?" Roberta interrupted.

"Better. Aaron has been kind to bring by the groceries. I know I owe him for those. I wish he would let me pay," Gracie said and turned to Aaron.

"Oh, no. We are glad to," Roberta insisted.

"Excellent squash casserole, and love the turnip greens," Pastor Ted complimented.

"Do you like the rolls?" Erma asked. "I made them." She fluttered her lashes and took a small bite of the yeast roll with her front teeth. "Is it okay if I call you Teddy?" Erma asked almost knocking over her tea cup; it dropped to the saucer with a loud clank. Her cheeks flushed. Gracie could have sworn that Erma's blouse was open an additional button.

"I always pictured Ben as a match for Gracie, but," Erma glanced toward Aaron and Gracie. "but you two make such a cute couple." Erma took a gulp of her tea rather than the earlier lady-like sips.

"Erma!" Roberta shot a glance across the table.

"Well, they do. They'd really have cute babies, you know. Aaron and Gracie both with that dark hair and as smart as Aaron is, they'd have such good genes."

Aaron and Gracie blushed in unison.

"Erma, that's enough," Roberta broke in.

"Oh, dear me." Erma pulled her hand to her chest covering the exposed cleavage. "I am sorry. I just believe that when two people are meant to be together, the forces are too strong for them to be kept apart." And with those words Erma looked directly at Pastor Ted who jolted in his seat as if something had bitten him under the table.

"Erma Franklin! May I see you in the kitchen?" Roberta ordered.

Erma placed her fork on the china and held the edges of the table as she fished beneath with her leg. Then she bent over, her blouse fell open providing a clear shot for Pastor Ted and Aaron. Aaron's eyes darted open, while Pastor Ted stood from his seat and placed his napkin on the table, excusing himself.

Raising her head from under the table, her hairdo disassembled, Erma held her left shoe in her hand. "Found it."

"No, Pastor, stay please," Roberta insisted following Pastor Ted to the door. Erma was on their heels jabbering about the nice evening.

Gracie snickered as she and Aaron traded glances, both realizing that Erma had slipped off her black, patent leather, high-heeled shoe and stroked Pastor Ted's leg with her stocking foot.

Ben leaned over toward Erma's tea cup, sniffed and said, "Something a little extra in that tea!"

*   *   *

Kage kept playing the conversation with Barney over in his head. Once, when his boss wasn't watching, he picked up the phone to call Gracie. After two rings, he caught his boss's evil eye and hung up. Kage stared at the clock on the wall as if it were a ticking bomb, counting down the minutes until he would explode from anxiety.

Chapter 19

Dr. Laben took Thomas' pulse once more and asked Gracie to give them a minute to talk. She tried to listen through the door but could hear only her own heartbeat. When Dr. Laben emerged from her Grandfather's room, she stepped toward him.

"Is he going to be okay?"

Dr. Laben put his hand on her shoulder. "He wants to talk to you."

Gracie turned toward her grandfather's room, leaving Dr. Laben to find his way out.

"Granddaddy?" she whispered, opening his door.

"Peppermint," he cleared his throat and nodded toward the chair beside his bed.

Gracie pushed it away and sat on the edge of his bed next to him. "What, what did the doctor say?"

"Said I was stubborn." His breath sounded hollow as he tried to muster a simple laugh.

Gracie tried to lighten the mood. "So am I. Is there a medicine to fix stubborn?"

173

Again, Thomas started to chuckle. It caught in his throat, raising his chest several inches off the mattress. Once he'd settled, he pointed to the closet door. "Open that ..."

Gracie stood up, not sure what he wanted her to do. "The closet?"

He nodded.

She opened the door to Marilee's closet. The musty scent of leather and linen met her, and she was six again. As a little girl, she'd crawled along the closet floor, over Marilee's shoes, passing her hat boxes and the shell of the Samsonite luggage to open the door at the closet's end, into another bedroom. It had been such a mystery to her young mind, a dark cave to be searched, a safe place to hide.

"What am I supposed to look for?" Gracie asked.

"The large bag with a zipper." Thomas tried to sit up.

Gracie thumbed through the clothes on the rack in the closet and came to a manila hanging storage bag, that she suspected once was white. Taking it out, she unzipped it slowly, not sure what she was about to uncover.

Gracie gasped, "You still have her dress?" She ran her hand carefully over the delicate lace overlay. The dress was no longer the bright white it had been in Marilee's wedding picture, and her mother's.

"Marilee wanted you to have it."

"Granddaddy, it's beautiful."

"Not like it used to be when Marilee wore it. She'd been so pleased when your mother had asked to wear it. Now, it's old, dingy, and wrinkled, like me." He shared a weak smile. "But I see it as it was," he reminisced and reached out rubbing his fingers together, wanting to feel the fabric against his skin.

Gracie edged closer, sitting next to him cradling the dress in her arms.

"Tell me about it, Granddaddy, back then."

"Her daddy didn't like me."

"Why?"

"They called me the King of the Charleston, and your grandmother was a fast learner."

"Really?"

"We used to twist and turn until our feet got tangled. I didn't mind getting tangled with her. They thought I was a bad influence."

"Not you, Granddaddy."

"Oh, they thought I had my priorities all mixed up. Her daddy said I spent too much time wiggling instead of working."

"I never knew."

"Oh yeah, I was young once, and your grandmother was the best thing that ever happened to me."

Gracie turned to look at their wedding picture on the nightstand. The dress in her hand bore only a resemblance to the shiny, silky one in the photo. Its waistline was embellished with lace and the hemline fell just below Marilee's knees. Small

175

cap sleeves delicately wrapped her shoulders, and her face was covered by a lace veil held by a beaded band that extended onto her forehead.

Gracie studied the picture of her grandfather in the photo and then looked at him beside her, his eyes closed and his breath uneven. He had aged as the wedding dress in her hands had aged, and he no longer looked like the man in the photo. But he looked like her grandfather, and she liked that better.

* * *

Gracie asked Barney to keep his voice low, her grandfather was sleeping in his room and sound traveled easily from the front room. His hair was slicked back, and his button-up shirt was tucked into his pants.

"Do you have Kage's work number like you said?

"Yep." He reached for his pocket. "I got them right here for you."

Gracie took the paper from him. "Thanks. I know he can't afford to be calling me a lot," Gracie said, making excuses for Kage.

"Well, talked with him yesterday, and he seemed to be just fine."

"You talked to him?" Gracie felt defeated.

"Yep, told him about your grandfather, like you asked." Barney placed his thumbs behind his belt buckle and pushed his shoulders back.

"You did?"

"Yep, he said he was doin' just fine. That Louisville was the life for him. He won't be back this way no time soon. Figure he's got all kinds of women watchin' after him now."

Gracie suspected he said that to be mean, though she feared Barney knew something she didn't. "Barney, you've been kind to come by this evening and sit with me. I'm awfully tired, though." Gracie clenched her fist at her side.

"You've had a lot on your mind, and I just want you to know that I'll do anything I can to help." Barney didn't move from his seat.

Gracie tried again. "I'm sure you have to be up early in the morning to work for Gene."

"Yep, but that don't matter none. I stay out lots later than this," Barney smirked.

Barney's earlier words bothered Gracie more by the minute, and she had to ask, "What did you mean by what you said about Kage?"

"What's that?"

"About other women!" Gracie shot back, then remembered her grandfather and lowered her voice. "About Kage.

"Honestly, you think he's ever coming back here?" Barney blurted, an obvious jest toward Gracie's naivety.

"Why are you talking like this to me, Barney? Why would you bring me Kage's number only to say mean things about him?"

"Gracie, you're a fine lookin' girl. You don't need to be waitin' for some drifter like Kage. You got to move on, find you the right man." Barney puffed out his chest, as if to suggest he was suitable.

Gracie scooted toward the edge of her seat, uncomfortably fiddling with the piece of paper in her hand.

"It don't bother me you ain't got no hand. It might bother some to see that there, but I'm okay with it," Barney went on.

Standing from her seat, Gracie felt heat rising from her chest up to her neck. "Barney, I'm not feeling very well. I think we are going to have to call it an evening."

Barney stood as well. "It has been a pleasure, Miss Gracie. Your company, as always, makes for a mighty fine evening. I'd like to visit again." The proper language Barney used clashed with everything about him.

"I am really not sure that's a good idea. I'm taking care of my grandfather and honestly not looking for anyone to be calling on me." Gracie was irked by the thought that she had allowed him to assume otherwise.

"I understand." Barney picked up his hat and held it in front of his chest. He bowed in what Gracie guessed was his attempt to show some sort of respect of her wishes. "Then I'll give you some time."

Pleased by the loud click the door lock made after Barney left, she sat on the couch and unfolded the piece of paper in her hand. There were his numbers, one she recognized as Pearl's and the other she had not seen before. She picked up the phone and dialed. The man who answered the phone at the gas station was not pleasant, though he did agree to tell Kage when he came in that she had called.

*   *   *

Though she imagined everyone else in Ridgewood was asleep, Gracie was wide awake, questioning her sanity. She glared at the hole in the curtain. On impulse, she threw the curtain to the floor, wildly stomping on it, tangling her feet and nearly falling. Catching her balance on the arm chair, she wadded the curtain up, tucking it beneath her right arm. When she found the hole again, she ripped the curtain in one restless motion. Though the insane behavior didn't make her feel better, it fit her mood perfectly. She had unevenly sewn the unraveling hem on the sitting room curtain and accidently cut the material when she removed the stitches. With the curtain in ruins, she stretched to hang a sheet she found in the closet over the window.

She tried to make her grandfather's favorite banana nut bread but didn't have the patience to follow the recipe. She guessed at the measurements and substituted ingredients. The curtain in the trash was now topped off with the half-baked banana nut bread batter. Her life at eighteen had turned into watching the phone, waiting for it to ring, and hoping she could get her grandfather to the bathroom quickly enough.

When asked how she was doing, Gracie never shared the truth, that sleep brought on nightmares and that she cried alone in the wee hours of the night, since her grandfather was no longer able to come to her room to comfort her. Maybe she didn't tell anyone because she no longer wanted to hear shallow words of encouragement and lame attempts to cheer her up. The conversations were the same: *It is all going to be all right. Things happen for a reason. It is the hard times that make you stronger. Everybody in this town loves you. We are your family too.* Not by a long shot had anyone in Ridgewood ever come close to finding the comforting words she needed. A long cry in her grandfather's arms would help her feel that someone understood, but his arms no longer had the strength to hold her. She felt him slipping away.

Chapter 20

"Did you get my letters?" Kage panted, out of breath from his jog to the nearest payphone on a short break. "How'd you get the station's number? My boss said you called. You okay?"

"Kage!"

"Gracie, I need to ask you something. Are you talkin' with Barney?"

"Not like that! Kage, I can't stand him. I'm so glad you called! He keeps coming by or calling and asking to see me. I told him no. He told me you've been talking to other women."

"What? That guy's a liar, and I've heard stories about him. When I called Gene, Barney grabbed the phone to tell me that you two were seeing each other," Kage raged. "Don't talk to him anymore, okay?

"Gladly!"

"Tell me about your grandfather."

"It's hard ..." Gracie's voice quieted.

"He'll be okay. He's a tough bird. He nearly scared me off."

"I think he thinks he did, and he's not too upset about it," Gracie said and attempted a laugh, but her voice failed.

"He's lucky to have you," Kage encouraged.

"He's not getting out of bed, and he lets me do things for him that he never did before without a fight." She sat quiet for a second and then sputtered, "I'm losing him."

Kage listened to her weep, feeling helpless.

*   *   *

Gene strung the Christmas lights, hanging them from the loft and winding them around the beams in the barn from the roof to the floor. *Joy to the World* from the Victor RCA radio filled the room. Willy and Barney dragged in an evergreen tree that must have been chosen more for being the closest and easiest to cut and haul than for its looks. Without any ornaments to hang, it didn't matter that one side was dry and crumbled at the touch. Gene hadn't decorated for Christmas in years. Actually, he'd never decorated for Christmas. Olivia had always done the hard work. He'd just supplied the biggest tree he could cut and pull through the barn door and stand upright without breaking his back.

"Why're we celebrating this year?" Willy asked staring at a blinking light like a deer in headlights.

"Always celebrated it," Gene answered pouring water into the bucket of rocks that was holding the tree steady.

"Well, why all the bright lights and music playin'?" Willy touched the colored bulb.

182

"She always loved Christmas," he swatted Willy away from the popcorn bowl and began stringing the popcorn with a needle and thread, "and so do I."

*   *   *

"We wish you a Merry Christmas. We wish you a Merry Christmas ..." voices rang outside. Gracie opened the door to Christmas carolers. Erma escaped from the singers and pranced to the porch to give Gracie a hug and then found her place again with the crowd tucked beside Pastor Ted. Gracie hadn't realized how much she needed the hugs and joyful sounds.

"Come in. I'll check to see if Granddaddy feels like having you sing to him," Gracie said. She opened the door wide and motioned for everyone to come inside.

Erma didn't wait with the group in the sitting room but instead followed Gracie into her Grandfather's room. "It's Christmas Eve," she spouted as she rounded the corner into his bedroom.

Thomas tried to adjust in the bed so he could sit up a bit as he agreed, "It is."

"We are here to wish you a Merry Christmas!" Erma leaned in to hug him.

"Go ahead and get everyone, Erma. Bring them in here," Gracie requested as she helped stuff a pillow behind his back and another under his neck as he worked to scoot himself up in bed to a sitting position.

183

Gracie sat next to her grandfather on the bed, straightened the sheets over his legs and placed her arm around his shoulders. She rested her head against him. He smelled like Erma's perfume.

"Joy to the World, the Lord is come ..." they entered the room singing, packing the small room. They sang three songs, and Pastor Ted prayed.

"You're lookin' good, Thomas." Pastor Ted stepped forward and extended his hand to place it on Thomas's.

"Doesn't he look great!" Erma gushed.

Gracie nodded her head and added, "First time I've seen him smile in weeks."

*   *   *

Kage wrapped the package with a brown paper bag he'd cut flat to fold around the box, inside he'd stuffed paper hoping the gift would make it through the mail to Gracie without breaking.

"What'cha got?" Pearl walked toward him from the kitchen with a cup of coffee, steam hovering at its rim.

"A present for Gracie."

"For Christmas?"

"More like New Years I guess. Still gotta get it mailed."

"She'll love it, I'm sure."

"Got you something." Kage pulled out a box wrapped in newspaper, not so much for safe packing but for lack of any Christmas wrapping paper.

"For me? From my little brother," Pearl cooed and reached for it.

"Are all big sisters so grabby?" Kage jested.

"Did you call me crabby? That's not nice, little brother," Pearl teased.

"Now that you mention it," Kage retorted as Pearl ripped open the package.

"Socks?" Pearl snickered.

"Not just any socks—knee socks. They'll keep you warm."

"And single," Pearl added and slipped off her shoes and socks and pulled on the knee socks. "Where's my purse? I got you something, too."

Kage pointed to the kitchen table, and Pearl shuffled over in her socks and pulled out a small paper bag.

"A Town's Tavern T-shirt. I like it. Did you steal it?" Kage flipped the shirt around to the back that read "St. Patrick's Day Beer Fest 1965".

"I did not!" Pearl squawked. "I pulled it from the trash where they'd tossed several from the stockroom."

"Even better," Kage chuckled and pulled the T-shirt over the one he was wearing. "Thanks, Sis."

"Stick around and next December I'll get you the 1966 St. Patrick's Day Beer Fest T-shirt for Christmas to go with this one."

"Who could turn that offer down," Kage teased. "By then I'll have saved up and can buy you several pairs of those knee socks."

"Please do. I'll have worn these out by then, you know," Pearl kidded. She lifted her leg and circled her foot at the ankle.

*   *   *

Gracie snuck into her grandfather's room, trying not to wake him. She set down the fruit basket she'd picked up at Franklin's Grocery. It was his Christmas gift from her. Erma had insisted on packing it with twice the fruit and charging half the price. Gracie knew not to resist and cooed words of appreciation, pleasing Erma.

"Gracie, can you reach in that drawer and pull out the book in there?" Thomas asked Gracie as she picked up his soup dish from the nightstand.

"Thought you were asleep?" Gracie set the soup dish back down and opened the drawer, "This book?" She pulled out the Bible.

"No, the other one."

Gracie reached further back in the drawer and pulled out a notepad with a floral cover. She handed it to Thomas.

"It's for you."

Gracie opened it. "There's a bunch of writing in here."

"I didn't have a way to get out and get you a present, then I remembered this."

"What is it?"

186

"Marilee's prayer journal. She used to write her prayers out every night once you moved in with us. Prayers for you. Even when she wasn't doing well, she'd write."

"Granddaddy, oh my!"

"Read me one. Don't care. Just pick one."

Gracie turned the pages. "There are so many. I don't know."

"Then read more than one. Just read to me."

Gracie flipped to the middle of the journal and her eyes fell on a page near its center.

"March 20—Pastor Ted preached today on Isaiah 45: 13-14. Though I've read through Isaiah more than once, this verse didn't stand out to me, and it wouldn't have for the reasons that it did today. He read to us: "For I am the Lord, your God, who takes hold of your right hand and says to you, Do not fear; I will help you. Do not be afraid, for I myself will help you declares the Lord, your Redeemer, the Holy One of Israel."

Dear God, please take care of my Gracie. Keep your grip strong. What we see from this earthly view is brokenness and loss. My heart is broken. Shattered into pieces that only you can put back together. In the same way Gracie struggles I do too. I am broken and it is like people expect the pain to heal as unrealistically as Gracie would wake up with her right hand again. Not on this earth.

God, please help Gracie do so well without her right hand that she knows that you have hold of it, helping her in every struggle. Can there be no more tears when she can't open the pickle jar? Will you give her as pretty handwriting with her left hand as she had with her right? Bring to her a loving husband to clasp her necklace for her when Thomas and I can no longer ....

Gracie blinked through the tears. She looked up and her grandfather was sleeping peacefully. Gracie flipped to the back of the journal where the pages were blank. She dug for a pen in the nightstand drawer and found one. She began to write.

God, please tell Grandma that I am writing this with my left hand, and she'd be proud. I know that I don't pray often enough. My mind wanders and honestly, I question if the prayers work sometimes. Pastor Ted's sermon a few Sundays ago was from Mark when the disciples woke Jesus in the boat during the storm. Jesus asked why they were afraid and if they had no faith. I opened her journal to the verse she'd written with a similar message. God was that you? Are you here? How do I not be afraid? Help me.

Gracie flipped the page and wrote in large letters: *Mark 5:36: Do not be afraid; just believe.*

Pastor Ted had said these words, spoken by Jesus, so many times that Sunday, that she had them memorized. She dated the next page for the following day. She planned to write her prayers until all the pages were full.

Chapter 21

The note in Gracie's hand postmarked January 3 was the most recent, Kage's ninth letter to her. She received this one tucked inside a package. She bought him a new pocket knife for Christmas, and he'd mailed her an Everly Brothers record with her favorite song "All I Have to Do is Dream." She pictured Kage in her mind. *At what point had the awkwardness given way to excitement, and the excitement extended to friendship, and now, had it become love?* She relived the feeling of his arms—the protection, the happiness, the love. It was nice to enjoy thoughts of Kage without having to admit that the distance and passing days made it difficult.

She jumped. The crash in her grandfather's bedroom sent her running. Along with his wedding picture, Thomas slumped against the bedroom floor.

*　　　*　　　*

Gracie imagined it was the fright in her voice that encouraged Dr. Laben to arrive so quickly. He and Gracie managed to get

Thomas back in bed, but he wasn't responding. Dr. Laben dropped his head, avoiding Gracie's gaze. "I'll call Pastor Ted."

His words caused Gracie's heart to nearly stop.

Gracie sank to the floor in the hallway as she pulled the ruffle around the neck of her nightgown to cover her face. The sting of the cool hardwood against her legs awakened the rest of her body which had gone numb. She wrapped her arm tightly around her knees, her body balled up. She didn't cry, only shook. She wasn't ready for this.

January 4, 1966
Thomas Edward Howard
joined his wife and son
in the peaceful arms of our
Savior, Jesus Christ, in Heaven.
He is survived by a sister and granddaughter.

It took everything she had to call her Aunt Elaine in Bellmont who was bedridden after complications with her hip surgery. The conversation altered between tears, comforting words and more tears. People drifted in and out of Gracie's house bringing food, envelopes of money, and more flowers than she knew how to care for. The evening passed in a daze, each hour colliding with the one before. Erma declared she would stay with Gracie for the night, while Aaron's mother insisted on taking Gracie home with her. In the end, with lots of assurance from Gracie that she'd be fine, they went home. She waved goodbye and closed the front door. Though Gracie hadn't wanted anyone to stay with her, she was aware of one thing that chilled her all over—she was truly by herself, alone, for the first time in her life.

*   *   *

Pastor Ted stepped toward the front of the church. Unlike at other funerals he had presided over, he had no notes in his hands. He just stood looking from where Thomas peacefully rested to where Gracie sat. He looked down, not yet speaking.

Every pew was filled, parents held young children on their laps. The church was a sea of black, the only color coming from potted plants surrounding the sanctuary and Erma Franklin's shawl. She wore the traditional black and topped the outfit off with a large black hat, the bow vying with the size of the ribbons hanging from the flower baskets. Her shawl, made of silk ribbons and authentic bird feathers, draped her shoulders. The bird feathers intertwined and tangled with the silk ribbons, creating a bright red, purple, and orange wrap. Her arrival had caused an outbreak of sneezing as she found a seat near the front. The shawl whipped against the kids' noses as she passed, tickling sneezes right out of them.

Pastor Ted seemingly struggled to begin the eulogy. His eyes focused on the floor, he started, "I've known Thomas my entire life, and through him I've learned more than any sermon that has ever passed through me to you." His voice was quiet, unlike

191

when giving the forceful sermons that Gracie had grown accustomed to over the years. He told tales of Thomas and recounted the amazing faith Thomas had maintained throughout a life that would have shaken the devotion of many others.

In the middle of the eulogy, when Pastor Ted had praised Gracie for her love and care for her grandfather, Erma had cried out, "Oh Gracie, Gracie, my Gracie!" and buried her face in a handkerchief.

Pastor Ted paused. He wiped a tear and continued. "Gracie wanted me to read something to you today." He reached beneath the podium and pulled out a thin book. "I'll close today with this Bible verse that Marilee wrote in a journal to Gracie. Marilee begins, 'On your toughest days, know these words. Psalms 34:17-18. The righteous cry out and the Lord hears them; he delivers them from all their troubles. The Lord is close to the brokenhearted and saves those who are crushed in spirit." Pastor Ted closed the journal, held it to his chest and bowed his head. The next few seconds passed with a rhythm of sniffles. "Amen," he concluded. Then added, "Those of you who wish to come forward for a final moment with Thomas are invited." Pastor Ted motioned for Gracie to come forward to stand beside him near Thomas.

Erma was first to their side, bird feathers that fell from the elaborate stole mapping her trail. She dramatically leaned her head back and held tight to her hat with one hand and the front of her shawl with the other and wailed. Gracie turned her head to avoid the feathered madness as Erma reached out to hug her. Seconds later Pastor Ted was smothered as Erma collapsed against him. The line of folks waiting behind her stood patiently for a moment until a rustling of hushed whispers began and children scurried to gather freed feathers.

Though the ruckus, Willy and Gene stood somber. For the first time Gracie noticed the slight resemblance between the two brothers. Willy's face seemed thinner without the goofy grin. He dressed in his best effort of a suit and tie, the varied shades divulging nothing had been purchased in unison. Gene kept his head down. Gracie wondered if his eyes were damp. This was the only time in Gracie's life that she would hug Willy and Gene. As she had suspected, it was awkward, but that had fitted well into a day full of uncomfortable moments.

*   *   *

Kage had arrived late for his shift. His boss hadn't spoken kind words to him all day. When the phone rang and he handed it over without reprimand, Kage knew something was wrong.

"Oh, Gracie!" Kage paced. "When's the funeral?"

"It was today," Gracie murmured.

"Are you going to be okay?" Though she was miles away and he could only hear her breath in the phone, he knew she was shaking her head, unable to speak.

Kage's boss, though considerate enough to let him talk with Gracie, banged shut the cash register drawer and stomped outside to pump gas, clearly sending a message for Kage to end his conversation.

Chapter 22

"No ma'am! You, my dear, don't have a choice." Erma picked up Gracie's purse and carried it out the door, assuming Gracie would follow.

Erma had forced Gracie off the couch and into the bath, insisting Gracie go shopping with her.

Gracie, who didn't view shopping as recreation, soon learned Erma had the hobby down pat. They stopped in a store in Hartington. Gracie lifted the price tag and wanted to apologize to the clerk for touching it. Erma twirled around, picked up several items and threw them over her arm. Then she waved her hand in the air.

"Toodles. Over here!" She sang out to the young man behind the counter.

Gracie looked at the garments hanging in the dressing room, as Erma went on about how the mini skirt was the new look that everyone would be wearing by the end of the year. Gracie tugged at the skirt of the dress on the hanger. She knew her grandfather would've had a great deal to say about this little escapade with Erma.

"Go on. Try it on. You have the perfect body for it," Erma encouraged Gracie. "It wasn't that long ago that I looked as youthful as you." Erma sucked in her lips, emphasizing her cheekbones, tilted her head toward the full-length mirror, and ran her hands over her stomach and hips.

Gracie thought the solid white dress with a simple silver belt buckle was pretty; however, she knew she would never wear it. She imagined Pastor Ted stopping Sunday service and dropping to his knees to pray thinking Gracie had gone into such poverty that she could only afford half of her dress.

Erma went on and on about the white dress but in the end, they left with a figure-hugging, pastel, wide-legged jumpsuit and a pair of flat-heeled boots. Gracie wondered if people in Louisville wore outfits like that.

*   *   *

Gene wished he could do more. Gracie didn't answer when he knocked several times, so he walked around Gracie's house to the back and into the cellar to unload the jars of canned corn, beans and apples.

He knocked on the back door. Waiting, he held two freezer cartons of strawberry preserves. He knocked once more, then leaned toward the door and called out, "Gracie?"

No answer. He jiggled the door knob, and it unlatched. He cupped his hand around his mouth like a miniature megaphone

196

and leaned into the cracked open edge of the door and shouted, "Gracie, I have a couple things for your freezer." He paused listening. No sound.

Strawberry preserves were Gracie's favorite, at least that is what Thomas had told him once. It had been Olivia's too. He crouched down low to the ground and covered his eyes with one hand and edged the door open with the hand holding the freezer cartons of preserves. "I'm sitting these inside," he mumbled. He pushed the door open just enough to push the preserves through. He peeked between his fingers. The preserves had slid along the floor and come to rest beside the refrigerator. He placed his hand on his knee for balance and stood up, finally uncovering his face. He pulled the door shut, making sure to hear it latch and tugged on it once more to confirm it was secure.

He hadn't been to Thomas's house in years, although he'd seen him nearly every day for the last decade either at Swirly's or at church. The stone steps beneath his feet appeared to shift; he felt off balance all of a sudden. At first, he thought maybe he was light headed from standing up. Then he looked up to see if it had started to drizzle. "I'm gone," Gene called back at the empty house. Through the blur, his steps felt weak and broken. He wiped the tears from his eyes and rounded the house toward his truck.

* * *

"Gracie?"

"Kage!"

"Your phone works! I dialed your number, knowing it was disconnected. I know that's crazy, but I wanted to feel the number on my fingers even if just to hear the recording, but you answered!" Gracie's voice rang into the phone.

Kage glanced at the clock. It was just past midnight.

"Pearl must have paid the phone bill," Kage sat up on the couch stretching his forehead to make sure his eyes were open, that he wasn't dreaming. "I miss you."

"I miss you! It's hard. You know, here without him," Gracie murmured.

"I'm sure it is."

"I need you."

Gracie's words tugged at his heart. "I can hitch rides to Ridgewood and be there."

"Your job, your sister?" Gracie's voice broke. "But I want to see you so badly. Sometimes I pretend you are here with me, because this house is so quiet," Gracie confessed. "I've read your letters over and over."

"I shouldn't have left."

Gracie interrupted, "But, your sister—I understand."

"Come see me, Gracie. Close up the ice cream shop and come see me."

"I haven't opened it since ..." her voice faded.

"Come, Gracie, please." Kage didn't recognize his own voice, begging.

"I have the money to buy a ticket and could afford to stay in the hotel. Is the hotel close by you?" Gracie asked.

"Yes. Do it, Gracie!"

"I want to Kage, I do." Gracie struggled. "But I'm scared."

"I'll meet you at the bus stop. I'll be the first person you see when you step off. I promise," Kage's words raced.

"Promise?" Gracie sounded like a little girl.

"Promise."

"Okay," Gracie whispered.

Kage sat staring at the phone, not believing that she had actually said yes.

When the phone rang again seconds later, he expected it to be Gracie—afraid she changed her mind.

"Is Pearl there?"

"No," Kage replied, relieved it wasn't Gracie reneging.

"Expect her soon?" The voice on the other end quizzed.

"Don't know for sure," Kage answered.

"Can you take a number down?"

"Sure." Kage leaned over the end table, turned on the lamp, grabbed a pen and rummaged for a piece of paper, "Ready."

"It's Cecil at 555-684-1186."

Kage sat silent, but then managed, "Cecil. Cecil Kage?"

"Yep, who's askin'?" Cecil's tone grew noticeably harsh.

"Benjamin Kage," he paused. "Your brother," his voice dropped off.

"Well, shoot me in the hind-end, I swear! Where'd you come from?" Cecil snorted. "I was scared it was somebody wanting us for money or worse. It's my brother Ben! Well, I ain't believin' this! What you been doing for, oh, the past what's it been, twenty years?"

"Been doing this and that to make some cash, traveled through both Georgia and Alabama wondering if I would ever find my brothers," Kage replied.

"Finished our last job in Alabama this week and we're headed off again in a couple weeks for another farther South," Cecil said. "You lookin' for work?"

"Got a job but always looking for good paying work."

"Well, from what we hear, there is lots of work in Florida. They are building up so many hotels and resorts that they can't get enough workers. Paying better than this road work, because they're on a tight schedule, and private companies with lots of money they say."

"Heard the same."

"Well, tell Pearl we're headed up to see her," Cecil said. "You gonna be there a while?"

"Plan to," Kage said. "I'll let her know."

As Cecil ended the call, Kage thought of questions he wanted to ask him. Some were easily answered, but others he didn't even know how to ask, like did they blame him for their mother's death.

Chapter 23

Gracie stepped into the bus station. She set down the overnight bag she'd pulled out of the bedroom closet and rubbed her hand against her hip. Self-consciously, she re-tucked her blouse as she walked toward the ticket office.

"Gracie!" Erma Franklin called from the bench in the waiting area.

Startled, Gracie jumped. "Oh! Erma, I didn't see you there."

"I'm waiting for Corporal Ben Franklin. He's home for the weekend. Don't you love the way that sounds?" She repeated it raising her chin, "Corporal Ben Franklin."

"That's great. Please tell him I said congratulations." Gracie took a step toward the ticket office window.

"Where are *you* going?" Erma asked with a coo.

Gracie looked down and then away, before confessing, "Louisville."

Erma raised her hand to her face and covered her mouth but didn't say anything. As if on the instant, Gracie's prayer was answered; Mr. Carrier called for Gracie to step to the ticket window.

While Erma was chatting away with the others waiting for the bus to arrive, Gracie grabbed her bag and snuck outside to wait for the bus.

She glanced toward the closed sign, hanging on Swirly's door, and knew that her grandfather wouldn't approve. She was going to see Kage.

When the bus arrived, the driver stepped off first. Two men in suits followed him, and one handed him a tip. The driver responded appreciatively, "Thank you, Mr. Myers." Gracie wondered what business they had in Ridgewood. When she saw Corporal Ben Franklin step off the bus, she turned away so as not to make eye contact and slid behind the two men in suits, so as not to be seen. Erma alone would be enough to spread the gossip of Gracie's departure.

The bus driver yelled out to board the bus, "Put your luggage under here. Hurry up now." He swung open the door on the lower end of the bus and two pieces of luggage fell out. Pulling Gracie's luggage handle from her hand, he yelled to her, "Go on, girl."

Gracie stepped onto the bus and walked toward the back sitting in the only empty seat. The older lady she had sat beside puckered her lips tightly, as if she had just sucked on a lemon, placed her hand on Gracie's knee, and said, "Sweetheart, this seat is saved. My daughter is meeting me at the next stop."

Looking around the bus, Gracie saw no other empty seats; her heart began to pound. She gave a timid smile to the lady who either did not sense Gracie's discomfort or simply didn't care.

Gracie stood and walked toward the front as everyone settled. As she looked from the bus window at everything familiar that she was leaving, she already missed it.

"You need a seat, young lady? You can sit right here on my lap," a man said as she passed.

Gracie could see from the corner of her eye his brute body jiggling with coarse laughter as he looked to see who appreciated his humor.

"Take a seat!" the bus driver yelled.

At that everyone on the bus turned their heads toward Gracie.

"I'm not sure there is one," Gracie answered, her voice too quiet for him to hear.

As she made her way to the front of the bus, the bus driver's stare pierced her. "There aren't any seats, just one, and she is saving it," Gracie muttered.

"Ain't no saved seats on this bus. What does your ticket say? You got a seat assigned to you. Can you read, girl?" The bus driver scoffed.

"Yes, I can read," she mumbled. Actually, Gracie hadn't realized there was a seat number on her ticket. She quickly struggled to pull the ticket from her sweater pocket. Not knowing where on the ticket to find the seat number, she handed the ticket to him. She could see the expression on his face as if he said, "So you can't read."

"31B," he said. "That's your seat by the lady in the back. Ain't no saved seats!" He called again to the back of the bus and pushed the ticket at Gracie.

Gracie turned again toward the back of the bus as it pulled away. Her body swung with the bus, and she nearly did land in a man's lap. He steadied her with his hand.

She mumbled, "Thanks." He returned a simple smile, and she noticed his U.S. Army fatigues.

Sitting down beside the lady, Gracie said weakly, "This is the seat I'm assigned."

The lady smiled, but it was not the gentle smile of the man in the service uniform. It was a familiar, condescending smile. "You can sit right here until the next stop. When Laura gets on, you can ride in her seat." She spoke as if it would be Gracie's privilege to switch seats with her daughter.

"I can do that." Gracie looked at her hand in her lap still clutching the ticket.

"You don't travel much, do you?" The lady asked, her voice sweet and condescending.

"This is my first time on a bus," Gracie said, knowing that wasn't news to anyone.

"How old are you?" the lady asked, twisting her head to take a good look at Gracie.

"I'm nineteen," Gracie answered, looking away from the lady. As she fiddled with the button on her sweater, she felt more like eight.

Gracie noticed the lady staring at her left hand as it rested on her right arm.

"You can't read?"

Gracie wondered if that was really the question she had on her mind.

"Yes, I read fine," Gracie countered, though she realized the lady didn't believe her anyway.

*   *   *

Kage twisted the metal watch band on his arm and glanced at the watch's face, not even registering the time. Standing outside the doors of the bus depot looking down the road, he glanced away and back again as if in that second the bus might round the corner. Because he couldn't sit still, he stood. When he could no longer stand still, he paced. She would be here, here with him, in just a few minutes.

Kage hoped that the rain would hold off until Gracie arrived, but soon it began to pour, and he could no longer see as far as the bend in the road. Kage backed toward the edge of the bus depot and then under the overhang that shielded him from the steady downpour. This worked until the wind picked up and a gust of rain blew over him, soaking him all at once. He ran inside.

The voices echoed in the bus station's lobby. Kage made his way through the crowd, as he heard someone yell, "It's here."

He dashed out the doors into the rain. A few people followed, standing beside him as the bus came to a stop.

*   *   *

Gracie spotted Kage as soon as the bus door opened. His hair was soaked, appearing two shades darker, and his clothes were drenched. He wore a lightly starched, white, long-sleeved dress shirt—wet now, clinging so that his skin showed through. She'd never seen him look so handsome, his dimple obvious and his eyes intense.

Gracie's new seat, once she'd traded, giving hers to the lady's traveling companion, was on the second row. With only six steps, she found herself in Kage's arms. He lifted her off her feet, his familiar arms tight around her waist. She could feel his cool skin through her blouse.

*   *   *

They looked like wet ducks when they arrived at Pearl's; Gracie showered first and then Kage. Though Pearl wasn't there, her apartment smelled of coffee and freshly sprayed floral perfume. The phone rang, and on its third ring Gracie decided to answer it.

"Hey, Pearl."

"She's at work."

"I keep missing that girl. She ain't called me back. This is Cecil."

"Oh," Gracie said. "You are Kage's brother?"

"Kage? Which Kage brother? There's several of us, little lady," Cecil snorted.

"Benjamin," Gracie said, liking the sound of his first name on her lips.

"Well, tell those two good-for-nothin's for one of them to meet their brothers at the bus station this afternoon."

As Gracie hung up the phone, she spotted a photograph of Pearl and what looked like one of Kage's brothers. She ran her finger over the frame and then touched their faces just as she had done so many times with her sister Sarah's photo. What she would give to be able to see Sarah again. At that moment with that thought, she was jealous of Kage. As she picked up more of Pearl's family photos, she thought of Kage drifting and alone while she grew up with her loving grandfather. But the simple truth was that he was uniting with his family, just as she had lost the last member of hers.

Chapter 24

From a distance, Kage watched the three men exit the bus. He knew as soon as he saw the first one step off that he was a brother. Not strictly because his jaw line resembled Kage's or because of the similarities of their deep-set eyes, but it was his expression. He didn't look the least bit enthused to be there, just about as excited as Kage had felt the first day he stepped foot in Ridgewood. The other two followed, one built with a frame similar to the first, but the other lighter and less stout. Kage released Gracie's hand and stepped forward but hesitated when he heard his name called from behind.

"Ben? I got off work early," Pearl yelled.

Kage motioned to Pearl to hurry up, then pressed the palms of his hands against his pants. He took Gracie's hand to pull her swiftly through the crowd in the bus depot toward his brothers.

The largest brother of the three turned to Kage when he heard Pearl's voice and motioned for the others. Many times Kage had pictured in his mind what meeting his brothers would

208

be like, but this was real, not just another concoction of his imagination.

"Little Ben?" called the smallest brother from a few steps behind the other two. "Are you Benjamin Kage? I'm your brother Cecil, Cecil Kage." Cecil jogged toward Kage. Kage, picking up his step, loosened his grip of Gracie's hand as Cecil reached out to pull Kage into his arms. "We never thought we'd ever meet you, little brother."

Pearl called out, "Carl!" She caught up with the largest of the brothers and gave him a bear hug. He lifted her and swung her around. She squealed.

The other extended his hand to Kage, "I'm Adam." Adam had a deep, gruff voice and a beard more from neglect than purpose. He was a husky man, similar in stature to Carl and his muscular physique, but with the addition of a beer belly. Adam, dressed in a T-shirt and jeans, held a heavy brown overcoat. Dark bikers' tattoos covered both arms. Kage recognized an intensity in his eyes similar to the other two, but beyond that and the physique, there was not much of a family resemblance.

Carl lowered Pearl to her feet and extended his hand to Kage, then followed the firm handshake with a hug and hardy slap on the back. Carl had a noticeable scar above his left temple, and his receding sandy hair exposed a fresher wound.

"This is Gracie," Kage turned to Gracie. Cecil extended his right hand. Gracie offered her left hand and he took it awkwardly at the wrist. Adam and Carl nodded "hello" to Gracie.

"You boys should have warned me sooner you were coming and maybe I could've scheduled time off. I had to beg and plead to get this afternoon off," Pearl teased.

"Well, show us this work place of yours," Carl said.

"Which, the hotel or bar?"

Carl raised his hand to his mouth as if he were drinking from a cup.

Pearl smirked, "Not sure why I even asked." She pointed in the direction of Town's Tavern.

"You got our room reserved, Sis?" Cecil asked, tossing his arm over her shoulders.

"Yes, through the end of the week," Pearl answered, nudging him in the ribs. "No crazy business or misbehaving, you hear? People there know me."

"You got all the connections." Cecil bowed to her.

"Wait a minute. I can set you up in this joint, but you're paying the bill."

"You got it. We might even buy you a drink for all your trouble," Cecil kidded.

*   *   *

Town's Tavern had drawn its regular weekend crowd. Kage whispered in Gracie's ear, "Let's take a walk. These guys don't look nearly as beautiful as you." Kage grabbed Gracie's sweater.

Returning the tender squeeze of his hand, she reassured him that she had been eagerly waiting for him to ask.

As the evening sky's crimson and violet canvas faded with the sun, an easy breeze picked up, and Gracie held the side seam of her ankle-length skirt with her hand. A paper cup scooted past on the asphalt, picking up speed. It spun, twisted and beat them to the fence which ran parallel to the riverfront. Gracie wrapped her arms around Kage's neck releasing her skirt to the coils and twists of the wind.

"You'd think the most exciting part of my day would've been to see my brothers for the first time." Kage glanced toward the water's edge.

In his arms, she felt a comfort she desperately needed after the uncertainty of the past weeks. Gracie lifted her face to the breeze as she sank further into Kage's embrace, allowing the wind to carry a lifetime of worries away.

Kage continued, "But honestly, after I'd met them," he shrugged his shoulders, "it didn't seem to matter so much. I mean, sure I'd always wanted to see them, but ..." Kage paused as if searching for his next words. "When I think of them right now, I still see them with the imaginary faces that I've always pictured," Kage paused again, looking over Gracie's shoulder, seemingly deep into the water.

Under the riverfront-park lights, Gracie watched his eyes and every expression as he spoke. Even the movement of his jaw line meant something to her—as if it were part of the story.

Gracie listened while he tried to absorb the events of the day.

"It's like their real faces, the men I met today, get in the way. I know that sounds weird. I had them, well, made up, I guess. They were," he paused once more.

"They were what?" Gracie asked, searching his face.

"I don't know. I feel bad saying it. I just felt like, well, they'd be," he still searched for the word, "more."

"Like what? More of them? Or larger? I'm not sure Adam could be much larger or was that Carl?" Gracie asked teasing.

Kage laughed at her lame attempt to be witty. He placed his hand on the back of her head as she looked up at him. "No, I mean," Kage struggled again to explain his feelings. "It just doesn't make sense. I feel disappointed, and I can't explain it. They just weren't what I expected, that's all, I guess. They're strangers. How can those strangers be my brothers?"

Pulling at his arm, Gracie indicated she wanted him to sit next to her on a nearby concrete platform. "It's okay, Kage. You just met them. You still don't know them. You've got time to get to know them better."

"I know. I just imagined it for so many years—my entire life. I guess I didn't really know what it would be like to meet them." Kage repeated himself, looking away.

"And you expected more—more than a hand shake and 'where's the bar?'" Gracie asked. "Maybe something about them missing you or asking about your life?" Gracie paused, turning his face to hers with her hand. She watched for any indication

212

that she was on track. "Or them wanting to just stare at you for a long time not believing that you were really, finally with them. Kind of like how I feel about you."

With those words, he kissed her. He nodded his head—their lips still touching. Gracie felt as if she had just met the little boy from the orphanage.

"How'd you do that?" Kage broke away from their kiss but kept her wrapped closely to him in his arms.

"Do what?"

"Know what I was feeling?"

Gracie hesitated before speaking. "I know I don't talk much about that night and the fire," Gracie whispered taking another second before continuing. When she spoke again her voice was raw. "I remember after the fire, I'd play with kids in the park after school, and I'd be swinging, running, and laughing, and I'd forget. I'd forget what had happened, you know—even what happened to me." Gracie looked down at her arm.

"Then all the kids would jump onto the monkey bars. I'd stop mid-step, and it would all rush back. The ache would make my throat tighten, and I'd try to swallow, but the feeling wouldn't go away. No one noticed me just standing there though, without a hand, unable to join in. They all kept playing, hooting and giggling as they swung from bar to bar, and I'd just stand there feeling like the world was closing in on me. Blinking as hard as I could, I hoped they would get worn out with the monkey bars so we could do something else. No one ever noticed that it hurt so bad to be left out and to be different—to be so incomplete."

Kage pulled her closer, tightening his grip, as if he could maybe protect her from the painful memory.

"It wasn't just that I couldn't play with them anymore. It was that not a single kid understood how I felt. They all just went on—normal. No one cared, and at the same time, I didn't want anyone to notice that I was left standing alone. I wanted to hide, to disappear. It all hurt." Gracie breathed in deeply. The simple words revived all the insecure feelings. She looked out into the river. That made it easier for her to talk about it—to almost pretend it was someone else's life.

"I'm sorry," Kage whispered. "I'm sorry for what you've been through. I wish I could make it all perfect for you. I wish I could fix it." He kissed her neck, and Gracie welcomed the tingling sensation.

"It doesn't matter that you can't fix it," Gracie spoke to the distance. "You can't. It can't be fixed." Then she looked directly at Kage and said, "But you do make it better. You have already made it so much better." Gracie shut her eyes and once more breathed in the cool night air. "As hard as I tried to go on and to escape it, nothing's really changed. I'm still and always will be the little girl who ran from that house the night of the fire, that was ... *is* me." Gracie said the words, though difficult, for the first time aloud.

Twisting her torso, she turned toward Kage and wrapped her arms around him and added, "No matter how many brothers and sisters you hunt up and find you're still going to be the little boy who grew up in an orphanage, but that's okay." Gracie hoped he understood. Before she had a chance to say another word, Kage's lips pressed hard against hers, and she knew he did. She knew he understood—her.

*   *   *

Aaron placed a bag of groceries in his passenger seat to deliver to Mrs. Laurel. He even included the pork rinds for her husband as she requested, though Aaron had attended Mr. Laurel's funeral a decade ago.

The visit always went the same—strange—but the same. Aaron would knock. She would call out for her husband to get the door. Aaron would wait. Then she would come to the door mumbling, "Well, I don't know where he could be. He's always sneaking off 'bout suppertime."

The first visit he'd accepted her offer to come in. He took a seat in the garden room and a root beer. She started telling him the story of how Mr. Laurel proposed. "It was so romantic. He told me to meet him at the entrance of the Lost Cave. We'd snuck off there a few times," she admitted, blushing. "When I got there, I didn't see him, but there was a flashlight at the entrance of the cave. I turned it on and started wandering in. Then I saw where he'd scratched the letters "*this way*" into the rock wall. Then several more steps and I saw the word "*here*" carved. There underneath the word, on the ground, was a small black velvet-covered box with a white ribbon tied around it. I opened it and inside was this ring." She held out her left hand. "He was watching and ran to me. We were married days later. He is the best husband a woman could ever have," Mrs. Laurel cooed. She paused only a second. "Sorry he isn't here right now. He's gone to the barber, I think. Yes, it is the barber today. He'll be back this afternoon for supper. I'm cooking."

Searching for an escape plan, Aaron had insisted that Mrs. Laurel needed to start supper before Mr. Laurel got home.

Now the deliveries were simpler since Aaron always mentioned he had several deliveries to make. She'd hand him several dollar bills for the groceries, each rolled perfectly like cigarettes. The first time he'd handed the bills to his aunt at the store, she held them in her palm at a distance, inspecting them. "Well, that's odd. That's exactly how Mr. Laurel used to roll his bills he paid with when I waitressed at the Starlight-Diner."

Aaron's pondering of Mrs. Laurel's antics was interrupted. "You got something for me there?" Barney asked, nodding toward the grocery bag in Arron's car.

"No!" Aaron spouted, sliding into his car.

"Oh, just givin' you a hard time, boy," Barney smirked, sticking his hands in his back pockets.

"I got a delivery to make, if you don't mind." Aaron took the keys of his parent's Ford Mustang from his pocket.

"You seen Gracie?" Barney asked, running the tips of his fingers against the car's hood leaving its clean exterior smudged.

"Why?"

"She ain't been answering her phone."

"Well, she's not in town."

"That right? Where she off to?"

"She's in Louisville. Why?"

"So, she's run off," Barney cracked. "Ain't that sweet?"

*   *   *

"I liked the movie," Gracie said as she walked with Kage. "Wouldn't it be amazing to be able to sing like that, and to have your whole world change overnight into such greatness?" They'd watched *The Singing Nun* starring Debbie Reynolds.

The lights in the hotel hallway were dim.

"Good," Kage answered.

"You aren't listening to me." Gracie nudged him with her elbow.

"Gracie," Kage leaned closer to her outside her hotel room doorway.

"What?" Gracie whispered as his lips brushed hers.

"Don't leave me," he mumbled his lips still on hers. "Don't go back." Tomorrow she was scheduled for the noon bus.

"I don't want to," Gracie lowered her face and nuzzled at his neck.

Kage pleaded pressing against her, "Stay."

Her back pressed against the door, she reached behind for the doorknob. "You, don't go," Gracie said and pulled him into the room.

Kage ran his hands from Gracie's shoulders, down her sides and to her hips. "Gracie ..."

"What?" Gracie mumbled, her lips on Kage's.

Kage, resting his hands on the curve of her hips, pressed forward as they kissed, causing Gracie to stumble. She bumped against the table in the room before catching her balance.

Between breaths, Kage whispered, "I love you."

Gracie twisted from his grasp and fumbled for the lamp, the light waking them from their spell.

She brushed her hair out of her eyes, her hand rested just above her forehead. "What did you say?"

"Huh?"

"What did you just say?" Gracie repeated now, seeing the intensity in his eyes.

"What?"

"Say it again. I want to see you," she paused, "when you say it."

"That I love you?" Kage reached for her.

"Yeah, say it again," Gracie repeated and watched him, her eyes dancing.

"I love you," he whispered, his nose touching hers.

Gracie leaned back, creating a distance between their faces. She now cradled his chin in the palm of her hand. Their eyes locked, and Gracie rubbed her hand along his face. Moving her fingers from his chin over his lips, she then grazed his nose and eyes, to his forehead and back down the side of his cheek. Finally, she pulled his face back to hers. "I think I love you too," Gracie whispered moving her lips closer to his.

"Think!" Kage exclaimed.

"Yeah," Gracie answered, tickled by his reaction. "I mean, I've never ..."

"Me neither, Gracie," Kage retorted. "But I know! Gracie, you are the most amazing girl I've ever known, and when I'm with you, I just can't describe it."

"It's like nothing else matters but for the two of us," Gracie completed his thought.

"Yeah, only you." Kage grabbed her hand drawing it to his lips.

Kage's lips first kissed the back of her hand and then her palm, then he met her eyes. "Do you love me, Gracie?" Kage now held her pinkie finger resting between his lips.

Looking into the face of a man, she saw instead the tender heart of a boy. "I do, Kage. I do love you," the words poured out. They had been bundled up for so long, and their release made Gracie feel like a woman and a little girl at the same time. "I love you," Gracie whispered again. This time more for her ears than his.

Kage picked her up in his arms, scooping her from her feet. His swift movements surprised Gracie, and she squealed.

Kage jested, "It's a good thing. Your pinkie was in grave danger." He bit his teeth together next to Gracie's ear. Setting her down on the edge of the bed, he bent to one knee and loosened her sandal. It dropped to the floor, and then the other. He ran his hand up the calf of her leg and leaned forward to kiss the top of her foot. It tickled; Gracie gasped.

"You, don't leave," Gracie proposed and tugged lightly at the neck of his shirt wanting him next to her. "Hold me. I'll fall asleep in your arms."

"Gracie, I don't think you understand." Kage peered at her bare leg exposed. His eyes lingering at her breasts tucked inside her dress, before looking to her. He shook his head. "No, Gracie," he paused. "I can't just hold you."

Gracie swallowed hard.

"Gracie, I have to go," his voice huskier than usual, "now."

Gracie started to say something, but Kage shook his head. He stood, lifting her legs to the bed. He brushed loose strands of hair behind her right ear. Gracie watched as he removed the jewelry from her wrist and placed it on the nightstand. Grazing her forehead with his lips, he whispered, "Someday, Gracie Howard, I want to buy you a ring for this finger," he said as he took her ring finger and kissed it just below the knuckle.

*   *   *

"You still up?" Kage asked turning on the lamp by the couch in the living room.

"Yeah, just got in myself." Pearl filled a glass with water. "You going to be okay, Kage?"

"What do you mean?" Kage adjusted the blankets on the couch.

"After she goes home, are you going to be okay?" Pearl repeated.

"Yeah," Kage answered, preferring not to talk about it.

"You're good to her, Kage. You're a good man," Pearl said, lighting a cigarette.

"Why do you say that?"

"You love her. It shows in the way you look at her and talk to her. I was just saying she's lucky. That's all."

*   *   *

Gracie, still awake in bed, traced the plaster design on the ceiling as she recounted the day. She couldn't calm her mind. So many feelings ran through her and all at once. For one, she thought about what it might feel like to have her sister to talk to. Then she thought of Pearl, though she'd spent only a short time around her, she knew Pearl well enough already to know Pearl would never have accepted the bus driver's attitude. She would have cut him off mid-sentence. Pearl would have told the lady to find a new seat. She admired how Pearl tackled life, boldly and full of color—evident in Pearl's style, from her red nails to her matte-blue eye shadow.

Then there was Kage. She heard his voice still in her head, his words and his face there when she closed her eyes. Before he left, he tucked her beneath the covers and leaned near her ear and whispered, "Good night." Gracie watched him, watching her. She didn't have to ask what he was thinking. Somehow, she knew. She had to be thinking the same things. He turned off the lamp on his way out, and she stayed until morning tucked under the covers in her dress just as Kage had left her.

Chapter 25

As Gracie rearranged the ice cream tubs to make room for a new one, she thought of how many ice cream shops the city of Louisville might have and wondered if it could use one more. On the bus ride home, she'd scribbled recipes to try a new flavor she'd call *Cozy Chocolate Crunch*–for Kage.

When the front door swung open, Gracie knew who it was without lifting her head.

"Chocolate swirl?" Gracie asked.

"How's Gracie?"

"Doing okay," Gracie answered and gave Gene a weak smile and shifted her eyes downward. Although she enjoyed mixing the new ice cream flavors, it was difficult to keep her mind off her grandfather. "Will you do me a favor?"

"Whatever you need." Gene was alone, no Willy, no Barney–no Kage.

Gracie went to the back room and returned with ice cream scooped on two spoons, resting between her fingers making her hand look like a lobster's claw. "I know tasting all the ice cream flavors is Willy's favorite thing to do, but I need some help."

Gene nodded.

"Try this first." She extended her hand for him to take the spoon held between her thumb and forefinger.

He nibbled at it at first. Then he held it at an arm's length looking closely at the chocolate ice cream. "What's in it?"

"Peanuts and marshmallows."

He took another bite, and Gracie wondered if the other spoon of ice cream she held would melt before he finished.

"Good. Ain't as good as Chocolate Swirl."

"Alright, try this one," and before he asked, she added, "sunflower seeds and coconut.

He handed it back to her. "Don't like coconut."

"Okay," Gracie ate the ice cream melting on the spoon. "One more, hold on." She stepped into the back room and returned. "Last one, cherries and chocolate chips." Gracie handed him the spoon, hoping he'd like it.

"Umm," he nodded his head.

"Good?" Gracie smiled unaware she was nodding along with him.

"Yep," Gene said and handed her the spoon.

"So, you want it? I'm naming it Cozy Chocolate Crunch." Gracie grabbed a cone.

"Nope. Chocolate Swirl," Gene answered and pointed to his favorite.

All week she asked the customers to taste the new flavors. So far cherries-and-chocolate-chips was the favorite, although marshmallows-and-peanuts was a close second. When Aaron was tasting he found a stool in the back and pulled it up to Swirly's counter. "Let me have another taste of that one." He pointed to the nuts and marshmallows. He savored the next bite for a second and then held up a finger, as he swallowed, "Needs peanut butter."

"What? How can all three need peanut butter?"

Gracie pulled the peanut butter jar off the shelf. "Here. Have some peanut butter."

Combining all the ice cream samples in his bowl, Aaron added a big scoop of peanut butter and mixed it all together.

"What do you call that?" Gracie asked, scrunching her nose.

"Gooood!" Aaron stuffed a big spoonful in his mouth.

*   *   *

Gracie brought home a quart of Cozy Chocolate Crunch and wrapped herself in the crocheted afghan on the couch. With the lights out, she nibbled on cherries and chocolate chips while she watched her favorite sitcom. Sally Fields played a spunky girl, full of courage and adventure, named Gidget.

What gave Gracie the idea or guts, she wasn't sure. It could have been an ice cream overdose or Gidget's influence, but Gracie set down the quart of Cozy Chocolate Crunch, pulled out the Samsonite suitcase and started packing.

Chapter 26

"Glue?" Kage's boss repeated. "Nah, ain't got no glue." He fiddled in the drawer and tossed Kage a roll of duct tape.

Kage wasn't sure his day could get worse. He'd lost against Pearl's razor, cutting his face in five places. Toilet paper pieces centered with red dots spotted his chin and cheeks. As he walked to work the sole of his left boot came loose flopping beneath his toes. He wobbled the rest of the way to the gas station, walking on his left heel and looking like an injured degenerate. Kage took off his boot and wrapped the shiny, silver tape around the tip of his boot several times and considered wrapping the other boot so they'd match.

"Can I help you, missy?"

"Is Kage here?

Kage stood from behind the counter, when he heard his name.

Gracie said nothing, just smiled.

"Gracie?" Kage rushed from behind the counter, wearing only one boot and on his other foot a dingy white sock. "How did you get here?"

"Bus." Gracie pointed to her bag.

"You didn't tell me." Kage couldn't believe she was there in front of him.

"I didn't know myself. Last night I was watching Gidget, eating this ice cream," she unzipped her suitcase and pulled out what looked like a bag of ice, "and I wanted you to taste it." She reached into the bag, dug around the melting ice, and pulled out a small container.

"You brought me ice cream?"

"No, I didn't just *bring* you ice cream. I *made* you ice cream."

"What?"

"Cozy Chocolate Crunch—try it. It's good." She extended the container to show him.

Kage pushed the dripping ice cream container across the counter toward his boss, who Kage had learned could be bribed. He pulled Gracie into his arms. "This is the best surprise ever!"

*   *   *

Gracie and Kage met Pearl, Carl, Adam, and Cecil at The Brown Hotel's swanky restaurant. Adam wore a long-sleeved flannel shirt that covered the majority of his tattoos. Cecil and Carl claimed to have 'conveniently found' the expensive, three-colored, striped British blazers they wore over T-shirts. Odds were that Carl's large Western belt buckle came from a similar unsuspecting source. Kage wore a pair of jeans and a button-up white shirt, the tips of its collar wrinkled and yellowed. Pearl's skirt was similar to the one that Erma had encouraged Gracie to buy, though it was black and a size too small. Gracie's modest, pastel-cotton, collared dress made her look like she could have been their mother but for the obvious age difference.

The gentleman greeting them pointed to Adam, indicating he needed to tuck in his shirt. Then he recognized Pearl and took a step back. "You look incredible."

Pearl blushed—her face only a shade lighter than her lipstick.

"This way," he said and waved his hand for the troop to follow. The restaurant, just opening its doors for dinner, was shared by only one other couple. "I think we can work you in at one of our special tables." He winked at Pearl, and she whispered, "Thanks, Harold."

Harold, demeanor intact, unlike his clumsy steps at Pearl's apartment, showed them to a table in the back corner near a fireplace. Candles flickered in the center of each table. The room was especially dim, adding to the delicate ambiance, and increasing Carl's difficulty in maneuvering his way through the restaurant to their table. He bumped and stumbled over several unoccupied chairs, with no regard. The server, dressed in black from head to toe, followed them, straightened each chair, and failed to hide his repulsion. Everything in the restaurant, from the folded cloth napkins to the soft music playing in the background, had been carefully curated.

"It's on me," Kage announced. He had received his check from Gene.

"Well then, I'm havin' the highest priced plate you got." Adam slapped Harold on the back.

Harold pulled out Pearl's seat, leaned forward and whispered something in her ear that caused her cheeks to outshine her lipstick.

"It's on the house," Pearl said, nodding toward Harold as he walked away. "I know people who know people."

"Sister! You sho' are something special. We's a celebratin'! We found our long-lost brother, Benjamin," Cecil told the server as he approached the table.

Carl and Adam yelled out their drink orders, but the server cut them off, "My name is Stanley, and I am your server. this evening ..."

Adam broke in, "Well, serve me a cold one. I'm dry!"

The server continued as if Adam hadn't spoken, "Our special this evening is a petite salmon smothered in ..."

"Ain't getting no petite nothin' tonight." Carl gave Adam a high five.

Stanley gave up and took the drink orders. Harold dropped a basket of bread on the table and gave Pearl a quick thumbs up sign and a wink.

The guys each grabbed a piece and crammed it in their mouths. Adam yelled, his mouth full, "Keep 'em coming, Stan! And get us a couple more of these baskets."

Cecil shared several stories about when they were kids and the crazy things they did growing up. With every piece of bread, there was another story, not a bite slowing him down. After one tale he laughed so hard that a piece of bread shot from his lips. He picked it up and popped it back in his mouth.

"So, remind me where you're from, Gracie?" Cecil asked, pulling Gracie into the conversation.

"Ridgewood, Kentucky, southwest of here. It's pretty there."

"Ridgewood, ain't never heard of it," Adam said. "They make 'shine there?"

"Shine? You mean, moonshine?"

"Yep, 'shine—the good stuff." Adam chugged his beer.

"I don't know." Gracie looked toward Kage.

"Probably," Kage nodded, "but word is that there's treasure buried there." Kage looked oddly at the butter knife.

"Treasure!" Carl exclaimed. "You a treasure hunter, little brother?"

"I knew he looked like a pirate," Adam interjected.

"Pirates search for treasures out at sea or something like that, Adam. Ben ain't no pirate!" Pearl exclaimed.

"I'd like to find me some treasure. Where is this Ridgewood?" Adam said patronizingly.

"I didn't say I believed there's treasure there. I just said that they *say* it has hidden treasure." Kage shared the story of the note written and published in the newspaper and the people who came to Ridgewood in hopes of finding it.

"Well, you keep on dreaming, treasure-hunting, little brother. You managed to dig us and your sister up from nowhere. You might just find you some treasure." Carl raised his glass for a toast. "To Ben, our lost brother, the Treasure Hunter." They managed to clank their glasses together with minimal spillage.

"If there's more pretty 'uns like her in Ridgewater, we might oughta pass through there." Adam winked at Gracie.

"Ridge*wood*," Gracie corrected, scooting her chair closer to Kage.

When Stanley returned with their order, the plates barely fit on the table. As if Carl's entrée were not large enough, he reached for Pearl's plate to grab a shrimp. She slapped his hand, knocking over his beer.

"My lobster's swimmin' again." Carl snorted.

Carl's lap drenched, he raised his empty beer mug, belched and broke into song. "Oh, say can you see, by the dawn's early light what beer we so proudly bear is on my crotch tonight."

Kage, Adam, Cecil and Pearl bent over holding their stomachs, choking with laughter. Gracie shared an apologetic smile with Stanley as he wiped the table and tried to salvage Carl's meal.

*   *   *

231

Adam, well past his liquor limit prior to supper, stumbled up the stairs and into Pearl's apartment. "Sis, where's the 'shine?"

Pearl groaned, "Do I look like I know any bootleggers?"

"You's probably one." Adam's words slurred. "How you afford this place?" He tossed open her curtains with his finger, letting the street light through.

"A regular job. Two jobs at that!" Pearl snapped.

"You didn't answer the first question," Carl pressed.

"Bourbon is as good as it gets around here." Pearl reached for a bottle in her cabinet.

Sitting around the table, they divvied it out. Gracie motioned she would pass.

"You too sweet for this kind of stuff, ain't 'cha?" Adam put his arm around Gracie and leaned toward her face. He tried to follow with a kiss, but she slid back in her chair. Adam fell forward, amusing everyone.

"Lookin' at 'cha, I could see you were a light-weight," Kage teased his brother. With Adam's eyes closed, his drink still found his lips.

"I'm ready for another." Adam pushed his glass to the middle of the table. Kage slid his glass to Adam. "You can have mine. I gotta work in the morning."

"You don't gotta do anything. You're with us now," Adam stammered.

"Cecil says you might be working with us, Ben," Carl swatted Kage on the back.

"Might do it. He says it's good money. How much we talking about?"

"Well, you can make enough in about six months to live the next six." Carl downed his drink.

"Depending on how much it takes you to stay drunk for the next six months," Adam snorted, swaying in his chair.

"But you're working day and night, sometimes not a day off the entire time," Cecil added.

"I can work those conditions," Kage assured him.

Carl took Kage by the bicep. "You look like you're developin'."

"Developing!" Kage pulled his sleeve back to show off his muscle.

Gracie's expression faded as their voices roared one over another. Her heart sank as she listened to him making plans for his future without her.

*   *   *

"It's a big hotel. There has to be a job for Gracie."

Pearl nonchalantly moved a dish towel along the kitchen counter, as she appeared to consider Kage's plea.

"You said the other day that the lady you work with got fired for being late again. You think you can put a few words in for Gracie?" Kage followed Pearl around the kitchen.

"Don't remind me. That could be me if I don't watch my step trying to keep these two jobs and have some kind of a social life hanging out with you idiots. That doesn't include you, Gracie," Pearl winked.

"Seriously, Pearl, I don't think you've had a full day off, but if Gracie got on at the hotel then you two could help cover each other's shifts," Kage pressed on.

"That makes some sense, but really, Kage, what do you think she can do?"

"She runs her grandfather's ice cream shop," Kage jumped to her defense. They carried on bickering, like brother and sister, as if Gracie weren't there.

Gracie pulled her sleeve down over her arm, covering the scars, and placed her left hand over her right arm.

"I never said I wanted a job here." Gracie broke in, shifting her gaze away from them.

Pearl interrupted, "I'm sorry. I didn't mean to be rude. You act like we shouldn't talk about it, but I can't ignore it." Pearl kept talking, giving no one an opportunity to break in. "She's very nice, but she doesn't talk about it." Pearl said to Kage and then turned to Gracie. "And then if a person does talk about it, then ..." Pearl slammed the cabinet door and leaned against the counter.

"I don't really think I want to live here." Gracie's voice cracked.

"Gracie, don't say that," Kage pleaded, sitting beside her. Kage looked toward Pearl. "She just doesn't like to talk about it, okay."

"I don't know that they'd hire me." Gracie added. "You know they'd be thinking the same thing. Kage, you're the only one who doesn't look at me like I'm different, and that's just because you're used to me now."

"Gracie, I never looked at you strange. I wouldn't!" Kage exclaimed.

Pearl whirled around to face them. "Both of you, be quiet!" Pearl screeched, her pitch by far the loudest of the three of them. "You can have your lovers' quarrel another time," Pearl snapped in frustration and threw her hands in the air. Pushing Kage's chair out of the way with unexpected strength that caught him off guard, she headed out of the room. He grabbed the edge of the kitchen table to keep from tipping over.

Instead of leaving though, Pearl came back to the table, and sat beside Gracie. "Listen, I didn't mean anything by what I said—not in a mean way. One thing I am is honest. Life for me isn't always easy either. I'm tired all the time. For the most part I just say what I think and do what I feel. That's how I make it these days. So, I didn't mean anything bad by what I said, and honestly if you ever plan to live in this town, you're gonna have to toughen up. Kage isn't always going to be around to tell everybody how great you are. No one ever was around to defend me. I had to do it for myself."

Gracie nodded.

Placing her hand on Gracie's, Pearl looked straight into her eyes. "So, can I ask you a question? If it upsets you, then it's okay to tell me that you don't want to talk about it. But I'd like to know what happened to you," Pearl said in a soft voice that hid its usual rough edge.

Gracie knew it was more the question of *could* she tell it. Gracie searched for the strength, and Pearl squeezed Gracie's hand tighter as if she sensed her struggle. Gracie explained how everyone in her town knew her story. They had known her family. Then when anyone new came to Ridgewood someone would always tell them, so no one had ever bluntly asked her before. "Even Kage heard from Barney who heard from who knows who," Gracie began.

Pearl still had her hand on Gracie's. Kage sat looking from Pearl to Gracie. Pearl's eyes filled with tears as Gracie talked about her family in greater detail than she'd shared with Kage. When she told Pearl, she included her feelings about what had happened and what it had been like for her as a little girl. She shared how that affected who she was now. She pulled up her sleeve and showed Pearl the burns on her arm and even pulled up her skirt, showing the burns on her upper thigh that Kage hadn't known about.

Pearl shared too, about the logging accident that had taken her oldest brother's life and about the day that Kage was born and their mother had died. She talked about what it had been like to live on the farm with her dad and four brothers, wishing every day that her sisters could come home. She admitted that she had been angry that Kage was ever born.

"But I know better now," Pearl reassured Kage. "I blame Dad for not getting someone else to help. He knew it was a difficult pregnancy. He waited too long to get help. I never understood," Pearl said, reaching across the table to place her other hand on Kage's.

"What was Dad like?" Kage asked.

"He could fix *anything* with a hammer and a wrench. He loved mama's canned pickles, gave hard spankings, and hummed when he was in a good mood."

They continued to talk for another hour until Pearl had to rush to work, and Kage realized that he was late for his shift.

*   *   *

Taking a running jump, Gracie climbed onto the mattress. The bed in her hotel room was twice the size of hers at home. Pearl, although not making the same impression as with her boss, had made friends with the woman who oversaw reservations, and she upgraded Gracie's room.

On her first visit, Gracie was awed by the marble statues in the imposing lobby and by daunting carved trees growing inside the hotel. She hadn't believed Pearl when she had told her about the executive suites. When she first stepped into the room, she touched everything: the magnificent painting above the bed, the lavender trim on the pillow shams, the plush lounge chair with wine-colored accents, the marble bathroom counters, and even the delicately designed light switch covers.

As she ran her finger along the bedspread's velvet-lined cording she imagined living in Louisville. Kage hadn't talked her into moving there, but he had persuaded her to stay another night. Though overwhelmed by the city's grand, polished buildings of ornate mortar and stone, Gracie felt right at home to be so near to Kage.

Later that night, cradled in the bed, surrounded by pillows like endless clouds, her mind drifted—her soul rested. A plaque mounted above the nightstand read *Sweet Dreams.* The soothing words filled Gracie's thoughts as images of Kage drifted in her mind.

She reminisced about her first visit and how Kage had eased her nerves after the terrible bus ride by sharing his own stories about his experiences at the ritzy hotel. "These people have their own language. I came by to see Pearl and the guy at the door said, 'Valet?' I thought he was saying hello in Spanish or something. Then, when I asked to see Pearl, he said, 'The concierge would assist me with my request just beyond the atrium,' and I had no idea what on earth he'd just said to me."

Still overwhelmed by the lobby's towering ceiling and the opulent drapes, flowing two stories, Gracie was surprised that in this strange world she felt safe.

Gracie decided she might not leave—ever.

Chapter 27

Kage grabbed and turned Pearl's apartment's doorknob so quickly that he walked face-forward into the door when it didn't open. He'd expected the door to be unlocked and Gracie waiting for him.

All day Kage had counted seconds passing along with the gas pump's ticking meter. Each count subtracted their time together. It was his last evening with Gracie, and he wanted it to be special. He pulled off his boots and stumbled over them as the door slammed behind him.

"You home?" Pearl called from her room.

"Where's Gracie?"

"I've been asleep." Pearl stretched as she stepped out of her room. "I'm not used to getting an afternoon snooze." Pearl squinted at the clock. "Thought Gracie was with you."

"No, I just got off work."

"Hmm? She left here a while ago," Pearl yawned. "Carl called and said you were with him." She buttoned her Town's Tavern shirt over the T-shirt she was wearing.

"Huh? I've been at work all day. She's with Carl?"

"No, I thought she was with you. She told me that Carl called and she was going to meet you. That's how I understood it, but I was half asleep when she leaned in the bedroom, so who knows?"

"Think you must've misunderstood something," Kage took in a deep breath, releasing it slowly. "So, you don't know where Gracie is?"

Pearl, looking at Kage with one eye partially shut and head tilted, snapped back, "Told you I thought she was with you. Quit the interrogation."

"Not meaning to make you mad, Sis. I'll call Carl." Kage picked up the phone and dialed the hotel and asked to be connected to Carl Kage's room. No one answered. He tried Gracie's room. No answer. Kage changed his clothes and tried again. Nothing.

*   *   *

At the hotel, Kage stopped first at Gracie's room on the second floor. No answer.

The hotel elevator was out of order, so he climbed the stairs jogging to the ninth floor. He could hear voices inside his bothers' room as he knocked.

"Who is it?" Carl yelled.

"Kage," Kage replied just as loudly, though short on breath.

Kage waited a few seconds. No one came to the door. He knocked harder. "Open up! You seen Gracie?"

"Nope," Carl yelled back.

"You know where she is? Hey, let me in!" Kage banged on the door.

"Hold your horses there, young feller ..." Carl fumbled to unlock the door.

Kage pushed his way in and saw Gracie sitting at the table with Adam and Carl.

*   *   *

Excited to see Kage, Gracie smiled. "You're late," she teased.

"She *is* here!" Kage shot his words toward Carl. "Why'd you say otherwise?"

"She just wanted to hang out with us for a while, I suppose. She's been havin' some fun," Carl said, lifting his glass filled with golden liquid.

Adam added, "For a change." Both men snickered.

Gracie repositioned herself in her chair, uneasy with the way Kage's bothers were treating him. "Carl called and said that you were coming here. When I got here, you weren't here. Then they said you'd be here any minute, and it's been," she looked at the clock, "an hour. Where have you been?" Gracie couldn't miss the tightening of Kage's jaw.

"No one called me to come over here. I came looking because I couldn't find you!" Kage glared at Carl.

Adam stood from his chair, lifted the liquor bottle in the air and swung it with his words. "Treasure Hunting Boy, you think you own this girl?" He stepped toward Kage clumsily. "Pretty

241

girls like this need lots of attention. She's been hanging out with us, and it ain't seemed to be no problem to her. Just you!" Adam stepped forward again toward Kage, causing Kage to automatically clench his right fist to his side pulling it up a couple of inches.

Gracie broke in, "This doesn't make any sense to me. What's going on?" She stood from her seat at the table and stepped toward Kage. His brow furrowed with anger.

"Gracie, you been drinking with these two?" Kage asked in a stern voice, the vein in the right side of his neck pulsing.

"Only a sip. I didn't like it." Gracie stepped toward Kage but stopped as the glare he had been giving Carl passed to her.

"You ain't never touched this stuff before," Kage scolded. "Did they make you drink it?"

"Who do you think you are?" Adam demanded eager to abet. "You ain't her Daddy, Treasure Boy. She's a big girl and can make her own decisions without you helpin'." He grabbed Gracie's shoulder and leaned in toward her, the liquor on his breath overwhelming.

Kage instantly raised his fists.

"Kage!" Gracie screamed putting her hand out between Kage and Adam. "Stop!"

As soon as Kage raised his fist, Carl pushed the chair he sat in backward and stepped in raising both his fists. "You ain't never fought another Kage before, boy," Carl challenged.

Kage pushed Gracie away from Adam's hold with a force that spun her to her knees. He stepped closer to his brothers and between clinched teeth said, "I don't know anyone else by the name of Kage." Kage swung the first punch hitting Carl on the left side of his face.

"Stop! Stop it!" Gracie yelled as Carl swung back, hitting Kage near his chin, knocking him back several steps.

Adam grabbed Gracie by the waist and pinned her arms to her sides. She struggled to get loose. "Carl's gonna kill him," Adam whispered in Gracie's ear and laughed.

Gracie's squirming caused Adam's grip to tighten. "Let me go. He's bleeding!" Gracie, with the heel of her shoe and all her might, stomped Adam's right foot, which had nothing on it but a dingy sock, and kicked him in the shin. She fought to get away as his grip loosened slightly.

"You think you can hurt me, little girl? You know who you're dealing with? Me and Carl here, we've taught many girls like you a lesson or two," Adam said with a chuckle.

She smelled the liquor releasing from his nostrils as he exhaled and felt his heavy breath on her ear. He turned her face toward his, and she bit his hand, tasting the nasty salt of his skin and the smoke from the cigar he'd been smoking earlier. Adam threw her against the floor, and Gracie kicked and screamed trying to push him off. She caught a glimpse of Kage before Adam crawled on top of her, his body three times her weight.

Kage, immediately turned his attention from Carl and reached around Adam's neck.

"Watch out!" Gracie screamed. From Gracie's angle on the floor, she could see Carl coming.

Carl hit Kage from behind with a huge blow to the back of the head. His hands fell from Adam's neck, as he collapsed and fell to his side.

"Stop! Please stop!" Gracie pleaded as Carl kicked Kage in the side twice.

Gracie bit Adam's arm with a force that took a plug from his skin and was able to push him away long enough to scramble over to Kage. He tried to sit up but groaned, gripping his side and the back of his head. Carl grabbed Gracie by the neck of her dress. It ripped exposing her slip. Kage struggled to reach across the floor for Carl, but then a second blow cracked against the back of his neck.

*   *   *

Cecil opened the stairwell door with his leg and began his journey to the ninth floor, his arms full of grocery bags. When he finally reached their room, he knocked with his elbow and found the door ajar. He heard what sounded like a chair crashing to the floor.

"What on earth?" Cecil said and cursed under his breath. The wrecked room drew his attention for only seconds before he recognized Gracie, trapped beneath Adam, kicking her legs fiercely.

Cecil dropped the grocery bags. Three apples rolled under the table and several beer bottles clanked. He shoved Adam against the wall with a force that caused the lamp on the table against the wall to rock until it tumbled over and its bulb broke, dimming the room.

*   *   *

Pulling her hand to her chest, Gracie held the ripped portion of her dress to cover herself. Carl swung at Cecil and the two of them exchanged blows. Gracie pushed herself across the floor away from their scuffle. When Adam became distracted by the ruckus between Carl and Cecil, Gracie edged closer to where Kage lay on the floor.

Adam began swinging at Cecil too, and after several hard hits, Cecil went down. Gracie scrambled to her feet and started to run, but then turned to Kage who was still motionless, his body sprawled across the floor. She couldn't see his face. Carl, in two large steps, grabbed her around the waist from behind and again she was overpowered. He threw her to the floor and straddled her. With one hand he unbuckled the straps of his overalls while pressing his other hand heavily against her throat.

Though fruitless, Gracie tried to scream. A muffled "Stop" came from her throat but didn't make it through her lips.

With a limp, Cecil walked to the drawer and pulled out a gun. Without hesitating, he pointed it toward his brother. "Carl, you best let that girl go. You hurt her; you die."

Carl turned his head slightly not concerned by Cecil until he caught a glimpse of the gun, then let go. Gracie crawled away from Carl, her throat sore from Carl's hand pressing against it. She'd been fighting so hard against his grasp that she hardly had the energy to move more than three feet away before she curled into a ball near the edge of the bed. Kage lay on the floor across the room motionless.

*   *   *

Adam pushed Town's Tavern's door open with his full body weight. The door cracked against the wall and the room silenced. The entire bar, which in the early afternoon was all of six people, turned their heads.

"What?" Carl challenged in a combative stance as he followed Adam in to the tavern. "Any of you here got a problem with me?" Carl looked to catch eye contact with anyone willing.

The manager of the Town's Tavern quickly put down the keg he was changing and stepped toward Carl with his palms out facing the men. "Ain't no fighting going on at this hour in this bar. If you got a problem, you gotta take it somewhere else."

"Where's Pearl?" Carl demanded, seconds away from breaking loose into madness.

"She's in the back, just got here. What you want with Pearl?" the manager asked.

"Tell her she's got company. Her brothers want to see her." Adam looked around, eyeing everyone staring, happy for a challenge.

"Pearl," the manager yelled. "They say you have company out here."

Pearl came around the corner, tying the strings of a black cloth apron around her waist. "Hey, guys," she nonchalantly called out and then took in the look on her boss' face.

"These two need to settle down if they're going to be served here. They came walking in like they wanted to take something up with somebody, and I ain't gonna have none of that," the manager said to Pearl and then looked to Carl and Adam. "You boys gonna behave, or you're out of here," he concluded turning toward two large men sitting at the bar. They stood up at his glance, clenching and unclenching their firsts.

"No, no!" Pearl called out, motioning for the two men to take their seats. "Charlie and Billy, sit back down. Don't kick 'em out. I know them."

Adam peered Carl's way and then at the two men and back to the manager. "We'd just like a drink."

"Fine, then have a seat, and don't cause no trouble." He directed a displeased look Pearl's way as he walked to the back of the bar to finish with the keg.

Pearl placed her hand on her forehead as she listened to Carl and Adam share their side of the story. How Gracie had been flirting with them. How she had thrown herself at Carl, telling him that she didn't think Kage was a strong enough man for her, and how Cecil had escorted them out, gun in hand.

247

"Ol' Ben didn't seem too appreciative of Gracie's affections for me," Carl chuckled elbowing Adam.

"Yeah, can't say Daddy would've had much use for him on the farm. He's as weak as a lame mule," Adam barked.

They then explained that Cecil didn't understand they were just having some fun.

"What about Ben?" Pearl looked ill.

"What about him? Left him for dead, as far as I could tell," Carl released a wicked snort. He raised his beer in cheers toward Adam.

"What?" Pearl squealed, her manager looking her way.

"Oh, he ain't dead," Adam snarled.

*   *   *

Cecil locked the door and put the gun on the table, careful to face it away from where Gracie lay curled on the floor. He placed his hand on her shoulder startling her. She instantly pulled away from him.

"They hurt you real bad?" Cecil asked.

Gracie didn't answer.

"Glad I showed up before they done what they intended to, but your pretty dress is torn and bet you have a few bruises turn up. Your neck's still red."

"Kage?" Gracie finally squeaked out, then coughed.

"I think he'll be okay. He's movin' over there. Carl or Adam hit him a hard one, I'd guess. They don't mind a fight." Cecil started to place the torn piece of Gracie's dress over her chest, but Gracie's hand bolted to stop him.

"No, no. I won't touch you. I don't mean to hurt you," Cecil assured her. He stood and took a few steps back as Gracie crossed her arms over her chest holding herself tightly, not taking her eyes off Cecil.

He stepped across the room and stooped down beside Kage looking closely at him. "Ben, you okay?"

Kage opened his eyes for a few seconds and grunted before closing them again.

"Hey, Ben can you hear me? Talk to me."

Kage touched his right side and moaned.

Cecil mumbled, "Might have a few broken ribs and your face looks like it's swelling. Got some color to your chin. Looks like a good bruise forming there."

Gracie sat up and leaned forward. "Kage?" she attempted before her words broke off in coughing.

Cecil gave Kage a few light pats with his palm on Kage's cheeks. Kage's eyes opened and he grabbed his side and mumbled, "Gracie. Where's Gracie?"

"She's here. She's okay. They didn't hurt her too bad a'tal. You going to be okay? Looks like they gave you a good kick or two," Cecil said. "You need to see a doctor."

"I'm fine," he said, trying to stand but then stopping midway to lie back on the floor. "They didn't hurt her bad?"

"Nope, I had to use the gun so they'd listen to me."

"You shot them?"

"No. That might've been too easy. Those two need to learn a lesson." Cecil chuckled as if this was somehow normal or acceptable by his standards.

Kage, holding his side, forced himself to sit up. "Cecil, there is nothing about this that's okay. Nothing! They hurt Gracie, and I think something's broken. I've met strangers I liked better than the three of you," Kage groaned speaking through clenched teeth. "To think that I spent my life wondering what you guys looked like and where you were. I wish I'd never met any of you!" Kage pushed himself up from the floor, his forehead wrinkled with pain.

Cecil opened his mouth in defense, but then said nothing. He dropped his head and walked toward the sack of groceries that had overturned, its contents now spread about the floor. "Sorry, Ben," he mumbled.

Kage crawled next to Gracie. "I'm sorry, Gracie."

"You didn't do anything. I shouldn't have trusted him. I just ..."

Kage broke in, "People aren't always nice like you've known your whole life."

"But they're your brothers." Gracie's voice was weak.

"No, they aren't. I don't have any brothers. I grew up in an orphanage, remember?" Kage muttered, his words cold.

"This is all my fault," Gracie apologized.

"What? Why would you say that?" Kage grimaced as he tried to take a deep breath.

"I should have been smarter and not listened to Carl."

Kage looked at her as if something had changed between them. Though her dress was torn and hair disheveled, his lips formed the words, "Still beautiful." He leaned his head against her shoulder. "You've got to go home, Gracie," Kage whispered and tried to stand. "You don't belong here, with me. I ..." Kage let out a breath. "Go back."

He kissed Gracie on the cheek, and then pulled away, holding his arms tight against his ribs. "Gene and Thomas were right. I'm not right for you."

Gracie reached out for him. "No," she pleaded softly, but he moved away.

"Cecil, take me to the hospital."

"Kage!" Gracie called, her voice finally clear.

Cecil dialed for a taxi. "We should take Gracie to be looked at too."

Kage nodded but didn't look her way.

"Kage, please don't do this," she pleaded.

Kage, his hand on the hotel room doorknob, turned around looking through Gracie, expressionless, and said, "We aren't right, Gracie. You belong in Ridgewood, not with me. That's all."

"But, Kage!" Gracie contested.

He was already out the door.

251

Chapter 28

Gracie pointed for Aaron to put down the groceries in the kitchen. She was on the phone when he arrived at her house.

Gracie called Pearl all week, finally catching her at home.

"He's not here."

"When he gets in, can you have him call me?" Gracie asked.

"I mean, he's no longer here, Gracie. He left."

"Forever?"

"As far as I know."

"What do you want to do with these?" Aaron asked as Gracie hung up the phone. Aaron took off his black thick frames and placed Thomas' spectacles over his eyes.

"I want you to take them off." Gracie reached for them.

"Sorry, Gracie," Aaron quickly apologized and removed them.

Aaron had been dropping by most afternoons, especially since he had found the molded bread, rotten eggs, and rancid milk in the refrigerator when his mother had sent him over with a banana pudding to welcome Gracie home from Louisville.

252

Gracie figured he had told everyone about that—and the bruises on her arms, neck and face.

Pastor Ted had brought supper the next night after she had returned and filled her car tank with gas. Chippy Martin, who owned the wood mill, and his wife came over and cleaned her house. They scrubbed the floors and did the laundry. Chippy worked outside on the landscaping. In a matter of two hours, the house looked as if it had benefited from a week's spring cleaning. Gracie fell asleep that night to the scent of Pinesol. In her dreams she saw glimpses of Kage, but every corner she turned, he had vanished.

The thought of not knowing where Kage was made her crazy, angry at him one minute and desperate the next. Their goodbye at Pearl's had been a simple, empty wave. She had felt encouraged when he'd stood, holding pressure against the wrap around his ribs, and walked toward her, but then he had taken the doorknob in his hand and pushed the door shut behind her. The distance he kept from her hurt more than the bruises that lingered.

*   *   *

"You need anything?" Pastor Ted reached for the sagging sheet covering the window and realigned the clothes pins, clasping the sheet firmly to the edge of the curtain rod.

"Not really." Gracie looked away, though she wanted to scream that without her grandfather she felt painfully vulnerable, and now not knowing where Kage had gone or if she'd ever see him again, she was falling apart.

"I can't tell you how many people have asked me about you. Every time Erma Franklin sees me, she asks how you're doing."

Gracie looked intently at Pastor Ted while he worked with the make-shift curtains. She was appreciative that he hadn't asked about the curtain—or her bruises.

"I know, I know. Aaron has been so kind to bring me groceries."

"They are friendly," Pastor Ted said as he finished clipping the last clothes pin.

"Helpful," Gracie added with a nod.

"Always waving and smiling," Pastor Ted said.

"Yep, always," Gracie agreed.

"Good people," Pastor Ted remarked.

Though Pastor Ted meant well, Gracie found the visits and conversations draining. But she knew that if he hadn't stopped by, she'd be sinking helplessly into the couch.

*   *   *

"I don't gotta taste today. Two scoops of that chocolate crunchy stuff," Willy spouted his order.

"No longer making it."

"Why? That was some good stuff!"

"Lost the recipe," Gracie lied, shifting her gaze downward.

Leaving Willy inside on his tasting frenzy, Gene stepped outside Swirly's and licked his Chocolate Swirl. The chocolate was smudged and he thought it looked the same color as the bruise on Gracie's upper right cheek.

"Today's got a nice breeze," Gene commented in an effort to make conversation with Mrs. Laurel and her daughter, Evelyn, as they approached.

"Don't tell me I got diabetes!" Mrs. Laurel barked. "I can have ice cream if I want."

Evelyn pointed to her own ear, indicating that Mrs. Laurel had misunderstood.

"How you doing, Mrs. Laurel?" Gene spoke louder.

"Huh?" Mrs. Laurel responded, leaning closer.

"She's fine," Evelyn answered. She cupped the side of her mouth and whispered to Gene, "I've moved in with her so she's not alone." Then she raised her voice and said, "Thanks for asking, Gene." Evelyn took her mother's arm and tried to direct her toward the front door of the shop.

"Hello, Gene," Mrs. Laurel said glancing up at Gene as if she had just noticed him.

Gene replied, "Looks like you're doing well." He nodded goodbye and stepped toward his vehicle.

"How's Olivia?" Mrs. Laurel turned to ask.

Gene stopped mid-step.

"Sorry. I'm so sorry, Gene," Evelyn apologized. She grabbed her mother's arm and pulled her toward Swirly's front door, scolding her, "Mother, you aren't thinking right again today!"

"Honey, what is wrong with you?" Mrs. Laurel asked looking genuinely concerned for her daughter.

It had been years since someone had said Olivia's name to him. In fact, he couldn't remember the last time. The sound of her name played over and over in his head.

There were so many days he would think only of her.

*   *   *

Pearl hit the snooze lever on her alarm clock as she rolled over in bed. She'd been dreaming about her brother, Ben. She dreamed he was outside knocking on her door. When he'd run off, he had simply left a note that read, "I'm gone," and a $5 bill. She contrasted in her mind the differences between Ben and her other brothers. The others had run out on the hotel having paid only a portion of their bill and none of the charges added for damages.

She cringed, thinking about the incident, still heartbroken over it. She had tried calling everywhere she could think of, dialing information in both Georgia and Alabama, looking for people where Ben mentioned he'd stayed. Ben's boss at the gas station said he didn't show up at work either. He'd left with no contact with anyone.

When her alarm clock rang a second time, she sat up in bed and picked up the letter on her nightstand. Though the handwriting was rough, it was addressed to Benjamin Kage. She imagined it was from Gracie as it was postmarked Ridgewood.

Chapter 29

Aaron rubbed the ointment on Gracie's left arm. "So, the doctor says these little bumps are a result of stress?"

Gracie nodded. She could easily spread the cream over the rough patches on her right arm, but she needed Aaron's help to cover the splotches on her left arm.

"First bruises and now this rash." His brow narrowed as he rubbed the cream in more thoroughly than necessary.

"What do you mean by saying that?" Gracie grabbed the tube from him, but when she struggled to screw on its top, he grabbed it back from her.

"I can't believe he exposed you to those heathens."

Gracie knew she'd regret telling him about what had happened in Louisville, but she had needed a friend.

"Those traveling folk aren't much different from wild animals. If I was to see him again, I think I'd have to take this one up with him." Aaron flexed his right arm as he socked his fist into the air a few times.

Gracie's eyes widened as she pictured Aaron throwing a punch at Kage. Aaron was built nothing like Kage. She imagined stocking detergent boxes on the fourth shelf at the grocery was about as labor intensive as Aaron's day got.

"Stop it with the traveling comments. You sound like my grandfather."

"Your grandfather was a smart man," Aaron said, working the ointment into his hands and between his fingers as if it were lotion.

"I know that, but that doesn't mean he was always right, you know. He once told me that you were a mama's boy," Gracie teased.

"What?" Aaron squalled, his voice instantly altering to a higher pitch.

Gracie knew that would get him, and she was surprised by how much she enjoyed the amusing sense of control as he became quickly worked up. "Yep, ain't nothin' wrong with being a mama's boy, I suppose," she bantered.

"I ain't no mama's boy. You see my mama around here anywhere?"

"Aaron, I said granddaddy wasn't always right. That was my point. I never once said you were a mama's boy." Gracie tried fighting off the giggle, but it escaped.

Aaron's face warmed. "You're cute when you laugh like that. I haven't seen you laugh much lately," Aaron said.

Gracie felt her face flush. She knew he was right. She hadn't.

Pearl awakened to the phone ringing, sure that she had over slept and Town's Tavern would be on the other end. When she answered she was already prepared to hear the irate shrill of her boss but instead heard Kage's voice. She bolted up in bed, wondering if she was dreaming.

"Where are you? Are you okay? I've been worried about you!" Pearl's words ran together.

Kage asked with a chuckle, "Is this what it's like having a mom? You sound almost like you care, Pearl."

"I do care," Pearl retorted gruffly. "You just up and left without saying a word. That ain't nice, Ben. Not nice to do to someone at all! Where have you been the last month?"

"I shouldn't have done that to you, sorry. You were good to me and let me stay with you."

Pearl broke in, her tone softer, "Why'd you run off?"

Taking a low breath, Kage hesitated. "Pearl, I'm not good enough for her. That day with Carl and Adam—" Kage stopped mid-sentence, his tone tense. "Look at me. I don't have anything. Not a steady job, not even a place of my own. How on earth could I think that I could take care of someone else? What happened to Gracie was my fault. She trusted me, and I exposed her to ..." his words trailed off.

"Don't tell yourself that," Pearl pleaded.

259

"It's true. I know now what Gene Carter was saying about me not being what Gracie needs though it made me so mad. He's right. And you didn't need me there either, causing trouble."

"If you were here, Ben Kage, I'd smack you silly," Pearl hissed through clinched teeth. Pearl began brushing through her hair. "You comin' back, Ben?"

"Nope. I don't like that place. It might be good for you, but there's nothing for me. I'm going south. I just best not run into anyone with the same last name as me."

Pearl didn't know what else to say, so instead she changed the subject. "Where are you now?"

"Georgia, but just passing through. I stopped at the Lamberts' home for a night. They told me you called."

"I just like to know where my brother is now that I know he's alive. Have you talked with Gracie since?" Pearl asked, pulling the receiver away from her ear as she pulled on her T-shirt.

"Haven't. She's home—safe— where she oughta be."

Pearl sensed from his confident tone that he believed that. "Well I've got to go. You'd better come back and see me sometime, mister." Pearl put her shoes on ready to run out the door.

"Will do, but no time soon I'm afraid. Take care," Kage concluded.

"Wait," Pearl called into the receiver. "Almost forgot something. I got a letter mailed here to you. Don't know who it's

from, but it has your name on it." Pearl searched for the letter
hoping she could find it.

Chapter 30

The bus couldn't have flown fast enough for Kage. Each minute further evoked his imagination which was running wild.

Taking the note from his pocket, he unfolded it. Its letters printed, not written—a joke, poking fun at him. He read it again, although he already had it memorized. Pearl had forwarded the letter to him in the mail. Once he received it, his plans changed.

The letter that he'd assumed was from Gracie, wasn't from her. There was no signature. The note simply read:

Treasure seeker? Are you a boy or a man? Enclosed was a bus ticket to Ridgewood.

Reading the words printed on the paper, his jaw taut, and his face red with fury, he wadded it up and pressed it back into his pocket. His brothers were taunting him. *Were they in Ridgewood?* With the thought of his brothers finding Gracie and no one there to protect her, he hit the back of the seat in front of him. The couple sitting in the seat turned around, and he apologized. Resting his head in his hands, he ran his fingers through his hair. All the anger of feeling that life hadn't been fair to him was nothing compared to the rage burning in his chest. They may not have expected him to respond, but he had. Especially when he realized that not only was there an enclosed ticket to Ridgewood but the postmark on the letter was from Ridgewood, Kentucky.

*   *   *

Gracie blushed at the sight of the flowers. She had agreed to go to a movie with Aaron. He had successfully guilted her into it. In the beginning it was easy to turn him down, but he was persistent, and she had run out of ways to tell him no.

He showed up early at Swirly's. His hair was styled differently. Gracie suspected that his mother had fixed it, although she was sure he would never dare to admit it. She bet his mother bought the flowers he carried as well. He extended his arm, pushing the flowers toward her, fidgeting like a kid at the doctor's waiting for a shot. Gracie tucked her washrag in her waist band, like her grandfather would do, and reached to accept them.

Aaron dressed as if he were attending a wedding—or a funeral. In his suit, he looked as he had the day of her grandfather's service, which made her stomach turn more.

"Thanks, Aaron. They're pretty," Gracie lifted them to her nose.

"I thought so. They reminded me of you," Aaron's words sounded as odd and strained as he looked.

"I know the movie starts soon. I'll be just a minute. I have to change in the back and lock up," Gracie motioned, noticing that Aaron was pacing and fiddling with his glasses.

"That's fine. Take your time," he encouraged, his head nodded, resembling a nervous twitch.

Aaron was a friend, a large leap from the guy who had bugged her at the grocery store. But the guy pacing in front of the ice cream case was not acting like *just* a friend.

Gracie changed into a dress that Aaron had seen her wear a dozen times. She felt sticky and tired from working all day and really wished she hadn't agreed to this—not tonight, not ever.

Aaron took her shawl from the coat stand and placed it around her shoulders, then insisted he take her keys to lock the shop. She rolled her eyes, not knowing how much more of this she could endure.

*   *   *

Kage rushed off the bus to find Gracie. He never expected to see this town again, and as he'd suspected, nothing had changed. Just seeing Swirly's, he warmed. It wasn't Gracie, but a part of her. The lights were out, and the closed sign displayed, so he turned on his heels toward her house. His thoughts drifted back and forth, from the fury he felt toward his brothers to how striking Gracie had looked in the moonlight, even wrapped in her scarf and coat that first night. With that thought, he ran faster.

He jogged up the steps to her front door and opened the screen, knocking hard on its wood frame. No lights were on. Though he knew it would be early for her to be asleep, he hoped it was possible and she was there. He hadn't thought what he would do or where he would go next if she wasn't. He rattled the doorknob, kicked the door, and turned away. His heart beat fiercely, not so much from the run but from the anticipation he had of finding her.

Facing the dark sky, he walked away from Gracie's, wondering what he would do now. He knew he wouldn't be able to sleep until he found her and made certain that she was okay—not that he had a place to sleep anyway.

*   *   *

Gracie pretended that James Bond's mission was to rescue her, not the woman in peril on screen. She sank lower in her seat as Aaron placed his arm on the back of her chair.

When they exited the theater, Aaron offered, "How about a walk near the orchard? Or maybe we can go dancing?" Aaron started singing and twisting his arms and hips off-beat to his own rendition of Chubby Checker's *The Twist*.

Without mincing her words, Gracie blurted, "There's no place to dance. Aaron, I just want to go home."

"Are you okay? You don't look like you feel good."

"I don't feel well. Maybe it's a headache coming on."

"You should've said something earlier," Aaron said and reached toward her as if he were going to feel her forehead.

She swatted his hand away. "It's just been a long day," Gracie apologized, wishing she could tell him that she didn't want this—whatever this was.

In the car, Aaron talked about the movie, the new products at the grocery, the cool features of his vehicle, and many other topics that Gracie ignored. Once she nodded off then quickly looked to Aaron to see if he had noticed. When she nodded off a second time, Aaron threw on the brakes, throwing Gracie forward. He gripped the steering wheel to maintain control, and the car swerved to miss something in the road.

"Watch out!" Aaron screamed at the window.

"What was that?" Gracie expected to see an animal in the road but instead the tail lights cast a glare on the figure of a man.

"That was close," Aaron piped.

"No doubt. What if you'd hit him?" Gracie exclaimed.

"Well, it wouldn't have been my fault," Aaron retorted.

"Thank goodness that didn't happen."

"You okay?" Aaron asked, looking over at her.

"Yes. You keep your eyes on the road," Gracie ordered still shaken.

Aaron pulled to the front of her house and insisted on getting out to open her door. He'd often opened the car door in the past, but just because he made such a big to-do about it tonight, it added up to another uncomfortable part of a miserable evening. When Aaron took her elbow to help her step out of the car, she sarcastically thought she should curtsey, though she was afraid he would think it fit right into a perfect evening.

"Thanks for the movie," Gracie said as she tried to break away toward the front door.

Aaron stuffed his hands in his pockets and shifted his feet awkwardly. He started to say something but was distracted. "Huh?" He squinted toward the distance.

"What?" Gracie asked. Then she saw the figure coming toward them. "Aaron," she pointed. "Someone's coming ..."

Aaron watched as the person approached, jogging. "Who is it?" Aaron yelled.

Aaron's car beams lit the face of the man they had almost hit as he drew closer to them.

Dropping the purse that she clasped, Gracie froze. "Kage?" she asked first in a whisper and then repeated his name louder, "KAGE!"

He reached his arms out, and she went running into them.

*　　　*　　　*

Kage had tried to imagine what it would be like when he saw her. As afraid as he was that his brothers had stopped in Ridgewood, he was also anxious about how Gracie would receive him. Gracie kept saying his name over and over. Her voice replayed in his head even after she stopped.

"You came back! You came back!" She exclaimed. "Wait, but I'm mad at you!"

"I'm sorry ..."

"You never called me. You didn't even really say goodbye," she scolded.

Kage's apologies rolled out. "Gracie, I don't have what you need. And then my brothers—" Kage stopped, embarrassed to admit his failures.

"You should've called," Gracie insisted.

"Are you okay?" Kage stepped back and looked at her in the car lights inspecting her piece by piece.

"Yes, I'm fine. What about you? Are your ribs better?" She grabbed beneath his lightweight jacket to touch his side.

"Yes, better. Not totally back to normal, but much better," Kage reassured her. "I'm so glad you're okay!"

Aaron's cheerful expression vanished like a kid with the candy taken from his hand. Stepping toward Aaron, Kage extended his hand. Aaron eyed him closely as if he would like to say something then didn't and tentatively accepted the hand shake.

"Have they been here?" Kage asked, looking over his shoulder.

"Who's been here?" Aaron got the question out before Gracie.

"My brothers, have you seen them?"

Gracie's back tensed. "Why ... why do you think they'd come here?" Gracie stuttered.

"Because, remember how they called me Treasure Hunter? Look at this." Kage pulled the wadded note from his pocket.

Chapter 31

Kage lingered outside Swirly's the next two days, describing his brothers and asking if anyone had seen them. He slept at the ice cream shop at night and helped Gracie get the shop open in the mornings.

Kage extended his hand to Gene Carter as he stepped out of the old cattle truck, stopping just short of hitting Swirly's front porch post. "How are you, Gene?"

"Well, doing alright, I suppose. Ain't had no good help these days, I can say that for sure." Gene didn't appear surprised to see Kage, but Kage knew Gene well enough to know an expression of any kind from Gene was rare.

"Well, it may be because you're working them into the night with no supper," Kage chided.

"Might be." Gene took Kage's comment in jest as it was intended. "You here for a while or just passin' through like you do?"

"Well, not sure. I might be leaving ... might not be."

Gene looked curiously at Kage, then beyond him. "I saw some bruises on Gracie. You do that?"

"I did not and would never!" Kage became defensive.

"Why you here, boy?"

Kage didn't like Gene's insinuation. "Sir, I do know where Gracie got those bruises, and I take full fault for it because it shouldn't have happened. I want you to know that I didn't lift a hand to Gracie and have never been anything but gentle with her." Kage took a deep breath not sure what to say next.

Gene didn't say another word but instead stepped around Kage and into Swirly's.

*   *   *

Evenings on the porch swing were Gracie's favorite—Kage wrapped in her grandmother's quilt with her. Gracie made sure he apologized more than once for the way they'd parted in Louisville.

"You have to understand what went through my mind. Seeing you and knowing what almost happened and that it was my fault, I hated myself. I couldn't understand why you didn't hate me. I think I wanted you to hate me. Maybe I thought it would be easier to let go that way," Kage explained.

"What hurt most was how it ended, nothing else. When I left, you said nothing."

They had talked late into the night. She had listened to his stories of when he'd first taken off on his own. He told her things he said he had never told anyone. She learned what made him angry, hurt, and sad. She didn't have to ask what made him happy, because when he talked about those things, his eyes lit up, and his dimple flared. It was the same look that Gracie had recognized when she stepped off the bus in Louisville, the one she had stored in her mind for whenever she thought of him.

She opened up to him as well. She had boxed up her many emotions, and in a way, talking about her family brought them back to her again.

"My Dad always kept his spirits up. They'd gone into debt on the farm, and the house, and the purchase of several prize horses. But when the horses got sick and their income slowed, I once heard him tell my mother that things like this happen. Farmers expect tough times," Gracie paused.

She remembered seeing her father hold her mother, and now thinking back to it, she understood more than ever what they meant to each other.

"There was no way my grandfather could keep the farm after the fire. Someone from out of town came in and bought it at the auction. They had no idea how hard it was for Granddaddy."

Gracie looked into the distance. "He stood and watched people bid on it. It went for less than he'd ever have sold it for. The owners came by Swirly's once, maybe twice. It's their second home. Crazy ... huh? The house they built; they call it their country house. They rent out the farm land," Gracie shrugged.

She tried to picture her house on the hill as it had been. She closed and opened her eyes. When her eyes were shut, it was there.

"Let's go."

"Where?" Gracie still lost in thought.

"To see the place where you grew up," Kage encouraged.

"Really?"

"Sure, we could."

"Tomorrow?"

"If you want ..."

Gracie instinctively kissed him.

*   *   *

The house that stood atop the hill was nicer than any house she knew in Ridgewood. Bushes grew large and well-manicured against it as if the home had been there forever.

The large horse barn was gone, but the smaller one remained. They had painted it bright red. There was a fence dividing the farm land and cattle grazed, several staring at Kage and Gracie as they approached.

"The trees!" Gracie pointed to the large trees that extended far above the roof of the house. "I see the trees!" she repeated. Her steps quickened.

The large oaks didn't sit directly in the back yard, as they had in Gracie's childhood. They stood to the left of the house, not near it. They were separate, at a distance, alone—two trees looking over the valley. Strong and healthy again, they'd recovered from the night of the fire. She thought of Sarah.

"We played so many times in these trees." Gracie reached out and touched one with her hand, and then hugged it like an old friend.

Kage took her hand and gave it a simple tug, suggesting that they sit beneath the tree. "You okay?" he asked.

Gracie nodded, and they were quiet. He pulled her near, his arm resting around her shoulders. She leaned closer and took in the spring air. The buttercups around the trees had bloomed and faded. The irises were awaiting their turn.

"It is beautiful up here," Kage spoke softly.

"I love it. See that fence down there? About once every few years it would rain so much that the water would get above the fence and you couldn't see anything but the tops of those trees. It would make mom so nervous. She didn't like us to play outside until the water went down. We'd cry and beg, and sometimes she let us play, but she watched us the entire time."

"I bet," Kage responded, looking at her and not where she pointed.

Gracie traveled her finger through the air along the fence row. "We loved to lie on our side and roll and roll down the hill. I'm not sure if we ever got all the way to the bottom, because we'd roll into each other. We'd giggle so hard we'd be out of breath from laughing, but then we'd hike back up the hill; as soon as we got to the top, we'd roll back down it again. Then one winter, Dad brought home two snow sleds. Sarah jumped up and down and hugged his leg. I jumped up on his back with my arms around his neck. He walked through the house, helping my mother gather mittens and scarves, us both hanging on him. That was the best."

"Wow," Kage mumbled.

Sorry, I'm rambling."

"I'm loving it," Kage reassured her. "I'm listening," he encouraged her to continue.

Gracie lifted his hand, touching her lips to his knuckles and intertwining her fingers with his. "You should have seen me when we played in the snow. I had on two pairs of socks, long insulated underwear, two pairs of pants, a T-shirt, a sweatshirt and a heavy coat. Then on my head was a hat that stretched over my ears with matching gloves and a scarf. Not to mention, the coat had a hat too that tied beneath my chin. I remember not being able to bend my arms or knees. I pretended to be a monster." Gracie made a futile effort at a scary face.

Kage laughed and she smiled—a weak smile. "Sarah was three, maybe four, I guess. She looked like a wrapped ball, but then she got hot and started to cry. Dad saved the day. He started playing with her, walking stiff legged like a monster. In a matter of seconds, she went from a sad ball to a happy monster. We were all happy monsters."

"Fun," Kage whispered.

"It was." Gracie quieted, reliving the day in her mind.

"Did you get to try out the sled?"

"Oh, yeah. Dad bought the sleds thinking I'd play on one and he'd take Sarah down on the other, but I wanted to be on Daddy's, too. All afternoon we all three played on one—me in front of Daddy, and then my arms around Sarah in front of me. It was my job to hold her really tight so she wouldn't fall off. I felt so important."

"Taking care of little sister ..."

"Yeah." Gracie nodded, her gaze traveling as she slowly imagined the sled making its way down the hill.

"At first Dad would pull the sled up and Sarah and I would hold hands walking up the hill, one of us falling down every other step. He'd run and encourage us to run, but we'd just fall more. Then Sarah got hot, again, and started complaining. So, I pulled the sled and he carried her. Mom took pictures of us playing that day. I wish I had those pictures," she trailed off.

"It was a fun house."

Gracie nodded, wiping the corner of her eye.

"Sounds like a happy life. Even with what happened, you have so many happy memories. I never had any of that."

She leaned forward onto her knees and scooted in front of him. "We can make our own memories," she whispered. She leaned her forehead against his, their noses touching.

"Here." He reached in his pocket.

"What?"

"It's for you ..." Kage pulled a box from his pocket.

"Me!" Gracie exclaimed, pulling back only slightly so she could see into his eyes. "A present?"

"Open it," Kage encouraged, and she could tell his hand shook holding the box out to her.

"What is it?" Gracie asked, sitting back on her heels.

"Stop asking questions." Kage pulled the string around it, beginning to untie the bow for her.

"What could it be?" Gracie asked again as she slid the lid off the box and looked inside.

"I wanted you to have it," Kage said as Gracie pulled the ring from the box. It was simple, but Gracie's eyes widened.

"You got this for me?" Gracie asked. It was silver with one small diamond.

"It kind of has a story behind it." Kage helped her put on the ring. It fit her ring finger perfectly. "Pearl gave it to me. It was my mother's engagement ring."

Gracie lifted her hand near her face to get a closer look and Kage leaned in as if looking at it for the first time. "Her ring?" Gracie processed the thought.

Kage cleared his throat. He looked shy and unsure, like the night they had first met. Gracie knew him so much better now and felt anxious for him as he searched for his words. "Well, remember the night that I left your hotel room?"

Gracie nodded, "I do."

"Well when I came home, Pearl kept asking me questions. She said some of the nicest things about us. Then she fumbled around in a drawer and pulled this out and gave it to me. She said that she had several things of our mother's and she wanted me to have this."

"Your mother's ring," Gracie repeated. She was overwhelmed by the moment. Kage sitting with her, the hill she had grown up on in front of her and on her finger she wore the ring of Kage's mother—the only thing he had to know her by—it was too much to process. Gracie knew she couldn't have imagined a moment like this if she had tried.

Kage took Gracie's hand and began, "That night in the hotel room, remember how I said that someday I was going to put a ring on that finger?"

"Yes." Gracie was the one shaking now. She felt her lips quivering as she listened.

"Well it was kind of crazy. After I said I wanted to put a ring on your finger, less than an hour later Pearl handed me this ring, and once I had it, all I wanted to do was give it to you," Kage said, leaning in to kiss her.

"Kage?" Gracie asked through their kiss. "I only have one hand to wear it on you know?"

"Good!" Kage chuckled, leaning forward toward her and taking them both to the ground in his embrace. Gracie laughed out loud. She wasn't sure why she was laughing, but she knew it was the best feeling she'd ever known. With his arms wrapped around her, she felt as if she could take on anything.

"Will you wear it until I can buy you a better one, one with a larger diamond—like you deserve?"

"No," Gracie jerked her hand from his.

Kage instantly pulled away.

"No, no ... I mean." Gracie sat up as she tried to untwist her words as she watched Kage's face drop instantly disheartened.

"I mean I want *this* ring, not another ring—unless you really don't want me to have it."

"I want you to have it if you really like it."

"I love it," Gracie held it close for another look and repeated, "I love it!"

"You know what I was thinking about the other day?"

"What?"

"Treasure."

"Hmm?"

"There *is* treasure in Ridgewood. I found it."

Gracie folded against his chest, pressing her ring up under her chin, feeling the diamond against her skin. She could hear his heart beating. Gracie closed her eyes, listening. Was his heart beating faster than usual? Hers was.

This day was special to Gracie for so many reasons: because she was with Kage, because he'd given her the special ring and a promise for the future, and because she had allowed herself to remember without sadness, but with joy, that this was her life.

* * *

Gracie, still in her Sunday dress, sat with Kage on the porch swing. Kage slowed the porch swing and showed Gracie the small scar on his chin, all that physically remained from the incident in Louisville with his brothers.

"They aren't here, Kage," Gracie urged, trying to reassure him.

"You're not hard to find, if someone's looking. Everybody in this town knows you and all someone has to say is, 'Have you seen that pretty girl who works at the ice cream shop, with the beautiful eyes and dark hair." Kage lifted his hand to touch her hair.

Gracie cut him off, pointing to her arm "And this." She felt comfortable with Kage— because he loved her, just as she was.

"Yeah, that," Kage acknowledged and glanced at her. "But if that letter is my brothers' idea of a joke, I'm not amused. I still get angry thinking about it. The word family," Kage paused, "just doesn't mean the same thing to me that it does to you."

"Look, Kage, I'm okay, and you're okay," Gracie said and turned his face toward hers. "If it keeps you here, I'll tell you I'm scared to death, and you can't leave."

Kage held her gaze. "We *are* okay, aren't we?"

"Better than okay," Gracie assured him. The ring on her finger made her feel like the woman she had once been scared of becoming.

"I haven't figured out the plan yet, but I want us, forever. Gracie ..."

279

"That's it," Gracie interrupted.

"What?"

"You remind me of—" she stopped short of saying her father, but that was honestly the person she pictured. She had many special memories of her father, and one came to mind. She remembered him once with all the past-due bills spread out on their table. Even with the extra work he'd picked up at the wood mill, there was no money to build the tree house he'd promised Gracie and Sarah. Sarah had crawled to his lap, the blonde hair that she'd gotten from their mother smoothly resting on her shoulders. In her young wisdom she told him, "Daddy, I don't need a house in a tree. This one is better anyway because you and mommy can play in it." She still remembered the look on her father's face, humble, yet proud as he took in every ounce of Sarah's big hug that followed.

"Of what?" Kage probed.

Gracie shook her head, "Nothing."

"I don't know, Gracie. I don't even know how you see me. I can't give you anything. I know... a ring. But I didn't even buy it. Aaron likes you. I can't imagine you and him together, and I don't want to, but he could provide you with ..."

Gracie interrupted, "With what? A boring life. A life I don't want."

"The kind of life you deserve," Kage said.

Gracie shook her head and said, "I just want you."

Kage stared into Gracie's eyes and again she saw it, the determined, proud—yet humble—look, like her father's, as he spoke. "I am not going to work from job to job and town to town for the rest of my life. I've seen what it does to people," his voice broke off.

"Not you, Kage. You'd never be like that, like them. Cecil isn't like that. He'd never have hurt me or you. The other two are just like wild animals," Gracie said using Aaron's words that seemed to fit.

"Guess people think that of me too. Gene Carter asked if I was the one who put those bruises on you. They don't know me, but I know how they see me, and I don't like it."

"Don't pay any attention to Gene Carter. He doesn't know anything about anything but ... Chocolate Swirl ice cream." Gracie giggled at her attempt to be funny.

Kage continued, still in deep thought. "You believe in me. Why? Why do you even want to be sitting here with me when I don't have any money left in my pocket and can't even pay for a nice dinner for you?" Kage asked, touching her face with his fingertips.

Gracie got right up in his face and said, "Because *you* aren't like anyone else I've ever met! You, Benjamin Kage, are the most exciting, amazing, interesting, fun, handsome, kind person I've ever met in my ..." and with those words he pressed his lips to hers.

She turned her body, cradled in his lap, and his arms encircled her. Their kisses lingered, broken only by taking breaths and staring into each other's eyes, sharing an unspoken message between connecting souls.

Kage finally broke the gaze, grabbed her and hugged her like she had clung to her teddy bear as a little girl. She gasped trying to get her breath as he rocked her in his arms. Still cradling her, he whispered, "You fix my heart, Gracie. You fix it."

Looking up at the stars, some of the same ones she'd seen the night he had walked her home for the first time, stars that had appeared so distant when he had left, she mouthed, "Thank you!" to the One above those vast skies Who had brought Kage to her.

Chapter 32

Gracie awakened, not from a bad dream but with an ice cream recipe in her head. She even had its name: *Sweet Dreams.*

At Swirly's, Kage helped her mix the vanilla ice cream with the strawberry preserves and add a faint chocolate ribbon swirl. Gene Carter peered as curiously at Kage as he did at the tub of Chocolate Swirl invaded by strawberry preserves, but he didn't say a word other than "Chocolate Swirl."

When they closed Swirly's that afternoon, Gracie watched Aaron pace outside the grocery store. She felt badly that she hadn't talked to him since the night they nearly ran over Kage. Gracie got in her car, on the passenger's side. Kage opened the door for her just as Aaron had done before, but now with Kage it felt natural. He scooted into the driver's seat, and Gracie slid across the vinyl to the middle of the car, her head coming to rest against Kage's shoulder.

"He's got it bad for you," Kage said as Gracie extended a wave in Aaron's direction. "Really bad," Kage repeated, causing Gracie to blush.

"You think?" Gracie asked.

"You're crazy if you don't see it."

Gracie nodded and mumbled, "What do I do?"

"Just don't go falling in love with him before I get back."

"What! You're leaving again?" Gracie deflated instantly.

"Gracie," he pleaded, "I don't have a choice. But you have to believe, I'll come back. I will."

"I'm tired of it, Kage!" Gracie said, shocked by her own honesty. "You know I thought that you had decided you didn't want to move around anymore—that you wanted to stay in one place. Why I thought this would be the place! You'll have to forgive me for assuming that I might be somewhere in your plans. Why'd you give me this?" With her teeth, Gracie pulled the ring from her finger and spit it from her lips onto the floorboard.

"Please put the ring back on," Kage pleaded. "I don't want to have to work my whole life for someone like Gene Carter. I could do it, but that isn't what I want. It isn't what I want for us!"

"Kage, I have a house and Swirly's. I need the help. It could work."

"I need a paycheck. I need to be the man you deserve," Kage insisted.

"Why do you have to always run off? That's what caused all the trouble in the first place!" Gracie put her hand over her face, trying to think of something to say that would make him stay.

"I don't want to leave. I don't want to run anywhere!" Kage's voice rose as well. "I wish I had the answer. I wish I knew I could support you and give you things a man should. If I could just work for one year down south in construction, I could save up enough money."

"Stop the car!" Gracie screamed. Even before Kage came to a complete stop, she had opened the door, and touched the toe of her shoe to the road as the car slowed beneath her foot.

"What are you doing?"

"What? You ask *me* what I'm doing? Kage, you're driving me crazy. I can't take it anymore. I can't do this." She threw her arms in the air and her sleeve fell, exposing the scars on her right arm. Covering it with her hand, Gracie pulled her arm against her chest. She glared at Kage then took off walking. For one quick second she thought about running back to him, afraid he might turn the car around and leave on the next bus. Too stubborn to turn her head, she listened hard, hoping to hear the car start up again and the motor hum behind her.

*   *   *

Kage sat stunned. How had he messed this up? He planned to come back, as quickly as he could, didn't she understand that? And his following thought was, *"Why did she have to be so gorgeous?"* He watched her from the back, her shoulders ticking

285

in beat with each step and her long hair swaying from side to side. His eyes drifted to the floorboard where the ring lay.

He drove slowly, counting his options with each individual pop of gravel under the weight of the tires.

When he arrived at Gracie's, she'd just stepped up on the front porch on her way inside.

"Gracie," Kage shouted, shutting the car off quickly and jogging her way.

Gracie kept her back to him when he stepped up on the porch. She answered weakly, "I can't tell you how many quiet nights I tried to remember the sound of your voice, or what I would have given for you to walk through that door."

He turned her toward him and grabbed her hand and right arm holding them up close together in front of him, and then brought his lips near, kissing her fingers softly. She looked up at him, tears pooled in her eyes.

"I don't care," he spoke calmly. "I don't care that you don't look just like everyone else. You're prettier than any girl I've ever met. I don't care that you're still angry that you don't have your grandfather anymore or your family. I know how the reminders every day never go away. Maybe it was easier for me or maybe I missed out on what really counted, I may never know. But I don't want you angry at me over it. Don't blame me and include me in all the list of things that have been unfair to you. Don't do it, Gracie." Kage looked at her for a sign that she understood what he was saying.

286

"Don't go!" Gracie begged. "Don't! This house is empty and all I'll do is think about you. I'm tired of all the pain. I'm tired of it all going wrong. I'm just tired." Gracie beat her fist against his chest lightly.

Kage pulled her close, snug, her face buried against him. "Okay, okay," Kage promised.

"I'm trusting you, Kage," Gracie said muffled against his chest.

"And I *trust* you," Kage mumbled, his lips against her hair. "Now what do I do?" He closed his eyes letting her scent intoxicate him.

*   *   *

"I was curious if you'd have any room for another hand these days?" Kage asked, noticing Gene had three men at work.

"Nope, can't say as I do. Got three lazy ones I'm paying right now." He pointed in the direction of the disinclined men. Barney waved, and Kage nodded, annoyed even at the sight of him.

"I understand." Kage took a couple of steps back. "Thought I'd stop by and ask."

Gene placed his rake against the truck and looked Kage over carefully. "I might," he paused, glanced toward the field and then focused on Kage, "be able to use you for a week or two when the 'baccer's ready."

"I really need something now and more permanent."

"Why, you planning to stay around here? This town ain't for everyone. Ridgewood ain't got the happenings I expect you're used to." Gene lifted his hat with one hand, scratched his head with the same hand before placing it back on his head, all in one well-constructed maneuver.

"That's what I like about this town, sir, the people. They're nice. I've met lots of them at the ice cream shop."

"Seems you show a liking to one of them more than the rest."

Kage quickly changed the subject, to avoid any chance for Gene to pass judgment on him again. "Well, if you know of any place that needs a hand, I'd appreciate it."

"Well, you're good at that travelin'. Seems you'd find something somewheres else just fine."

"Yeah, I figure that might be so. Just wanted to—" Kage stopped not wanting to share his plans with Gene and changed the subject. "Several shovels there." Kage pointed to one of the shovels leaned against the truck bed. "Sure you don't need some help?"

"Took those from Willy last night. I caught him and Barney sneaking out again on some kind of ridiculous treasure hunt. Last time they did that they got scratched up in a briar patch from head to toe and attached to a hundred or more cockleburs. Willy's got it in his head that it is somewhere on that hill over there." Gene pointed over his shoulder without turning his head. "They ain't never goin' to find it, none of 'em," Gene shook his head.

288

"Willy once told me that he stays awake at night trying to think up where that treasure is." Kage return a wave from Willy.

"Yep. Lost treasure sure will keep a person up at night," Gene quietly murmured under his breath while fumbling with a loose wire on the rake. "You ever find your sister you's lookin' for?"

"Yes, sir, I did."

"Well, I think she called here lookin' for you. Got her number, if you need it." Gene piddled with the rake tines, his back now to Kage.

"When was that?"

"Been a couple months, I guess. She said she found my number at her place and was tryin' to hunt you down. She also left another number—one for your brother Cecil. That number's in the house too." Gene pointed toward the old barn where Kage had stayed. "It's scribbled on a piece of paper tucked under a glass trinket on the buffet, if Willy hasn't moved it."

"You mind if I get it?" Kage asked.

"Go ahead."

Kage stepped toward the barn, however Gene continued—looking more like he was talking to his rake than Kage. He dragged the rake against the dirt. "Well, I suppose you could try to find some work at the wood mill. Don't know for sure, but you can check with 'em," Gene said then took hold of the rake and headed toward the shed, no good-bye.

*　　　*　　　*

Gene Carter rarely had a reason to stop at Franklin's Grocery, but recently he'd found one of the finer things in life that he decided was worth the splurge. Once a week he would stop in for it—toilet paper. Gene would come in and pick up several rolls at a time, but nothing else, just toilet paper. He carried his toilet paper to and from the outhouse each visit, still requiring the others to use old newspaper.

"That Kage boy's back in town. He used to work for you, right?" Aaron asked, trying his best to act as if he were just making casual conversation, though Gene knew better.

Gene nodded.

Aaron continued as he rang up the toilet paper, "Figure he's just passing through again. He seems to take a liking to Gracie Howard every time he drops in."

"Yep," Gene agreed.

"You like him much?" Aaron asked.

"He was a hard worker," Gene answered, pulling his cash from his pocket.

"Well, there ain't no work in this town for him. I know you've got three helping you, and I figure he can't do much more than shovel dirt." Aaron took Gene's cash.

"Nope, don't got no need for him at my place."

"Hello there, Mrs. Martin," Aaron said with a nod hello to the lady behind Gene in line. "How's Chippy?" Aaron asked, sounding more as if he were asking about a young boy instead of her sixty-year-old husband.

"He's doing great, just working too hard as always."

"Looks like you're loaded up with groceries. You got company coming over?" Aaron asked, making his usual conversation.

"Yes, guess you could say that. I got a young man staying at our house tonight. Chippy has him working at the wood mill starting tomorrow and seems he doesn't have a place to stay. He's a handsome boy—just handsome," Mrs. Martin said as she unloaded her groceries onto the counter.

"Is that right?" Gene asked.

"Yep, Chippy brought him to our house at lunch today and he nearly ate everything I had on the table. He's a hungry one, and he likes my bread pudding. Loves it!" She leaned in toward Aaron. "So, I'm making him some more for tomorrow."

Gene probed, swifter than Aaron on this one, "Who might this young man be?"

"His name is Ben Kage. A handsome thing, I tell you. And loves my cooking!" Mrs. Martin cooed.

Aaron almost dropped her jar of pickles on his foot.

*   *   *

"Hey," Kage burst through Swirly's door. "I did it. I got a job—a good one, Gracie. Listen, Gene suggested I talk to Chippy Martin." Kage shifted from one foot to the other. "He hired me on the spot!"

"Really?" Gracie squealed, dashing from behind the counter.

"It gets better. He invited me to stay on his property. You know the nice house on the hill just down the road from the mill? Well it has an apartment over the garage. He's letting me stay there. I'll have my own place," Kage cheered.

"You know the mill," Gracie paused, "that's where my father worked ... the year before ..."

Kage ran his palms over Gracie's ears, then held her head between his hands. "I know," he said quietly.

"I like that you are going to work there."

Kage agreed. "Gracie, he even mentioned maybe retiring in a few years and said he needed somebody to run the business. If I prove to be a hard worker, learn fast, and pick up a good deal of the responsibility, he might consider me. He was so nice to me!" Kage's voice rose again.

"Of course, that could only work if you stayed in Ridgewood?" Gracie asked hopeful.

I told him I was planning on staying, and then he asked about you!"

"What?"

"Yeah, kind of surprised me too. He said, 'Does Gracie have enough help at Swirly's?' That's what he asked."

"Maybe he saw you here. Maybe he thinks you were working here?" Gracie speculated.

"Yeah, I guess."

"You know, Kage, you could. We could work together every day," Gracie said, liking the sound of it.

"I don't know, Gracie. You fit here. You enjoy what you do, but it's not me. I want what Mr. Martin was talking about. I want to learn about what he does," Kage said, still wired. He began alternating his weight from leg to leg again, bobbing back and forth.

"Kage, I've never seen you like this, you're ... so happy."

"I am, Gracie." Kage placed his hands on her shoulders.

"Happy to be in Ridgewood?" Gracie asked checking to make sure.

"Yes, and happiest to be here with you."

"Promise?"

"Yep. Gracie, I love you." Kage leaned toward her.

"Promise?" Gracie whispered.

"Promise," Kage repeated softly, inches from her face. "Would you do something for me?" Kage asked.

"What?"

"Call me Ben."

"Okay ... Ben," Gracie mumbled leaning into him, their lips touching.

With all the bad timing in the world, Gracie heard Swirly's door open. Gene Carter sauntered in, Willy in tow.

Chapter 33

Gene Carter had been stopping in the grocery store ever since he had overheard at the stockyard that Gracie had come back from Louisville with marks and bruises. He hadn't just missed the Chocolate Swirl when Swirly's was closed, but he'd missed seeing Gracie's cheerful face. When Kage left, she didn't look like her joyful self. For Gene the ice cream didn't taste the same served without her warm smile.

Then when he heard that something happened to her in Louisville, he, as everyone else, had assumed it was Kage. A young girl shouldn't be traveling alone, they all said. But thanks to Aaron and his ability to make conversation with anyone and everyone, her story didn't stay a secret for long. At the stockyard, Gene heard that two men, brothers of Kage, whom Kage didn't even know well, had forced themselves on her. Gene, too old to go after them, had even thought of finding them. So, he began buying toilet paper, mainly to walk around the grocery store and hear what Aaron was saying. He wanted to get the story straight from Aaron, instead of the version that had made its way to the stockyard.

He heard Aaron say, "Yep, they held her down but another one came in with a gun and ran them off before, you know ... anything too bad happened. Heard that Kage boy got it pretty good, too, broke his bones and stuff."

To get that piece of information it cost him fifteen cents for two rolls of toilet paper. Then when he visited Swirly's several days later and someone asked Gracie how she was doing, she'd just shrugged. That's when he went back for more toilet paper and learned that Gracie was in love with Kage.

"Yep, she's pining away for that boy and he's miles from here," Aaron told Mrs. Laurel who was there with her daughter.

"Well," Mrs. Laurel cooed, "Love will find a way, dear boy. Love will find a way."

Gene could tell Aaron wasn't keen on Mrs. Laurel's optimism. She turned to Gene, who was behind her in line holding his two rolls of toilet paper, "You believe that, Gene?"

Gene changed the subject. "Glad to see you're out and about. Mr. Laurel behavin'?"

Mrs. Laurel nodded, batting her eyelashes in appreciation. "Oh, yes. I'm cooking his favorite supper tonight."

By his third visit to the store, Gene was hooked. He stood in the grocery line with four rolls all for himself. But as Gene listened to Aaron go on and on, he knew what he had to do. Especially once he'd received the call from Kage's sister. Pearl had explained she was looking for Kage. She confirmed the unfortunate incident in Louisville, but she also shared her admiration for Kage and his love for Gracie. She left Cecil's number, saying he wanted to talk with Kage, if Kage came that way again.

After Kage had visited Gene asking about work, Gene had made a run to town—for some toilet paper and another quick errand to see his buddy, Chippy Martin, at the wood mill.

"Well, hi there, Gene," Chippy welcomed Gene as he walked into the mill. "It's a pretty day, figured you'd be hard at work on the farm trying to catch up. I know everyone else is."

"Just took a quick break this morning to run by. Got a favor to ask," Gene said.

"Anything for you buddy," Chippy Martin said, putting the plank he was holding aside.

*   *   *

On the porch swing, Gracie and Kage made wedding plans together, deciding to keep it simple. Erma hassling Gracie to buy a fancy wedding dress, and Roberta endlessly debating calla lilies or garden roses had exhausted Gracie. The Franklins wanted to help make it perfect. For Gracie, none of those things would make it perfect.

Pulling her hair back from her face, Gracie slowed the swing and turned to Kage. "I wish so badly my family could be with me," Gracie admitted, coming to grips with the true source of her downhearted spirit. "Even as young as I was, looking at my

296

mother's wedding pictures in the album, I had an image in my mind of what it would be like for me. My sister, next to me, my mother's eyes red, swollen like my grandmother's had been in the pictures—and my father standing beside me. How can I be so happy and so sad all at once like this?"

"So, let's get married ..." Kage ran his finger over the ring on her hand, "On your hill."

"What?"

"I know you've been talking about a church wedding, but maybe we can get married there ..."

Gracie interrupted connecting with his thought, "under the tree."

"It's just a thought. You might not ..." Kage reverted.

"No, it's perfect, but I want it to be just the two of us and, of course, Pastor Ted." Gracie said visualizing it. "And I have the perfect dress!"

"Only if that's what you want," Kage agreed.

"I do," Gracie said and giggled after her words. "Just practicing." She leaned her forehead against his.

*   *   *

At Gracie's, Kage picked up the phone and dialed Pearl. "Glad to catch you in," Kage said and shared their good news.

"You gave it to her!" Pearl squealed. Kage pulled the phone away from his ear.

"Twice actually," Kage snickered but didn't explain. "Now I'm saving up for a band to go with it," Kage added, and Pearl squealed again. Then she asked to talk to Gracie.

Kage could hear Pearl's voice erupt from the receiver as the two talked. "You take care of him. He ain't had much. He needs you."

Now that Ridgewood was his home it felt like a place he'd never seen before. He'd never been to *this* place in his life before, and he liked it.

After talking with Pearl, Kage hesitated before calling Cecil. Even though Pearl shared that he split from his brothers, he wasn't sure he wanted to hear Cecil's voice either. The phone rang several times, and Kage started to hang up.

"Hello," Cecil said on the other end.

For a second, Kage said nothing, and Cecil repeated his hello.

"It's Kage," he said and then followed, "Ben."

"Well, bloody about time I heard from you," Cecil said, relief in his voice. "Where are you? Pearl said you ran off, nothin' said to anyone. I wondered if you went off looking for Beth Ann and Ruby hoping for better luck, since we weren't much of a find."

Kage asked Cecil about his brothers visiting Ridgewood, but Cecil didn't know if they had circled through Ridgewood or not.

"Listen here, brother. I ain't going to apologize for those two again. I up and traveled in a different direction. I'm down here in Florida, alone. I might be lucky as to not meet up with them. Wondered if you wanted to join me?" Cecil asked.

"Thanks, but no," he said and let out a long sigh, trying to consciously release the anger he held toward Cecil. "I do appreciate you helping Gracie and me out, you know ... when."

"Brother, let me tell you something. Those two are going to get themselves killed someday, and I don't want to be there to see it. They ain't got no sense when it comes to living right. Sorry for what you and that girl of yours went through. You seen her again since?"

Kage summarized what he'd done the last few months and how he found his way back to Ridgewood. Also, he boasted about his job and his plans with Gracie.

"I'm proud for you brother. Ben, you're a good man. Mom and Dad would be pleased."

Kage nodded his head, not that Cecil could see, or know how much those words meant to him.

Chapter 34

May 4, 1967

On a Sunday afternoon in early May, Gracie stood beside Kage on the hill under the tree where he had given her the ring. It had been over a year since Kage had placed it there. He'd saved not only for their wedding bands but also enough for a trip to see the ocean.

There with Pastor Ted, Kage took Gracie's hand and slipped the wedding band onto her finger and, without Pastor Ted prompting him, he kissed her. Though the entire town was gathered, waiting at the Franklin's home, Gracie stood still, hoping somehow that this moment would never end. It had been Kage's idea to marry on top of the hill, but it was Gracie's choice that it only be the two of them. She appreciated the celebration awaiting, but the anticipation of seeing the ocean for the first time and being alone with him that night was nearly more than she could bear.

*　　*　　*

Gums showing from cheek to cheek, Gene smiled. He looked around the barn, wanting to show the newspaper to somebody, but he was alone.

He leaned back in his chair and reached in the desk drawer for a pair of scissors and felt around the bottom of the drawer until he was sure they weren't in there. He instead carefully ripped the announcement from the newspaper, making sure not to rip the picture of Gracie Howard or the words below. His eyes were beginning to fail him, but there was no mistaking the gleam on her face in that wedding photo. He remembered the feeling himself from decades earlier on his own wedding day.

He pulled his Bible from his top dresser drawer. Two brittle newspaper clippings and an old black-and-white photograph fell out of it. One clipping had the headline, "Treasure to be Discovered in Ridgewood," the other clipping read, "Missing Treasure Somewhere in Ridgewood." As he picked up the old photo, the upper left corner chipped off into his hand. It was a photo of a young man and woman. She wore a simple knee length white dress with a lace collar, her long hair meeting her shoulders. She had rarely worn it down like that. She was beautiful, absolutely beautiful. Their thin bodies were close, and his arms embraced her around the waist as they posed. The girl, nearing sixteen at best, looked every bit of a sophisticated twenty-five-year-old. She was leaning forward in the photo; it caught them both laughing, their faces bright and youthful. He remembered how she had felt in his arms that day, how he had

301

been the happiest man alive at that exact moment, and it had been caught on film.

He brought the photo closer to his face. The sight of it caused his huge smile to thin. He looked at his image in the photo knowing it was from a lifetime ago, but to him Olivia had not changed a bit. The picture had captured her intense beauty that she had carried with her always, every day that he'd known her. He touched her face in the photo and then tucked it away in the book and placed the neatly-cut newspaper clippings, published decades ago on top of it. Then he placed the freshly torn wedding announcement atop the others, shut the Bible, and returned it to the drawer.

Chapter 35

With the interstate complete, Ridgewood prospered, now with more commerce than any city in a seventy-mile radius. In a single decade, hundreds of families had moved there along with a sizable automobile factory and with another one under construction. Everybody was pleased about the new opportunities, which didn't leave Gracie much room to pout over the interstate exchange running right over where Swirly's had stood for thirty years.

Gracie hadn't thought much about it when she heard that Gene Carter had passed away. She was a little embarrassed by her natural reaction. She chuckled, although she didn't mean any disrespect. Since they had closed Swirly's, she didn't see him as often. When she did, she shared a friendly wave, and he still pointed and clicked. Just at the mention of his name, she pictured his mud stained blue jean jacket, his optional teeth, as if they were accessories, and his devotion to Chocolate Swirl.

"You getting that?" Ben called to Gracie, hearing the doorbell ring.

Gracie opened the door, surprised to see two men in suits standing in front of her. Their greeting was followed by an introduction; they were attorneys.

"Mrs. Kage, our names are Robert Meyers and Thomas Murphy of Meyers & Murphy Law Firm located in Louisville, Kentucky."

She had only dealt with a lawyer once and that was during the forced sale of Swirly's, which had led her to be somewhat wary of the men on her doorstep. Gracie yelled for Ben, who pulled on a shirt as he walked into the living room and saw the two men seated near the fireplace.

"Mr. and Mrs. Kage, we'll get straight to the point as we are sure you are wondering what brings us to your home today," the heftier of the two men said. He pulled from his leather bag a large manila envelope. "Mrs. Kage, as I said, my name is Robert Meyers. I'm here to deliver to you several things at the request of your friend, Gene Carter."

"Friend?" Gracie asked. "I did know Gene Carter ... heard recently he passed away. It's been several years since we've spoken."

"Well, he'd been quite ill, in and out of the hospital, refusing surgery that might have lengthened his life. He spent his last year in the nursing home after his brother passed away. Tom and I," he nodded toward the gentleman with him, "we've been fortunate to represent him in his business dealings."

Tom spoke up, "Gene's property went for a mighty fine price. We figure he sold it for at least ten times what it would have sold for before the interstate. He invested a great deal of the money too, and it has done quite well." Tom then turned to Robert. They had their system down.

Robert added, "Mr. Carter wanted us to deliver this package to the both of you upon his death. Sorry it has taken several months to process."

He handed the package to Gracie. She looked at Ben, questioning whether she should open it.

"Open it. Go ahead," Ben encouraged.

Gracie slowly unwound the string that clasped it shut. The document inside looked official, typed on Meyers & Murphy letterhead. She pulled the letter from the envelope and another piece of paper came out along with it. She gasped.

"Dear God, it's a check." She stared at it for several seconds without saying another word. Ben, sitting beside her on the couch, leaned toward her to see.

"Gracie!" He gasped aloud.

She laid the check on her lap and covered her mouth.

"$200,000, for us?" Ben asked looking from one attorney to the other.

"Yes, Gene wanted you to have it. He also included a few other items for you." Robert gestured to the same envelope now on the floor. It had slid off Gracie's lap when she unintentionally jumped at the sight of the check.

Gracie's head was swimming as she leaned down to pick up the envelope. She pulled out what looked like a bus ticket receipt, then squinted looking at it more closely. She flipped it over to see if anything on the back helped to explain. She then flipped it back over and said, "It's dated ten years ago."

Grabbing it from her hand, Ben studied it. Shocked by his interest in it, she now looked as intently at him as she had the receipt.

"This is the ticket. This is it!" Ben stood from the couch. The $200,000 check now slid from his lap to the floor. Tom bent down to pick it up and placed it on the coffee table in front of him. Everyone's eyes now on Ben.

"Remember when you asked me what brought me back here, and I said I had to settle a score, you know, with my brothers. Remember, the note. I thought it was from them. I must have been wrong, but how? Could it?" He was not making sense to Gracie.

"I don't understand," she mumbled.

Ben paced across the living room floor, muttered a few words and then shook his head. She tried to follow his rambling.

"Remember, I never planned to return to Ridgewood. I was in Georgia and headed south. You know, after what happened when you came to see me in Louisville. I wasn't going to ever go back there or come here again. If it hadn't been for the note, I might have never returned to Ridgewood. I got the note. That is why   I   came."

Gracie nodded, and Ben repeated, "I wasn't going to come back."

"Yes," Gracie wasn't sure where this was going. He was making her nervous.

"Well," he said and swooped his hand forward toward Gracie, "I only came back here because of the note. Remember it mentioned all that treasure crap? And being a man?"

"Yes, I guess." Gracie remembered him telling her about a note.

Ben paced. "Maybe it wasn't my brothers playing a joke on me. It never made sense to me that they'd sprung for the bus ticket!"

"It wasn't?" Gracie asked still trying to keep up.

"No, it was from Gene. Gene Carter!" He held the bus receipt up in front of her. His fingers held its top corner and he gave it a dramatic shake.

"What makes you think Gene wrote the note?"

Ben looked at the two attorneys to see if they followed him. They nodded him on, and Ben reacted with a snap of his fingers. Gracie wondered if they understood what Kage was saying better than even he did. "Well, when I got back to Ridgewood and didn't find them, I figured my brothers had already hit the road. You know Pearl didn't get the letter to me right away. It sat around for ... I don't know how long. The enclosed ticket had expired." As Kage spoke, he shook the ticket stub again. He turned on his heels, breaking his pacing routine and biting his bottom lip in thought.

"Ben, you never told me all this, about an enclosed ticket," Gracie responded, confused.

"I know, I know. It didn't matter," Ben said and paused thinking for a second. "Wait, I even went to Gene Carter for work, and he turned me away. I don't get it. Why would Gene Carter do this, why would ...?" His forehead creased, Ben looked from Gracie to the attorneys.

Tom spoke up, "Maybe I can help." He pulled from his briefcase a copy of a newspaper article. It had yellowed over time, especially around the edge where it had been cut out.

"You are both familiar with the rumor that went around about Ridgewood years ago?"

Gracie and Ben nodded. "Guess it still makes its way around," Gracie said, remembering overhearing someone talking about it recently.

"Well, this note," and he read its reproduction printed in the paper: *I am writing because in Ridgewood there's lost treasure. We got riches yet to find. Come seek them with me* was written by Gene Carter and mailed to his wife Olivia Carter in Hartington where he suspected she was living with her aunt. Included in the envelope was a ticket for her to return to Ridgewood. Our best guess is that Mrs. Carter carried the note with her to a hotel, for what reason we don't know. Was she considering coming back or did she meet someone there? We

308

won't ever know. After Gene's death we did a quick search for her. I suppose that piece will remain a mystery forever."

Gracie couldn't believe it. She was still trying to picture it. She had a difficult time believing the connection between what she knew of Gene, what these gentlemen shared, and what Ben concluded. Could it be true that Gene unknowingly ignited the treasure rumor? Then when everyone was going senseless over it, never said anything to anyone? Could he really have played a role in bringing Kage back to Ridgewood—to Gracie, for Gracie?

"So, ol' Gene was a big romantic?" Gracie murmured to herself, but the attorney answered.

"Seems to be so," Robert continued, "We did find that Mrs. Carter had indeed remarried a man named Wendell Michem. She passed away several years ago, and when we asked Mr. Michem if he'd ever been familiar with the—" he pointed to the newspaper article. "He said he'd read it in the papers just like everyone else."

Tom piped in, "He had never seen the original and had no additional information. He also denied ever staying at the hotel where the note was found. So that leaves us to assume that for whatever reason, Mrs. Carter stayed in that hotel room and left the note behind, and then we all know the rest of the story as to what happened to the note from there."

"Who would've thought that of Gene Carter?" Ben sat amazed. "Could Gene have encouraged Chippy Martin to hire me?"

"But why?" Gracie, still having a hard time accepting it, looked to Ben and asked, "Why would Gene do that? I mean, write you and send you a ..." she shuffled around searching for the receipt, but Ben was still holding it, "bus ticket so you'd return here? It just seems, well, odd."

Turning to the men, Ben said, "You know, if I had to pick one word, just one to describe Gene Carter," he then looked at Gracie, "it would be—odd."

Tom nodded his head in agreement. "Odd certainly would be fitting, but I would suggest that there was a lot more to Mr. Gene Carter than any of us may ever know."

Chapter 36

Gracie's left index finger rested between Ben's teeth and his quirky, yet charming, grin. As she tugged her finger free from her husband's playful grip, his arms tightened around her beneath the sheets. A tear spilled from her thick lashes. She wiped the tear with her hand—her only hand. Though her right arm lay by her side, forever etched with scars, she had never felt more beautiful and complete in her life. Nestling close, Ben's body enfolded hers under the sheets, his chest against hers. She remembered how she had felt the first time he had held her in his arms, and especially she remembered the encompassing peace that had lingered. Gracie wrapped her leg around his lower half; she could never hold him tightly enough. She tucked her toes under his leg to secure their embrace.

In her husband's arms, Gracie tried to process all that had happened: the money—which was enough to dwell upon by itself—and the fact that it had been Gene Carter whom she had to thank for Benjamin Kage being a part of her life. His involvement in their second chance baffled her. She couldn't imagine her life without Ben, and at the mere thought, tears filled her eyes.

Gracie had so many questions—questions without answers. Eyes closed, her fingers placed against her lips, her thoughts turned to prayer.

Dear God, I have no words for You. I am so overwhelmed. The way You watch out for me. Why me? And the way you have always cared for me. You've placed so many people in my life. Those I never had the chance to thank. Those I never even knew to thank.

Her grandfather's voice played through her mind, as if he were still alive encouraging her. "I know your climb in life is tough, but you won't be one to miss the view from the top of the mountain, little Gracie. Keep climbing, my little girl. Keep climbing." Though she'd filled the pages of her grandmother's prayer journal years ago, she wanted to find the page again where her grandmother had prayed for God to bring Gracie a husband to clasp her necklace. She was going to write *thank you* by her grandmother's handwritten prayer for her.

"How amazing!" Gracie whispered and even at a murmur, her voice broke, emotion tickling her throat.

"What 'chu say?" Kage muttered rolling her to her back. He kissed her cheek and grazed her lips.

She tasted the salt on his lips from her tears. As he kissed her chin, her throat, and above her breast, she cringed, not from his kisses but from the cool breeze that flowed under the covers as he moved down her body, until his chin came to rest on her stomach.

"Love you," Gracie whispered.

His head rose and fell with each of her breaths. He kissed her belly, gentle kisses, then several noisy ones, and his head bounced with the ripple of her giggles.

Another tear escaped, even as a smile rested on her lips. Gracie was thankful her tears didn't alarm him. After years by her side, he knew the difference between her painful tears and tears of joy.

Ben stopped the silly kisses, when he heard footsteps scooting down the hallway toward the door.

"Mommy," called Thomas Kage. Gracie could tell he had his lips pressed to the crack underneath the door, trying to peak underneath. His view couldn't have been much more than a glimpse of the brightly colored rug spread on their bedroom floor.

Then under the door, Gracie saw a little hand emerge, his tiny fingers wiggling. She gasped out loud, taking in a deep breath, her final effort to control the tears. Ben tucked his head near her neck, placed his hand on her cheek, and whispered, "I love you." His breath tickled her ear.

Completeness washed over her from head to toe. "Thank you," Gracie said closing her eyes. She thought: *Thank you, Benjamin Kage, for loving me. Thank you, Gene Carter, well, for everything! Thank you, Granddaddy, for reminding me to keep climbing—and thank you, God, for peaceful dreams and the view from the top of this mountain!*

Little Thomas, wiggling those fingers under the crack of the door with no intent to cease, mumbled, "Mommmmmyyy ..."

The tears flowed once more as she heard the tiny voice again.

"Wuv you, Mommy ..."

Ben stood from the bed, pulled on his robe and opened the door. Thomas grabbed his daddy's leg and bounced with excitement. Ben picked him up and tossed him into the air. Thomas squealed, then, with his arms outstretched, made sounds like an airplane engine as his daddy flew him into the bed next to Gracie, draped by the white sheet. As Gracie cuddled him, she saw, in Thomas's sweet eyes, a small piece of her grandfather again.

Thought from the Author

What is it about us that we take such inspiration from the lives of those who triumph over tragedy? Is it as simple as that we love a story with a happy ending, or does it go deeper than that? Could it be because we never really know if, within ourselves, we have the strength to bear such tragedy and survive such intense grief? Or is it that we too actually do know pain—and along with more than a few tears—we know from experience, that after the pain, there does again come a time for joy, because *we* have our own story. And could it be that for everything we've been through, that no one really knows us—especially, if we keep it all a secret.

WHAT DID YOU THINK OF **TREASURE ATOP THE MOUNAIN**?

If you enjoyed this book, please provide a review on Amazon and Goodreads so that others will be encouraged to read it too. Your review helps gain exposure for the book and may connect it to someone who needed to know that there are Gene Carters in this world, and God always has his hand on our lives.

Please share **TREASURE ATOP THE MOUNTAIN** with friends and family by posting on your social media platforms. Its sequel, Roxie Applesauce will be released in 2020. Get updates by following Haleya Publishing on Facebook.

Acknowledgements

I thank God for being with me through this process as I depend on Him every day. What a great joy to be sharing this book with you. I hope somehow that you, reading this today, might be yet another part of His great plan, and that in some way, this book encourages you.

My special thanks must be mentioned to a handful of friends, family and professionals that helped me along the way. My sincerest thanks to Kristen Lester who—after reading the book in its first and roughest draft—called me crying. Her tears provided the encouragement I needed to push forward editing and rewriting. I am especially appreciative for all the feedback from those listed online at **haleyapublishing.com.** Each of you mean so much to me! Thank you to the WOW Women of Bowling Green Christian Church for adding me to the book club's authors list and providing such great suggestions. I must mention a very special thank you to the best beta reader I could hope for, Cari Small. Your review inspired me, as well as provided a clear direction for significant improvements. I also have great appreciation for Lynn Wilton who professionally edited the final copy. She is everything and more than the professional reviews you'll find posted on Thumbtack. I look forward to our future projects. And finally, to the man who supports me, loves me and sees me as greater than I will ever see myself, I thank my husband, Todd Matthews.

Foster care - Adopt

To make a significant difference and help one of the thousands of children annually who get misplaced and shuffled, who travel a scary, unpredictable path in their rightful desire to have what comes so easily to so many—a loving family, call your state's Child Protection & Permanency Agency.